The
Bard &
The
Barman

An Account
of Shakespeare's
Lost Years

MERRILL HATLEN

Content compiled for publication by Richard Mayers of *Burton Mayers Books*. *Cover Design by Martellia Design (Ukraine)*.

First published by Burton Mayers Books 2022. All rights reserved.

A CIP catalogue record for this book is available from the British Library

ISBN: ISBN-13: 9781838345990
Typeset in **Garamond**

www.BurtonMayersBooks.com

DEDICATION

To my parents—Theodore Hatlen, who taught me
that make-believe isn't just for children, and
Edna Endicott Hatlen, who encouraged me
to follow my heart.

~ CONTENTS ~

Acknowledgments   vii

Preface   Pg 1

Chapter One   Pg 3

Chapter Two   Pg 14

Chapter Three   Pg 22

Chapter Four   Pg 31

Chapter Five   Pg 50

Chapter Six   Pg 79

Chapter Seven   Pg 109

Chapter Eight   Pg 128

Chapter Nine   Pg 139

Chapter Ten   Pg 148

Chapter Eleven   Pg 163

Chapter Twelve   Pg 194

Epilogue   Pg 214

About the Author   Pg 217

AUTHOR'S NOTE

While living in France many years ago, my wife and I had a view of Henri IV's chateau, at the base of the Pyrenees. When I finally realized that Henri and Shakespeare were contemporaries, it seemed likely that they could have crossed paths. Indeed, the Bard's attempt at comedy, *Love's Labour's Lost*, was clearly based on "Good King Henri." So ask yourself, if you were the King of France, wouldn't you want to meet the playwright who immortalized you? This is the story of how they met.

ACKNOWLEDGMENTS

First and foremost, I would like to thank Deborah Piston-Hatlen, the love of my life. She witnessed my fledgling efforts to write, encouraging me to fail better each time, until I finally got the hang of it. She also provided support during our sojourn in France, which inspired so much of my work.

I would also like to thank Peter Guardino and Ian Woollen, both friends and authors, for reading my drafts and coaching me to keep writing. Longtime friend Kerry Hampton has also been in my corner, egging me on. Thanks as well to readers Cynthia Fox, Sally Murphy, and Russell Youngman.

The Bard & The Barman

PREFACE

While excavating the Chunnel between London and Paris in the late 1980s, an alert workman unearthed a ceramic jug hidden behind a brick wall in a latrine near the White Cliffs of Dover. Disappointed that the jug felt empty, but intrigued by the fact that the stopper was sealed with beeswax, he stashed the jug in his satchel. He must have known that confiscating such a find was against company policy, but he wasn't about to turn over his treasure to his bosses.

When the workman got home after a hard day's work underground, he used a candle to melt the wax seal, and was rewarded for his efforts when he found a scroll concealed in the jug. Carefully unspooling the parchment, he was delighted to find it covered in writing, in the neat hand of a surprisingly literate barman. Unfortunately, the moisture in the air when the jug was sealed had curled the edges of the parchment, but most of the scroll turned out to be legible. However, the workman was unable to decipher the meaning of the words, which were written in Early Modern English from the Elizabethan Era.

The workman hesitated to show the scroll to anyone else, for fear of having to explain how he found the manuscript. Curiosity soon consumed him, and he contacted the British Antiquities Museum (BAM), which proved to be a huge mistake. They immediately confiscated the scroll under the National Treasures Act, but agreed to provide the workman with a translation "in the fullness of time." To the workman's credit, he insisted that BAM at least provide a receipt for the scroll.

After several months of waiting to hear from the British Antiquities Museum, the workman consulted an attorney, who rolled his eyes when he saw the receipt. "They might as well have given you a coat check, for this scrap of paper is worthless in a court of law. My advice is to forget the matter, and count yourself lucky they didn't prosecute you for opening the jug. Can of worms, if you know what I mean."

As any Egyptologist could tell you, the wheels of the British Antiquities Museum turn slowly, so several years passed before anyone got around to transcribing what is now known as the Chunnel Scroll. Thus, thanks to the hapless donor and a volunteer translator at BAM, the written testimony (admittedly hearsay evidence) of William Shakespeare's unknown confidant has been preserved for posterity. Far from being a glowing account of the man, the candid remarks confirm that the Bard was a complex character in his own right. Indeed, the critical observations lend credibility to the barman's account, which has been rendered into contemporary language (ed).

CHAPTER 1

God willing, some fortunate soul will find my journal someday, but if not, I can go to my grave knowing that I did my best to shed light on a most mysterious man, none other than William Shakespeare, though he used several aliases. How ironic that such an esteemed writer couldn't spell worth a damn. Not even his own name, for God's sake; Shapeshifter is more like it. While I make no claims of being a writer, I am a student of human nature, recording my observations honestly, if sporadically. To my credit, I noted his appearance as a person of interest in my journal, on the 23rd of April, 1589:

Now have a regular customer who perches on the stool at the far end of the bar, as if he were a king who likes to be waited on. Comes in early for lunch and stays all day, nursing a beer and scribbling on scraps of paper, as if he were writing his last will and testament, oblivious to the world. Yet he claims to be a man of the world, talking my ear off when he's not scribbling or muttering under his breath. Often enough, he will suddenly bolt from the bar to embark on what he calls a constitutional, a long walk for his health. He claims that his best ideas come to him when he stretches his legs. Spoken like a country bumpkin from Stratford, but he seems determined to make his mark on the world in London.

As the barman at the Bankside Inn for almost twenty years, I believe I'm entitled to some of the credit for Shakespeare's work, if you can even call it that, for he sat on his butt most of the time. Indeed, he invariably

3

occupied his favorite barstool, next to the kitchen door, so he could slip out when a creditor or an irate husband tracked him down. He also took advantage of his roost at the far end of the bar for assignations with some of the kitchen help and barmaids, who should have known better, for he had a reputation as a womanizer.

Like the fish that got away, his reputation grew larger with each lie he told, spinning them into yarns that made him famous. Those of us who really knew him saw a very different side of the Bard, which is why I want to set the record straight. Mind you, it's not his money that I was after, which he wasted on gambling. I should know, because I was his bookie for a time, placing bets for him while he sat at the bar, sipping warm beer and ogling every woman in the place. As is well known, he had an eye for older women, but he wasn't very picky when opportunity presented herself. You'd be surprised how many maidens fell for his usual pick-up line, "Shall I compare thee to a summer's day?"

To his credit, Will had staying power, frequently sitting at the bar for hours on end, scribbling away with his quill, but spattering the bar with ink that I had to mop up. In that respect, I knew that he would amount to something because he kept at it. Yet the same could be said for many a gravedigger. Still, I don't begrudge him his success, for which I give myself some credit for serving as his sounding board. As a matter of fact, when he told me about his convoluted story of Romeo and Juliet, I warned him that the tragic ending would never fly. "People go to the theater to escape the wicked world," I told him. "The news is already depressing enough. Why heap more misery on their plate?" Obviously, I underestimated the public's taste for tragedy, but I was glad when he turned his hand to comedy.

As I see that I'm getting ahead of myself, let me go back to the beginning, because I helped give Will his start. The secret of success for a barman is being a good listener, which is my strong suit, if I may say so. To give credit where credit is due, I didn't just humor him, like I had to do with some patrons who are blowhards. He had a knack, no doubt about it, for lying through his teeth. I was never bored by his malarkey, but took it in stride, realizing that the man couldn't help himself. He just had to embellish the truth. He told me as much in so many words, claiming that his teachers hated him because he was a quick study, able to regurgitate the rubbish they taught him without really having to work at it. What passed for history was mostly stuff and nonsense, useless facts of doubtful origin, which he was forced to repeat ad nauseum. Like the Romans, with their reputed vomitoria. He resolved to make up his own stories, using his imagination instead of his memory, which we knew would be eroded. What passed for truth changed with the tides. What's the point of learning something if it's not intrinsically interesting? The point of recounting stories is not to tell the truth, but to entertain yourself and others, with words that have the ring of truth.

In that respect, Will was an honest man, who made no bones about his penchant for make-believe, which he valued more highly than mundane facts. Mind you, he wasn't one of those writers who pull things out of thin air, like Aesop. The Bard leaned on the truth like a crutch, which is why he wrote so many historical plays. He used facts to guide him, but had no qualms about bending the truth to his will. In that regard, he was well named, for he was a willful man if there ever was one, despite his insecurities. He was determined to prove that he would amount to something, afraid he'd end up like his father, whose fortunes faded in front of Will's eyes.

By the time he finished school he was yet another weight on his father, whose promising first act in life showed no hint of the decline of his reputation in his later years. Making a living as a glover is difficult in the best of times, but the plague devastated the economy, and his

Catholic sympathies made him an outcast. It was bad enough to be fined for having a rubbish heap on his property, but losing his position as alderman was the low point. Not the way to make an exit.

In truth, there was no point in Will learning his father's trade, for he had no aptitude with a needle, nor any patience for the life of a provincial tradesman. He longed to see the wider world that he'd only heard about from Cicero and Virgil. Their words, which he'd been forced to memorize, seemed like fossils to Will. He wanted to see things with his own eyes, feel them with his own hands, and taste them for himself. Worried that Will would fall prey to the "black arts," drama and music, his father wrote to distant relatives in France, hoping that they might be able to find work for his son. One less mouth to feed, with the hungers of a young man.

His father must have been desperate, for Will suspected that his mother's side of the family were Huguenots, who were concentrated in southwest France. The tension between Catholics and Protestants had been heating up in France, so his father was sticking his neck out to ask these kin for help. When they responded with an offer to put Will to work on their farm, his father crossed himself twice for good measure. Will had no idea where his father came up with the money, but for his fifteenth birthday his father gave him a one-way ticket to Calais. Both a gift and a kick in the pants.

Will had been taught that mankind was separated from paradise by death, so imagine his surprise when he discovered France, a mere twenty-two miles across the Channel. In truth, the rough crossing proved worse than death, but all his heaving was soon forgotten when the ship landed in Eden. The port of Calais itself was nothing to look at, but he had never seen so many pretty girls in his life. He'd been to London before, when he was ten, long before girls held any interest for him. He confessed that he was in no hurry to get to the village where his French relatives lived, near Bergerac, which is where he cultivated his taste for wine. So he took his sweet time, spending most of the little money he had on French pastry until his pockets were empty.

French maidens, alone, made the journey worthwhile, but the devil had his due when Will tried to speak their language. He wished that he had learned more French, but he quickly found his tongue under the guidance of his country cousins, three sisters who took it upon themselves to show him the ways of the world. The oldest, Claudine, took him under her wing and under her bed covers, determined to help Will make up for the time he'd lost in a Puritan country. He conjugated until the cows came home. Because of his family connection, both of them knew that they had no future together, but there seemed little point in resisting their mutual attraction while it lasted. He remembered the little bit of Latin he learned in school, *carpe diem*.

~

Such confidences were typical of Will, who acted as if he were confiding in me, but was actually bragging. I have to admit that I took vicarious pleasure in hearing about his escapades abroad, for I have never left the shores of England and likely never will. Yet I was troubled that he seemed to ignore the fact that he was no longer a rambling rake, but a married man with a family to feed. Merely earning a living as a writer would have been hard enough in any era, but we were living in a time of the plague. Supporting a family using only his wits seemed miraculous to me, but the man didn't measure up to the writer in my estimation. From what I could tell, he led a double life, a carefree bachelor in London and a married man who rarely saw his much older wife or his three children in Stratford. I couldn't understand how he juggled the pieces of his life.

Since Will seemed to lead a charmed life, I confess I found some comfort in hearing that things sometimes went awry for him. Yet even as he told me how things unraveled during his foray into France, he seemed to emerge from any trouble unscathed; like a dog who shakes the water off his coat and lies down to warm himself in the sunshine.

I doubt if anyone in the world has ever spent a more idyllic year than he did in France, working alongside his cousins in the vineyard during the day, discovering French food and wine, and venturing into Bergerac to explore the city from time to time. He could see why the English and the French fought over the place for so long. After dinner he played cards until the grownups went to bed, then had French lessons, if you follow my drift. However, for a number of reasons, the milk of human kindness began to sour.

First, he began to suspect that his relatives had not invited him to live with them out of the goodness of their hearts, but because they saw Will as a suitor for one of their daughters. He came from what was once a prosperous family, before his father's business began to fail. Despite being a blood relative, he was a distant cousin who might be a potential son-in-law. However, the more they got to know him, the more they realized that he had no inclination towards marriage, nor any prospects of getting a job. The only sign of talent he showed, for playacting, endeared him to their daughters, but not the parents.

Second, when his French got good enough, he tried his hand at writing skits, discovering that he could woo women with words. But he hadn't reckoned on the jealousy among the sisters, not only for his attentions, but for juicy parts in his little plays. Playing a lover in his own work only fed the fire of their jealousy, so he began to cast himself as a villain, which came naturally to him. Indeed, he played his part so well that his cousins began to cool off towards him. He tried pandering to them by writing more comedies, but the damage was already done. By the time their parents found out that his father was deep in debt,

Will had worn out his welcome.

Lastly, he discovered that he had a knack for cards, as he was able to remember which ones had been played with startling accuracy. His memory had always been his strong point, though it eventually became a burden because there was much he would have preferred to forget. At the time however, his sharp mind and youthful appearance opened doors for him as a gambler. His first taste of success came in Bergerac, where Will tried his hand in a card game and walked away with a pocketful of money. Beginner's luck, perhaps, but he was hooked. Best of all, he could go where the winds blew, without being tied down by anyone or any place.

Little did he know that he'd soon become a father and married man, but he made the most of his freedom to extricate himself from his relatives and set out on his own. A good actor soon learns the importance of making a graceful exit, though he stumbled badly in his first attempt. He wrote poems to each of his cousins, trying to convey his gratitude for teaching him the arts of love, and expressing his regret at taking his leave. Will should have known that they would compare notes, and that his favorite cousin, Claudine, would never forgive him for his sappy verses. He should have stayed in character, as the villain he fancied himself to be.

~

Vintage malarkey from Will, whose account of his travels was meant to entertain, not to inform. Nor did I have any idea how much truth he told. He painted himself as a pirate with a good heart, who couldn't help himself for his success with women. Poor Will, whose gift as a wordsmith won over women from all walks of life. I don't doubt his claim about gambling, for a playwright is nothing if not a gambler. Who in their right mind would write plays for a living?

~

Having spent so much time with cards in his hand, Will

couldn't help noticing that French playing cards were much more colorful than English ones. He shouldn't have been surprised, since French food is so much better than English slop, but he was curious to see where they came from. So he set off for Rennes, in Brittany, a handsome town full of handsome women, but the weather tended to keep them under wraps.

His quest led him to the workshop of the noted artist, Pierre Maréchal, whose work was a revelation to Shakespeare. Maréchal's studio was covered with playing cards from throughout the world, showing the superiority of French design. When he saw the cleverness of their four suits, with hearts running through the deck of cards, he was embarrassed to be English. Why didn't we think of that, he wondered? Perhaps Maréchal was genuinely flattered by his admiration, but he was also a shrewd businessman—unusual for an artist I must say. He offered to let Will sell his cards on commission, confiding that he hoped to corner the market in England. But he wanted to see what the competition was up to in Italy, and asked him if he knew any Italian.

He had learned a few useless phrases in school, so he replied in the best Italian he could muster, "I have a knife in my boot." Maréchal laughed, "Spoken like a gambler, my boy. How soon can you leave for Genoa?" While he took a liking to Will, Maréchal was no fool and didn't advance him any money for his trip, but gave him a bundle of cards to sell on his travels. "Your first test," he said, looking Will in the eye. Maréchal also gave him a letter to the captain of a ship in Vannes, authorizing his round-trip passage to Italy. Will gathered that this was a business arrangement, rather than a favor, but he had no idea what their arrangements were. As he learned early in his life, some things are better left in the dark.

~

Note how Will gave credence to his yarns by leaving things unsaid. Had he pretended to know what was behind the truth of the relationship between Maréchal and the ship's captain, he might have meandered so far from his tale that he would have lost me. He was economical with the truth, as he was with everything in his life. Stingy is more like it. Yet I could always count on him for a full helping when he talked about himself. As you can tell from his account of his travels, it was if he knew it might be the last time in his life when he was a free man. He reveled in the adventure that awaited him.

~

As Maréchal had instructed, Will followed the Vilaine River towards the Breton coast, ensuring that he wouldn't lose his way in the wilds of Brittany. Its connection with his homeland wasn't lost on him, including the rainy weather, but when the sun came out, he found himself in paradise again. The beautiful countryside, awash in cream and butter, had everything a young man could desire. He made much of his first encounter with a milkmaid, who was singing as she walked across the green pasture with a cow and her calf by her side.

"How I wished I knew the Breton tune she sang so lustily, for I would have joined her in raising our voices in the Eden around us. All I could do was hum along, which brought a smile to her face. 'I gather you are a stranger, for everyone around here knows this song. Nonetheless, you can carry a tune, which is more than I can say for most lads, who are afraid to raise their voices.'"

One thing led to another, and before he knew it, they were sleeping together in a hayloft. Will was glad to know that he had a musical bone in his body, even if he wasn't much of a singer. In the morning they picked the best strawberries he'd ever had in his life, and covered them with thick Breton cream. There's no telling how long he might have stayed there if the sun hadn't disappeared. The memory of that milkmaid has stayed with him ever since. Though he's forgotten her name, she's the model for some of his most colorful characters, even if they only play a small part in his works. He liked to say that ordinary people, not kings or queens, gave his plays the common touch.

~

As you can tell, Will loved to pontificate, praising himself in his inimitable self-deprecatory way. I couldn't help wondering how differently Will's life would have turned out if he had remained in Eden with the milkmaid. I'm sure his French must have been pretty good, but I can't believe he would have ever reached the heights he achieved in English, even with the nimble tongue he bragged about.

~

Fortune continued to smile upon him as he caught sight of a farmer driving a team of horses in his hay wagon. Catching up to him, Will asked the old man where he was going. "Off to the port before it starts raining again," he said. "Around here you can't wait for opportunity to present itself. If I'd waited till the sky cleared and the sun was up, I would have missed many a boat. You have to make your own luck, my boy. Never forget that." Will took this advice to heart.

He probably could have made a fortune in the port of Vannes, relieving sailors of their valuables, but there was no time for gambling. Will was determined to prove worthy of Maréchal's trust in him, and to carve out a niche for himself as an entrepreneur. He also had something to prove. That he was more than a gambler, capable of making an honest living. Having witnessed his father's decline, Will was desperate to avoid the same fate.

~

As you can tell, Will could speak from his heart from time to time, or give the illusion that he was doing so. In that respect he was underestimated as an actor. People forget that he wasn't just a playwright, but a jack of all trades in the theater. He knew all the tricks, including how to pull the wool over the eyes of his audience. If you ask me, that was his genius, to tell people what they wanted to hear. He knew how to dress up the truth to make it more palatable, and more interesting. For all of us could tell a tale or two about coming-of-age, but Will had the advantage of living in a remarkable time. Who else but the Bard could brag about being born during the Black Death?

CHAPTER 2

It was easy enough to find the *Dragon*, one of the ships of the East India Company, commanded by Captain Montague, whose origins are shrouded in mystery. His French sounded a little fishy to Will, but he immediately liked the man, because Montague minded his own business. When Will showed him the letter from Maréchal, the Captain had no questions. He asked his steward to show Will his cabin, which was so cramped he could barely stand up. The steward informed him that the ship left at midnight, and offered to let Will leave his belongings in the cabin, but he was determined to keep his things in sight. With some time to kill he ventured into town to see if he could find a good place to eat, because he doubted that the food on the ship would amount to much. Wise beyond his years, Will remarked.

While walking through the town square, he happened to see a most unusual sight. A handsome older woman was sitting on a blanket on the grass, with cards spread out before her. He was immediately intrigued by her of course, not only because of her dark beauty, but because of the Tarot cards on display. While he didn't know much about Tarot, he couldn't help noticing the Hanged Man, whose plight was obvious to any fool. The tears streaming down her cheeks confirmed that she was a damsel in distress.

"Is there anything I can do to help?" he asked, without the slightest idea of what service he might render her.

"Let this be a lesson to you, young man. I have compounded my bad fortune by using the cards to see my future. I should have known better. Though it is beneath my station, I have a gift for helping others foresee their future, but I am blind to my own fortune. Not only have I been robbed, but my own cards have turned against me. They insist on showing me that I've brought this calamity upon myself."

~

Telling me that he didn't want to bore me with the details, and admitting that he might want to use the woman's words in a play, Will abbreviated the story for me. The unfortunate woman claimed to be a Duchess from Barcelona, on her way from Paris to Genoa to visit her Italian cousins. Her carriage was stopped by robbers who seized her possessions and threatened to kidnap her. When she began cursing them in Catalan, they decided she was more trouble than she was worth, and left her stranded in the countryside. She had to walk the rest of the way to Vannes.

While Will thought it odd that she would travel so far west to catch a ship to Italy, he knew that she was either telling the truth or was a remarkably good actress. Either way, she was not a woman to be ignored. "Have you ever met a woman who could be ignored?" I wanted to ask, but held my tongue. He left off his condensation and continued his tale, unable to resist embellishing it with a measure of veracity.

~

Carpe diem, Will said again, seeing the opportunity to prove himself a gentleman and to gain the favor of the Duchess, whose Duke was nowhere to be seen. "Put away your cards, your highness, and put your trust in me. Young though I am, fortune has favored me, for I been given safe passage to Italy this very night. Let me speak to the ship's captain, to see if you can have my cabin, and I will gladly sleep on deck. You will not put me out, for my body is still

15

supple, and I can sleep standing up if I have to. Honestly, I would rather sleep under the stars, and I should warn you that the cabin is likely to be uncomfortable. Though it is beneath a Duchess, I can offer you nothing more, for I have yet to make my fortune in the world. Indeed, I have much to learn, and hope that Italy will make a man of me."

Of course Captain Montague agreed to his offer, partly because it was no skin off his nose, but mainly because he was pleased to have the company of a beautiful woman. For the *Dragon* was no usual vessel, merely carrying cargo. The crew doubled as actors, performing plays throughout the world. According to Will, they performed *Hamlet* in Africa, of all places. Never in his wildest dreams did he imagine that his fame would spread so far.

~

At this point I was ready to strangle him, for he had left me hanging, wanting to hear more about the Duchess, not the blowhard Bard. The man was full of himself, like any genius I suppose, but as an ordinary mortal I had no patience with his strutting. I wanted to hear what happened on the *Dragon*. Unfortunately, he continued to string out the story ad nauseam. All I can do is provide an abbreviated account of his journeys, for unlike most writers, I have to earn my living.

~

His fear about the food proved unfounded, but Will had the advantage of having dinner in the Captain's quarters. Rather than having fish like the rest of the crew, the officers were served ravioli, stuffed with sheep's brain, as they do in Provence. It soon became apparent that Captain Montague had eyes for the Duchess, but who didn't? In addition to being beautiful, she was a delightful conversationalist, entertaining her host with stories of life in the Spanish court. Somehow, she managed to avoid any mention of the Duke, which made Will wonder if he even existed.

After dinner they were entertained by the theater

troupe, who managed to avoid learning any lines by improvising sketches, like the Italians. As the captain explained: "There's no point in performing the same play over and over again, especially on a ship, where things go stale quite quickly. So if you have any suggestions for the actors, don't hesitate to throw them a bone. They thrive on challenges."

The Duchess took him at his word. "How about a story with star-crossed lovers?" Will was surprised by the alacrity of the players, who put their heads together for less than a minute before ordering everyone on deck at sword point, slipping into character as pirates. They began acting out the rescue of a man walking the plank on a pirate ship. With a sword held at his back the man was challenged every step of the way, ordered to jump in the air, do a dance, and sing a song.

Each performance was greeted with boos, until the unfortunate man was left standing at the end of the plank. Offered a chance for one last word, he called out "Dulcinea." Suddenly, a woman swung towards him on a rope, knocking his tormentor onto the deck. Wrapping her arms around the man, they swung across the ship to the tiller. The woman ordered the helmsman to "Return to port, or I'll run you through your bowels."

Will said that he would have added a wedding scene, with the captain presiding, but for a bit of after-dinner theater, he thought it worked pretty well. Obviously, they must have had some practice in acrobatics, which would have been useful in battle. In the meantime, the motley crew of sailors doubling as actors captured his imagination. "I had half a mind to join them, but my proclivity for seasickness brought me back to reality."

He thought it unfortunate that the man walking the plank was an invalid, with one arm in a sling, but he didn't let his disability stop him from being an actor, among other things. Sad to say, Shakespeare spoke no Spanish, so his account of his encounter with Miguel de Cervantes was sketchy, to say the least. Having heard that Will was a cardsharp, Cervantes wanted to test his mettle. Indeed, the Bard was surprised that his shipmate proved to be quite a gambler, able to shuffle a deck of cards with one hand.

According to Will, the crewman who offered to translate proved to be unreliable, whether because of mistranslation or counting cards, wasn't clear. At one point, Cervantes accused the translator of cheating, leaving Will in some confusion about why Cervantes had been banished from Spain as a young man. Trying to piece things together by asking other members of the crew about Cervantes' colorful life, it was clear that the Spaniard never tired of telling how he was injured in battle, captured by pirates and imprisoned in Algiers for five years until he was ransomed by nuns.

Great material for a play, of course, but Cervantes bragged that he would someday be known throughout the world, which gave Will pause. He had yet to write anything of note, but Cervantes took a liking to him. "Fortune has favored you with fair face and form, young man, but you have no future as a gambler. I observed that you never fold, but try to make something out of the cards you're dealt. I admire your daring, but you can't bluff your way through life. The look in your eye betrays your thoughts, for you are a dreamer at heart. I know what I'm talking about, for I have faced death several times, even in my dreams, having dreamt of my own funeral.

"In the dream I am lying in my coffin, pretending to be dead, dying to know what people will say about me. I'm afraid that I won't be able to refrain from replying, but it's not my tongue that betrays me. It is my nose that threatens to give me away, for the smell of the tapas in the adjoining room almost brings me to tears, knowing that I can't move a muscle.

"People can be cruel when they think no one hears them, and even crueler when they have onlookers. That was the hardest part, because I obviously couldn't see anyone with my eyes closed. I had to rely on my ears, which have begun to fail me. Fortunately, I am sensitive to touch, so I could tell when someone held a mirror to my face, to see if I was really dead. I held my breath as long as I could, but I almost choked when I finally had to inhale. But the unkindest cut of all came from a critic whose voice I knew all too well. 'I don't like to speak ill of the dead, but let's face it, Cervantes fancied himself to be a poet, playwright, raconteur, soldier and sailor. More like a jack of all trades and a master of none, if you ask me. He should have stuck with being a tax collector.'

"If I still had the use of my left arm I might have strangled him, pulling him into the coffin just to hear him scream. I would have said, 'Critics are nothing but parasites, living on the blood of their host. You, of all people, who can barely string words together, should be buried in this coffin instead of me. I have stories coming out of my ears, just waiting to be told.'

"Even in the dream I regretted my little prank, which did not amuse me as much as I expected. I considered sitting up in my coffin just to startle everyone, for the sheer drama of the moment. What a story it would have made for the witnesses, who could tell their grandchildren that they had seen Lazarus rise from the dead. Although no one remembers my plays, they would have remembered this scene for the rest of their lives. But for once in my life, I held my tongue.

"As if God appreciated my gesture, he rewarded me with the presence of a beautiful young woman. Of course, I couldn't see her face, nor verify that she was young, but I knew that she was an angel sent from heaven above. Indeed, she waited until the procession of mourners died down, after the food I had smelled was brought out for those in mourning, eclipsing any thoughts of me. After all, even grief must be fed. Who can mourn on an empty stomach?

"From the rustle of her dress I was sure that some

unseen figure was giving the sign of the cross, blessing me not only with her presence, but with the sacrament of the Holy Church. How I would have loved to hear the blessing that she whispered, but her words fell on unreceptive ears. Yet at that very moment I had an epiphany, so difficult for an author to accept, that words don't matter. I felt the first tear fall on my cheek, like a drop of rain signaling that the drought is over. Soon her tears began to stream down her face, falling onto mine. Then came her torrent of tears, washing me clean of my sins. If only my death could be so beautiful, I would gladly die a thousand times.

"I awoke to find my pillow soaked with tears, proof that dreams are as real as everyday life appears to be. It would have been easy enough for me to dismiss such criticism as the result of envy, but there was a grain of truth in what he said. The dream was a warning to me. With so many talents I could easily become a dilettante, spreading myself thin. Likewise, I could spend my life searching for the beautiful woman who shed so many tears for me. But she is an angel, dwelling in my heart, rather than the world of appearances. There is no point in chasing her, for she reveals herself when she chooses, when the time is ripe. It is my muse who brings me to tears. My dream was not a call to action, but reflection. Learn to listen to your dreams, young man."

~

Will's story didn't fool me for a moment, as his tale about meeting Cervantes was obviously a distraction, to avoid telling me the hard truth. He didn't want to admit that the Duchess dumped him for the captain, if she ever had any interest in him at all. While I don't doubt that such a troupe of riffraff could improvise a scene from a tale of pirates, the Bard's boast that he could have improved on the sketch didn't hold water. At that point in his life, he hadn't even stepped onto a stage, for God's sake. Even a genius has to draw upon his own experience, so I think

Will added this bit about the *Dragon* after the fact.

His loose talk about star-crossed lovers was but a bluff, pretending he had a hot hand, when his cards let him down. Yet I see that my asides are beginning to cast a shadow on my journal, nor do I have the time for my own thoughts anymore. With the plague in abatement for the moment, I have more customers than I can handle. All I can do is scribble down my recollections of Will's words catch-as-catch-can.

CHAPTER 3

Gallantly leaving his cabin to the Duchess, Will managed to stretch out on the bottom of the only lifeboat on the vessel, which tossed and turned even more than he did. When he finally managed to drift off to sleep, he was rudely awakened by waves breaking over the bow of the ship. Splashed with cold water, he retreated below deck, where the rocking motion only made matters worse. Will threw up what was left of the ravioli, glad that he hadn't had another helping. He regretted the captain's generosity with the wine, which continued to slosh around in his stomach.

In truth, he knew that the abundance of wine was a ploy to overcome what few qualms the Duchess may have had. In that respect, he was glad to find the Captain passed out on the passageway to her cabin, where Will ventured with half a hope that she would invite him in. The sound of heavy snoring quickly dispelled any thought he may have had about knocking on her door. While he found it hard to believe that such a lovely woman could snore so loudly, he didn't want to take the chance that she might have company. In any case, it was clear that he had missed his chance, if there ever was any. The Duchess and the Bard were not destined to be star-crossed lovers.

Mercifully, the weather improved by the time the ship put in at the port of Royan, where Will gawked at the barrels of cognac piled high on the wharf, as in a drinker's dream. While he had hoped to see the troupe perform for the public, the sailors were too busy loading barrels, which they hoisted with gusto. He was surprised to see the Duchess sketching the scene, since he had no idea that she was an artist. Yet it made sense that a beautiful woman would have an eye for beauty. Indeed, she caught the essence of the scene remarkably well, without gilding the lily. Nonetheless, he couldn't help wondering where she got her sketchbook, for she had supposedly been robbed of all her possessions.

Captain Montague rewarded the crew for their hard work by providing a couple of rounds of cognac, giving Will his first taste of the heavenly elixir. He was reminded of the fact that there was nothing comparable to it in England. Will counted his blessings for following his instincts to France. What a pity he didn't have time to see the source of so much pleasure in Cognac, but the captain knew better than to let his sheep venture too far afield. As was his habit, Montague set sail at midnight, ensuring a fairly sober crew and leaving stragglers to their fate. In that respect, actors and sailors are replaceable, and they know it, helping them toe the line.

Once underway, the ship was again buffeted by what are commonly called sea breezes, a euphemism for the gales that plague the Atlantic coast. As Will was about to discover, there's a good reason why the West coast of France is so sparsely populated, for the constant wind would drive most people crazy, and topple any trees planted for protection from the elements. It was no wonder that Bordeaux was set back from the coast, for had it been a port, the city would have been overrun by the sea, not to mention pirates.

Instead of a leisurely dinner and entertainment, it was all-hands-on-deck, taking down the sails that had been raised to get the ship underway. Captain Montague was intent on getting to Arcachon, whose natural harbor provided shelter. It was also the breeding ground for some of the best oysters in the world, but the very thought of shellfish made Will's stomach queasy. While he was eager to set foot on land again, the ship hadn't gone very far. At this rate, it would take forever for them to reach Italy, and he began to wonder if he wouldn't be better off traveling on foot. At least he could keep his food down.

Spending the night on deck again was out of the question, despite access to the lifeboat, which he knew would be overrun if the ship began to sink. That seemed like a real possibility, with rain falling faster than the crew could bail, and a howling wind that froze his fingers. Will admitted that he was tempted to go below and take his chances with the Duchess, but he doubted she would welcome him with open arms. Even if she did, he wasn't sure that he could rise to the occasion. Fortunately, Captain Montague managed to put in at Arcachon before the ship went under. The very thought of losing the barrels of cognac made Will shudder.

Mindful that the ship's precious cargo might tempt thieves, the captain ordered the crew to remain on board. Relieved to have found safe harbor, they refrained from grumbling about being stuck on the ship, and most of them were glad to get a good night's sleep. That was not Will's fate, since he had to stand guard throughout the night, but he counted himself lucky to still be alive. With too much time on his hands, he indulged himself with thoughts of spending the night with the Duchess. Will resolved to sneak into her cabin, which rightfully belonged to him, as soon as his watch was over. He figured that the worst that could happen is she would ask him to leave, but at least he'd give himself the chance to avail himself of her charms. How could she turn down such youthful exuberance?

At the break of day Will made his way to her cabin, feeling the flutter in his chest. There was no point in knocking, as he didn't want to give her time to get dressed. So he turned the doorknob as quietly as he could, hoping that he might be able to slip under the covers with her as if in a dream. A snore might have put him off, but he heard nothing, not even her breathing. Slipping out of his clothes, he gently pulled back the covers, only to realize that her bed was empty. Feeling like a fool, he got dressed and lit a lamp, finding the cabin completely deserted. Will immediately suspected that she had succumbed to Captain Montague, who had clearly demonstrated his commanding presence in a crisis. Will was but a mere boy.

Looking around the cabin, he noticed a trunk at the foot of the bed. Once again, he wondered what the Duchess was doing with any possessions. Will remembered that he'd already seen her wearing a couple of different dresses, which were hard to miss on such an alluring woman. Surely a robber wouldn't have overlooked such valuables, easy to carry and quick to sell. Will opened the clasp on the trunk, finding it full of dresses. He realized that she must have been carrying a small fortune in garments, which made him think there must be jewelry as well. To his credit, he had no intention of stealing from her. Will may be many things, but not a thief, even if he wasn't above borrowing.

Finding nothing but frocks in the trunk, Will tried tapping on the bottom of it, discovering a hollow sound. Turning the trunk upside down, he shook it, loosening the compartment that had been inserted into it. Slipping the compartment from the trunk, he found a leather case secured with a dark red cord. At first he was disappointed to find that the case contained empty sketchpads, but then he found another layer of sketchbooks, filled with nothing but seascapes. Skimming through the sketches, he noticed that all of them were scenes of harbors, including the one in Royan.

Will didn't have time to ponder why the Duchess would bother to conceal her sketches, which were well done, he thought. Why hide your light under a bushel? He was suddenly afraid that she would return from her escapade, which he didn't want to know anything about. Putting her things back as quickly as he could, it struck him how pathetic he had become. Instead of being able to disrobe the Duchess with his fingers, all he had seen with his own eyes were her empty frocks. He put everything back as best he could, ashamed at his folly, and slipped out of her cabin before he made matters worse.

While he was curious to see if the Duchess would resume her sketching, he was more interested in poking around Arcachon, whose attractive harbor was surrounded by trees and flowers. Finding a path along the water's edge, he explored the coast for most of the morning, until hunger drew him back to the port. Trying to save money, he settled for fried eggs at a place along the harbor, but there was no sign of the Duchess. Curious to see if she was still on board, he headed back to the ship, which was still under close guard.

Will found Captain Montague arguing with an official from Bordeaux, who claimed that there was a local tax on exports. Fuming, the captain replied that he had already paid tax on the cognac when he bought it. "I am a citizen from France, for God's sake, not some foreigner using the port for free. I thought Arcachon was a safe harbor. Now you tell me that I have to pay more tax? At least pirates don't pretend to be honest."

"When you enter any port, you have to play by their rules. You should know that by now, Captain."

"I have sailed this coast for years, and have never encountered such double dealing."

It was at this point that the Duchess emerged in response to the argument. "Excuse me, gentlemen. Let me speak to the Spanish Ambassador, as the cargo is bound for Spain."

The tax collector replied, "You can speak to anyone you like, but this ship is not leaving here until you pay the port tax."

Seeing Will, Captain Montague said, "Find someone to

take us to Bordeaux. Something suitable for a Duchess, young man." Having already looked around the port, Will knew where to find a carriage, and quickly brought it around to the ship. The Captain rewarded his success by telling him that he could accompany them. "You might as well see the city while you're at it. But don't get any ideas about gambling. The sooner we leave this place, the better."

The only large city he'd ever visited was London, so the sight of such a tidy, sunny place as Bordeaux enthralled Will. He'd never seen so many houses with gardens in the back, as if people actually had opportunities to sit outside. Not something one does much in England, to say the least. He was doubly glad to have something to look at other than the Duchess and the Captain, who acted like lovers on holiday, despite the urgent matter before them. For a woman headed for an impromptu meeting with an ambassador, she was carrying a heavy valise.

Rather than having to endure watching them flirt, Will took advantage of his youthfulness to sit on top of the carriage. At first he was delighted to find himself on top of the world, well aware of how far he had come since he left school. However, he soon discovered that the swaying of the carriage made his stomach woozy. While nothing like the seasickness he felt on the ship, it was all he could do to keep his breakfast down. Most of all, the constant motion of the carriage made Will realize how vulnerable he was to forces beyond his control. He would have much preferred to walk, for there's nothing like having your feet on the ground.

Indeed, Will might just as well have walked all the way to Bordeaux and back, for all he did was wait for the Captain and the Duchess to meet with the Spanish ambassador. Will was certain they must have had lunch with the ambassador, because the meeting took forever. As hungry as he was, he was afraid that if he ate anything, he'd throw it up on the way back. He comforted himself with the thought that he was saving money by skipping lunch, but it was cold comfort.

It did not help his spirits to see the Duchess basking in her success with the Spanish ambassador. It seemed to Will that she had also lightened her load, making him suspect that she had somehow sweetened the deal with her sketches. As much as he admired her artistry, he didn't think her seascapes were exceptional, but who was he to judge? After all, Stratford-upon-Avon was miles from the sea. What irked him the most was that the Duchess had somehow managed to ingratiate herself with the Captain *and* the Spanish Ambassador, without ever mentioning her debt to Will. Without his assistance, she would have been left stranded. Once again, he felt like a boy, thrust aside by grownups.

Once back on ship, Will was dying to slip into her cabin again to see if his suspicions were well founded, but there was no opportunity to open her trunk again. It occurred to him that he might be able to get away for a few moments during dinner, but he couldn't take the risk. After all, he reminded himself, her sketches were none of his business. She was a grown woman, who could do whatever she pleased, and he had no reason to suspect her. Perhaps he was just jealous, especially knowing that the Captain's generosity in letting her have Will's cabin had paid off in spades for him.

Will's inkling that something might be amiss proved prescient when the ship arrived in Hendaye, on the French border. Indeed, with the Spanish port of Fuenterrabía just across the bay, they seemed to be surrounded by the Spanish Armada. Of course there was no way he could have known that the Spanish were already making plans to invade England. Indeed, the scheme was happening under their noses, as Captain Montague and the Bard found out the hard way when the Duchess disappeared, along with Cervantes.

The last Will saw of her, she was walking along the

lovely beach at Hendaye, with her sketchbook under her arm, looking for a good place to catch the scene. When she didn't show up later in the afternoon, the Captain asked Will to go look for her, but there was no sign of the Duchess anywhere. He walked all the way to the border before turning back. Before he told the Captain, Will went to her cabin to see if her trunk was still there. The hidden compartment was empty, of course, confirming his suspicion that she must have given them to the Spanish Ambassador.

Before Will had a chance to deliver his bad news to Captain Montague, a messenger boy arrived to steal the Bard's thunder. Breathing hard from running, the messenger took the wind out of the Captain's sails, while offering a glimmer of hope: the Duchess had had to leave for Madrid immediately, for her husband had been killed in a duel. Will didn't have the heart to tell the Captain that her sudden departure sounded fishy, but the Bard had to hand it to her: in one bold stroke she finally acknowledged that she was married, while making it clear that she was a free woman. A widow to be sure, but after a period of mourning, she would have a new deck of cards.

As he could see the conflicting emotions course through the captain's body, Will didn't have the heart to tell him about her sketches, especially because he had no proof that they were anything more than they seemed. Certainly a woman with her artistic talent had every right to sketch what she wanted, but why conceal work that she should have been proud of? Innocent as he was at the age of sixteen, it didn't occur to Will that her sketches of harbors might be useful to the Spanish, who were intent on conquering the world. The possibility that she was a spy, doing reconnaissance on Spain's arch enemies, England and France, never occurred to him. Not until years later when the Spanish Armada met their fate. It was only then, when he was twenty-four, that Will realized that the Duchess had betrayed him. Even harder to swallow was the fact that Cervantes was a double dealer as well. Will was left wondering why the Spaniard had bothered telling him his dream. So much for trusting your muse. But Will was not the only one who failed to see which way the wind was blowing.

CHAPTER 4

The very thought of continuing on the *Dragon* all the way to Italy made Will sick to the stomach, for that would mean sailing all the way down the serpentine coast of Spain and Portugal, and running the risk of being blown into the treacherous straits off Africa. While the prospect of seeing Gibraltar was tantalizing, it seemed like an awfully long way to go just to see a big rock sticking out of the sea. And to be perfectly honest, he dreaded the thought of watching Captain Montague moping around without the Duchess; even if it did serve him right for intervening before Will had a chance to win her over. He couldn't say as much to him, of course, for the captain had done him a favor, but Will had cleared the debt by bringing her into Montague's life.

In any case, Will realized that he needed to depart from his original plan of sailing all the way to Italy, as he explained to the Captain: "I thank you for your hospitality, Captain, but fear I cannot continue on your voyage to Italy, for it has already revealed my weakness as a sailor. Clearly, I was not meant to spend my life at sea. I am not cut from sailcloth, but from cardstock, having discovered that I'm a gambler at heart. Indeed, I'm a man on a mission, having been charged by Monsieur Maréchal to expand his business.

"Truth be told, your crew are already wary of my cardsmanship, having discovered that my youthful appearance masks a formidable gambler. Not only am I unlikely to win any more money on the *Dragon*, but there are few opportunities to peddle decks of cards or to see what Maréchal's competition is up to. As I discovered at the border, my Spanish is very limited, and I would be completely lost in Portugal. Therefore, I have decided to take a shortcut to Italy, cutting across France at the base of the Pyrenees, where I can at least speak the language. If all goes well, I can catch up with you in Perpignan, sailing the rest of the way to Italy in calmer waters."

Captain Montague replied with the kind of advice Will would have liked to have heard from his father before his gloves unraveled. "I seem to have lost a lover and a son at the same time, but I trust that you will rejoin the *Dragon* in the Mediterranean, whose calmer waters may fit your disposition better. Indeed, it seems fitting that I met the Duchess in the Atlantic, which shares her stormy nature. I have you to thank for bringing her into my life, but I don't blame you for being a landlubber at heart. You have proven yourself to be a resourceful lad, so I don't doubt that you will find your way to Italy, with or without me.

"I'm certain that you will face some challenges along the way, for the world is full of thieves and cheats, so I advise you not to travel alone. Yet beware of bad company, for it's easy to be led astray, especially when you're young. Gambling and greed go hand in hand, so watch your back. Remember that your strength contains the seeds of your weakness, so your sharp mind can also harden your heart. I predict that by the time you get to Italy, you will be able to call yourself a man. But don't be in a rush to lose your innocence, or take advantage of the innocence of others, for experience can cloud your conscience if you're not careful. How I regret that I never had a son like you."

His kind words gave Will pause, for his jealousy of the captain and the Duchess seemed so petty. In his heart of hearts, he knew that he never had a chance of being her lover, so there was no reason for him to begrudge whatever happiness they had. Will also realized that he could never fall in love with a woman with something to hide. In that respect, he felt that he would always be a boy at heart. Even if the Bard tried to put his boyhood behind him as fast as he could.

~

Having never seen such peaks before, Will was astonished by the beauty of the Pyrenees. He soon discovered that by following along the foot of the mountains he couldn't get lost. All he had to do was to keep the Pyrenees on his right, taking the path of least resistance wherever possible. This sensible approach soon ran afoul, however, once he left the coast and headed inland, where he found himself in Basque country. Without knowing a single word of the language, and being unable to read any signs, he had to rely on the network of trails that ran through the mountains, guessing the best way to keep heading east.

Finding himself at a crossroads near the peak of La Rhune, he stopped to admire the view of the coast, with the beautiful port of St Jean-de-Luz below him. Seeing a priest coming from the Spanish side of the Pyrenees, Will was glad to find that he spoke French. "Excuse me father, for I'm trying to get to St Jean Pied-de-Port. Can you point me in the right direction?"

"God has smiled on you, for that is where I'm headed. I'm buying a donkey to travel through the mountains. Slower than a horse, but surefooted. I'm in no hurry, for I'm returning from a pilgrimage to Santiago, the high point of my life."

This struck Will as an odd thing to say, since the priest seemed so young. Indeed, Will would have guessed that he was a novitiate, as he had no beard. The priest also averted his eyes, often speaking with his back turned, as Will followed along like one of his sheep. Indeed, the priest's account of his pilgrimage did not pique Will's interest in such a journey. He observed that Catholics seem to enjoy suffering, but he didn't consider a blister a badge of honor. Nor did the priest have anything to tell about the food, which made his tale too Spartan for the Bard's taste.

Having to spend the night along the trail to St Jean Pied-de-Port, Will regretted that he hadn't brought more food. He had come to equate food with France, so he assumed that there would be places along the way to pick up some bread and cheese. He hadn't realized how sparsely populated the mountains were, especially in the Basque region, where people were hard pressed to eke out a living. So it seemed appropriate that Will's dinner consisted of some dry bread that Brother Jean had brought along, which he thought would go well with the Bayonne ham he had packed, but Will discovered that his guide didn't eat meat.

As he shared the dry bread, he regretted his decision to part company with Captain Montague, who was probably having ravioli again. Will soon found consolation when the wind began to blow, and he knew that the *Dragon* would be pounded by the Atlantic. While the hard ground kept him from sleeping well, he was in no danger of getting seasick. Instead, he was soaked by a deluge, reminding him that he faced a different set of hazards in the mountains. Just what he needed to become a man.

To his surprise, St Jean Pied-de-Port was full of pilgrims stocking up for their journey to Santiago, as it was their last opportunity to indulge themselves before crossing into Spain. From listening to Brother Jean, Will gathered that the pilgrimage wasn't supposed to be enjoyable, but was something to be endured. It occurred to him that he might be able to count his sea voyage as a pilgrimage, but he didn't dare ask if there was any such thing as a Protestant pilgrim. When Brother Jean told him that many pilgrims used donkeys to carry their belongings, that seemed self-indulgent to Will, but what did he know? Will had never even heard of Santiago before, nor the Way of St. James. Brother Jean took it upon himself to enlighten the Bard, providing an opportunity to fill an empty vessel.

Nonetheless, Will thought it odd that a priest avoided any contact with other men of the cloth. Indeed, Brother Jean seemed intent on finding a donkey until he discovered how expensive they were. He complained that the pilgrims had driven up the price, and told him that they would have to look elsewhere. While he wasn't eager to accompany the priest, Will recalled Captain Montague's advice about not traveling alone. So he agreed to go with Brother Jean to the next town of any size, Mauléon.

They hadn't gone far when a group of soldiers on horseback overtook them, demanding to know if they had seen any Spaniards. It was then that Will heard about Henri of Navarre. As Will was to learn, the king had created many enemies because of being a Protestant. Indeed, the region he now ruled had been a hotbed for Cathar heretics, igniting the Inquisition. The feud between Catholics and Protestants had continued to simmer, with Henri's little country surrounded by Catholics on all sides.

When the commanding officer demanded to know what they were doing in Navarre, Brother Jean spoke up as if he had rehearsed his answer. "I am on my way to the Cistercian monastery in Marciac to work in the vineyards. At the moment I am in need of a donkey, so if you can direct me, I would be much obliged."

The officer shot back, "You may find what you're looking for in St-Palais, just up ahead, but I hope you have money. Beggars are not welcome here, for everyone is expected to lend a hand. I should also warn you that the monastery is under guard, for the monks have provided refuge to imposters posing as pilgrims."

Turning to Will the soldier asked, "What do you have to say for yourself?" It did not seem like the right time to admit that he was a gambler, so Will explained that he was a merchant on his way to Italy, but his vague answer did not satisfy his inquisitor. "I'm glad to hear that you are just passing through Navarre, but what are you peddling?"

"The finest playing cards in the world, designed by Pierre Maréchal of Rennes," Will replied, starting to open his rucksack to show him a pack of cards.

"Wait," the officer commanded, dismounting from his horse. "Let me see for myself." Pulling out his valise with packs of cards, Will held them up to show the other soldiers. The officer said, "Looks as if we caught a gambler, but there's no harm in that. You have an honest face, lad, but I have my doubts about your companion."

As he stepped over to see what Brother Jean was carrying, the priest grabbed the officer by his shoulder and spun him around, holding a dagger to his throat. "If anybody moves, I'll slash his throat. Get off your horses, one at a time, and leave your weapons at the base of the tree."

Each of them slowly dismounted, putting down their swords. Brother Jean instructed Will to take the reins of a couple of the horses and to slap the rumps of the others, scaring them away. There was no way Will could refuse, and nothing he could say. He was afraid to break the spell, for he knew the soldiers could turn on them in a flash. Before they could do anything, Brother Jean told him to get on one of the horses, and to tie a rope around the officer's neck. Then the priest mounted the other horse, while Will held onto the rope, practically choking the officer, until Brother Jean got on the other horse. Slowly, they made their way along the trail, keeping an eye on the soldiers until they were out of sight. Dropping the rope, the priest let the officer go without saying anything, and took off on his horse. Will had half a mind to go his own way, but he was already compromised and didn't see any point in throwing himself on the mercy of the soldiers, who were madder than hornets.

It didn't take long to catch up with Brother Jean, for as a country boy, Will knew a thing or two about horses, and had picked the best one for himself. When the priest left the trail and headed for the mountains, the Bard never took his eyes off the priest. So imagine Will's surprise to find Brother Jean taking off his robe, revealing that he was actually a young woman.

Untying the scarf that held her tresses in place, she shook her long hair as if flaunting the fact that she had fooled him. "What are you looking at?" she demanded, as if Will had a choice. "I'm not an imposter, but a woman taking advantage of male privilege. Besides, I'm as dedicated as any monk. More so, in, fact, for no priest would dare take such revenge. God himself condones my quest, for his commandments do not apply to avenging angels." Will wanted to ask why she was telling him this, but he didn't want to interrupt her soliloquy.

"I'm following in the footsteps of Joan of Arc, eager to avenge her death. I have a bone to pick with Henri of Navarre, who has imposed Protestantism on his subjects, aligning himself with the Huguenots. His whole family is infected with heresy, beginning with his grandmother, who wrote sacrilegious books. Then there's his own mother, Jeanne, matron of the Troubadours, who sang the praises of profane love. She turned him into a two-faced monster by baptizing him a Catholic, then raising him a Protestant. Is it any wonder that he should have become such an opportunist?

"While he has distinguished himself on the battlefield, few know that he spends much of his spare time collecting butterflies. Though many people find such a despicable pastime innocuous, they ignore the fact that God's most beautiful creations are impaled on pins, shut between the pages of books, and displayed as trophies for all to see. Imagine what it must be like to be a butterfly, flitting from flower to flower in God's good time, spreading joy throughout Nature, only to lose your freedom and your life. And for what? That is the lesson I mean to teach King Henri. Are you with me, or against me?"

Will felt like a butterfly, trapped in a net. He saw no

way to escape except to play along, as he had done instinctively. When she had pulled her dagger on the officer, he didn't ask himself, whose side am I on? Having accompanied her on the journey so far, it seemed only natural to go the distance with her until they were pulled in different directions. Besides, he realized that as far as the soldiers were concerned, he and Brother Jean were two peas in a pod. Claiming that he didn't know he was traveling with a lunatic wouldn't hold water, especially when he acted as her accomplice. His best hope of getting out of the mess was to keep an eye on her, before she had a chance to carry out her mission.

Indeed, it was hard not to stare at Rose, whose beauty was only matched by her thorny nature, for she was as contrary as a shrew. Barking orders at the Bard, she insisted that he scatter the horses as they crossed a river. "They will be of little use to us in the mountains, and will leave a trail that's easily followed. We will follow the riverbed until we're well clear of any paths. Stealth will be our salvation. If we run into anyone, let me do the talking. Your English accent will raise too many questions. I shall say you are my mute brother, soft in the head."

It seemed to Will that mute would have sufficed, but he knew she must have some reason for painting him as an idiot, for all of her actions seemed calculated. Clearly, she didn't invite him along for company, but to use him for some nefarious purpose. He knew that if he didn't play along, she could turn on him in an instant, as he'd seen her do with the officer. So he needed to keep his wits about him, and vowed to watch every card she played. Sooner or later, she would make a mistake, and he would seize his chance. Yet Will found her intensity compelling, and he was eager to see her next move.

He hadn't traveled at night before, so Will was not prepared to walk through the forest in darkness. He was surprised how well his eyes adjusted, as if he were tapping into an animal instinct, but it was his hearing that he found to be most useful. By listening to the sound of the river, they could stay close to it, without having to scramble over rocks or getting their feet wet. The quiet also reminded him to stay in character as a mute, using only his hands to communicate with Rose. She insisted on following him, forcing Will to find the way rather than relying on her.

She didn't have to tell him to keep climbing, because Will knew she was seeking the safety of the mountains. It was the only place they could elude the soldiers, who would be scouring the countryside. But they were looking for two young men, not knowing that one of them was an imposter, who could have easily shed his disguise as a monk. Nonetheless, the possibility that one of them was a woman would never occur to the soldiers. Even if it did, they would never admit to anyone that a woman had disarmed them.

The Irati Forest turned out to be a great place to hide, for the vast tract of beech trees was practically uninhabited. Yet he might as well have been lost, for Will had no idea where they were or where they were going, except up. So when they finally reached the summit of the mountain, he discovered that they had almost crossed the border into Spain. There were no signs, of course, just a pile of stones to mark the border, but Rose obviously knew where she was going.

"We need to get some sleep before dawn, because we still have a long way to go. I will explain what you need to know in the morning. Do not even think of escaping while I'm sleeping. You are now a wanted man, and without my help you will easily be caught."

With those comforting words Rose disappeared into the mist which was blowing across the mountain, obscuring the sky so that Will was utterly disoriented. He wasn't even tempted to escape, but found a clearing where he could try to grab some sleep. Piling up some leaves, he made himself a bed as the mist swirled about him. As bewildered as he was by this turn of events, Will was glad to be on solid ground. His encounter with the Duchess seemed like a dream to him, and he regretted that he hadn't asked her to tell his fortune. Just as well, he thought, as he drifted off into a dreamless sleep.

Will was awakened by a thunderclap, as the cloud in which he found himself unleashed a torrent of rain. He wrapped himself in his blanket and sought cover underneath a large beech tree, but the rain was relentless. It wouldn't take long for his wool blanket to get soaked, so he knew he had to seek shelter. Without any idea where Rose had gone, he wasn't about to wait for her to boss him around. If nothing else, he needed to get moving, to stay warm until he could find someplace to get out of the rain. Figuring that there would be less rain on the Spanish side, he crossed the border, hoping to find an overhanging rock or shepherd's refuge as he descended the mountain.

Spotting a tree downed by the storm, he broke off a branch to make himself a staff. He knew that going downhill would be hard on his knees, and he wanted to have something to defend himself with. Having seen Rose brandish her dagger, he had no doubt that she had him at a disadvantage, but a sturdy stick would even the odds. Although Will knew that she could have killed him by now if she had wanted to, she needed an accomplice. For what, he didn't have a clue, but she was obviously a dangerous woman. Not only did she have God on her side, but she was bent on avenging one of his innocent creatures.

"Do you really think that stick will protect you?" she asked, coming up behind him. "I could have killed you while you were sleeping." With that, Rose threw her dagger at a tree near him, making Will recoil before he even had a chance to raise his staff. She pulled the blade out of the wood and put in her belt. "So where did you think you were going?"

She dismissed his explanation with contempt. "Even you must know that the Spanish have no love for the English, so what do you think they would do with you?

Imprison you, in the hope of gaining ransom. Anyone who has managed to come so far obviously has means, whether your family is rich or not. The fact that you're a Protestant certainly wouldn't help your case, for the Pope has declared open season on heretics. With God's blessing, I shall find a way to send Henri to hell, where he can join the rest of his family."

Rose seemed to have overlooked Christ's teachings about turning the other cheek, but Will didn't want to say anything that might rile her, so he held his tongue. Like a schoolboy who knows he's at the mercy of the headmaster, he waited to see what she had in store for him. "We need to find a place to hide until Henri passes through the mountains again, for he won't be able to stay away from his mistress for long. He fancies himself a ladies' man, which gives me one more way to get to him. But I need another lure. Let's see what God has in store for us."

Will didn't like the sound of this, for it implied that their fates were intertwined. Taking advantage of the fact that Rose spoke Spanish, they headed east along the border, ready to escape from Henri's soldiers if necessary. She didn't say much, but he'd played cards long enough to recognize a gambit when he saw one. Rose was hedging her bet, throwing in with the Spanish if it suited her, but trying to find a way to get within striking distance of Henri. That would never happen with any Spanish forces around, for Henri was pushing his luck by having a lover in Aragon.

Will knew that God moves in mysterious ways, but he was surprised to stumble upon a couple of donkeys, as if in answer to Rose's prayers. As they climbed higher in the Pyrenees they passed the timberline, finding themselves on a plateau perfect for foraging. Though covered in snow during the winter, the area turned green in late spring, when shepherds on both sides of the border took advantage of the abundant grass to feed their flocks. Rose and Will found themselves in a kind of no-man's land, where the border was anyone's guess. Attempts to mark the boundary with stones or signs were useless, as snow and ice undid human efforts to claim territory. Likewise, the few caves and man-made shelters that survived Mother Nature's tempests didn't belong to anyone. Whoever got there first had an unwritten claim to refuge.

In that respect Rose was not surprised to find a flock of sheep so high up in the mountains, but seemed to take it as a sign. Though challenged by the shepherd's Great Pyrenees, Rose managed to hail him by waving her red scarf. Will had expected a grizzled old man, so he was amazed to see that the shepherd was quite young. He thought to himself, 'Here's another job I could do without anyone looking over my shoulder.' But the thought of living in the mountains quickly wore off when it began to get dark, and Will realized what a lonely life a shepherd leads.

Indeed, the Basque shepherd, with a name Will couldn't pronounce, seemed quite happy to have company. Although the Bard couldn't understand much of what was said, Rose was able to carry on a conversation with the young man, managing to acquire a couple of donkeys that he used to carry supplies. Will suspected that he was a smuggler, trying to pull the wool over their eyes, but we all know that Shakespeare had an overactive imagination. While the shepherd didn't have any use for money, he was glad to barter the donkeys for a silver necklace that she wore around her neck, biting the silver with his teeth to test its quality. Will was surprised that she wasn't wearing a St. Christopher's medal, but she clearly was not a conventional Christian.

The long climb through the Pyrenees had whetted Will's appetite, but he was well aware that they had brought little to eat, so he was delighted when the shepherd started a fire to cook some lamb. Will said it was the best mutton he'd ever tasted, fresh from the shepherd's flock and simply grilled over coals. He fried potatoes in the fat, which they also used to dip their bread, washed down with good Spanish wine. The prospect of being a shepherd began to appeal to Will again, but he knew their host spent most of his nights alone. A solitary life was not for the young Shakespeare, having just begun his awakening.

Nonetheless, the prospect of romance seemed distant to him in the mountains, despite Rose's presence. Well aware of the company of two men, she took her belongings well away from them, along with the two donkeys. Will supposed that she wanted to ensure that he wouldn't slip away in the middle of the night, but such a precaution was unnecessary. He would have been lost on his own, and he was curious to see what she was up to. Did she really think she could kill the King of Navarre and get away with it, or was she prepared to be a martyr like Joan of Arc? In either case, Will didn't want to get involved with a mad woman. Yet here he was, further from Stratford-upon-Avon than even the Bard could have imagined.

In the middle of the night, he was awakened by the braying of one of the donkeys. There was no way he was going to see what all the commotion was about, because Rose was clearly dangerous, so he called out to her. In response he heard her laughing. "I didn't know donkeys had dreams," she said, as if some mystery of the universe had been revealed to her. "Go back to sleep. We have a long day ahead of us." That sounded ominous to him, and he wondered what she would do if he refused to go. Will doubted if she would kill him in front of a witness, but all she had to do was wait for him until he tried to escape. Such thoughts filled his head as he tried to get back to sleep, but he spent much of the night watching the stars. He thought to himself: 'Whatever happens, it was worth it just to see the heavens. We don't have stars like this in England.'

In the morning he awoke to find that the shepherd had already moved his flock, barely visible in the distance. Rose was busy reviving the campfire, burning sheep dung, as there was no wood to be found. The earthy smell didn't bother him, as a breeze carried the smoke away. With a commanding view of the magnificent countryside, Will was well aware that he was in a different country. Not only was the landscape more dramatic, but everything about the place seemed larger than life. He was the only thing that hadn't changed in scale.

Watching Rose stoke the fire, Will was mindful that he was at the mercy of a complete stranger, who could turn on him at any second. Yet he found himself emboldened by the suspense, breaking the spell by confronting her. "There must be some good reason for bringing me along. I think you owe me an explanation."

"I owe nothing to any man, including my father, who abandoned my mother before I was born. It is just as well, for I answer to no one, free to live as I please. If you must know, I saw something about you that intrigued me, but I was not looking for an accomplice. What I am bound to do is my choice alone. I don't need your help. On the contrary, I can help you grow up, for you are as innocent as a lamb being led to slaughter. I have enough guile for both us. You call yourself a gambler, but you know nothing about taking risks. You could learn a great deal from me, but only if you're willing to put your life on the line."

What she said made complete sense to him, except that he knew he was dealing with someone who was insane. Moreover, what seemed like a heart-felt invitation revealed nothing about her plans. Although he knew she had it in for Henri of Navarre, it was clear that she considered the King to be a pawn, caught up in a web of heresy rooted in the past. Killing him would do little to untangle the family history that put a Protestant on the throne in the midst of a religious war. It seemed to him that converting Henri would be a coup worthy of a woman like Rose.

As if reading Will's thoughts, she began to enlighten him. "God has not seen fit to reveal his plan for me, but I know that I will understand my mission when I look Henri in the eye. That is almost impossible for a woman on her own, let alone a man. The King is closely guarded, for good reason, and Henri isn't an innocent like you. Indeed, he is as slippery as the devil, which I would cast out of him if I could. For it is not the man I loathe, but what he stands for. I do not blame the centurions for slaying Christ, for they knew not what they did.

"Henri has an ally in your Queen, though she seems suspicious of him, despite being professed Protestants. My hunch is that he would be glad to meet one of her countrymen, particularly a lad with an open face and a gambler's verve. Let me see your deck of cards."

He retrieved a deck of cards from his rucksack and handed it to her. She fanned a handful of cards with a flourish, with the same swiftness she had shown with a dagger. "They are handsome cards, I will give you that, but the face cards lack distinction. The king and queen appear regal, but resemble no one. I suppose they are meant to be universal, so you can use them anywhere. But I expect that Henri would be glad to see his face in every deck of cards in Navarre, and France for that matter, but that might provoke a war. What better way to get close to him than to appeal to his vanity?"

Will was in awe of watching her mind at work, just as he was to see her brandish her dagger. Seeing the deck of cards, she quickly pictured Henri's face, perhaps because she was obsessed with him. Yet her sudden inspiration amazed the Bard. Why didn't I think of that? Not only did she realize that Henri would be unable to resist her idea, but she must have grasped that he would be drawn into her scheme as well.

From Will's perspective, her stroke of genius was a boon to him at the same time. Here was an opportunity to prove that Maréchal's trust in him was well founded. With cards tailored to Henri's kingdom, they could corner the market in Navarre. Though it seemed a pity that Henri's domain was so limited, at the moment it seemed like the chance of a lifetime. Little did the Bard know that Henri was destined to be King of France.

While Will realized that Rose had presented this opportunity on a silver plate, she had neglected the details, like a lot of bold thinkers. She was also mad, of course, but that also seemed like a minor detail. He hesitated to bring her back to reality, but he couldn't help asking the obvious question. "An inspired idea, Rose, but where are we going to find a picture of Henri?"

"You're obviously a foreigner, with little knowledge of French history. Monarchs invariably have multiple artists paint their picture, ostensibly for posterity, but actually to remind themselves and their subjects of the divine right of kings and queens. You'd be surprised how much time monarchs spend siting for portraits, but what else do they have to do? In this case, I have no portraits to show him, but he is bound to be impressed by my drawings of butterflies. Once he has seen my artistry, he won't be able to resist my offer to paint him. On second thought, I'll let him come up with the idea on his own. I'll turn his vanity to my advantage."

Will was fascinated to see how her mind worked, but he wondered if Henri would be so easily taken in. He was known for his cunning on the battlefield, so Will suspected that Rose had underestimated him. Knowing that their paths would soon cross, the Bard realized that he needed to escape before this mad woman drew him any deeper into her plot. Yet he found himself being drawn into the flame like a moth, unable to resist the light.

To her credit, Rose laid her trap well, finding a place along the trail through the mountains that Henri's entourage would have to pass through along the border, near Lescun, in the Vallée d'Aspe. As the trail followed along the river, Rose picked a place where she knew there would be butterflies, in a meadow where she had spent a great deal of time drawing them. Rather than just pretending to draw, she set up her easel in a place that overlooked the valley, giving her time to see Henri coming down the trail.

To ensure that she was ready to intercept him, she had Will stationed on a hill above the meadow. By this time he'd resolved to play along, partly because he knew that she wasn't going to risk assassinating him in front of witnesses, but also because he was curious to see what Henri would do when confronted with a dangerous, but beautiful woman. In effect, Will had placed his wager on her, but he wasn't sure what he had to gain.

It occurred to him that Rose's plan could easily have gone awry if the weather turned bad, because thunderstorms and squalls in the mountains were quite common. But it could not have been a more beautiful day in the Pyrenees, so when he saw Henri's party coming down the trail, Will headed down the hill as quickly as he could on his donkey. He had half a mind to shout, but restrained himself, fearing he might scare away the dozens of butterflies gathered on the meadow, flitting between the wildflowers.

Once he had caught Rose's attention, he wasn't sure what to do, so he quickly retraced his steps to make sure he didn't get in the way. Will didn't want her to have to explain his presence, and he feared that the soldiers were still looking for them, so he wanted to make himself scarce. Nonetheless, he was dying to see Rose in action, in what he imagined would be a kind of mating dance orchestrated by a black widow. Unfortunately, he was too far away to hear anything, so all he could do was watch the action unfold from a distance.

Two soldiers arrived on horseback as the advance guard, but took little notice of Rose, who must have appeared harmless as a plein air painter. Little did they know how dangerous she was. However, Will quickly realized that he must have looked out of place, sitting aside his donkey on top of a hill. As the cavaliers charged up the slope, he dismounted, trying to think of a good excuse for being there. He was especially proud of himself for his quick wittedness, picking a handful of flowers which he could pretend were for the artist he admired from afar.

As soon as he saw the faces of the soldiers, Will dropped his bouquet, for he recognized the officer who has accosted them. The recognition was mutual. "You're under arrest," he said, grabbing the Bard by the collar. "Stealing a horse is a capital offense in Navarre, so start saying your prayers. Now tell me what happened to the imposter. Your cooperation is the only thing that can save you."

The worst of it was that he couldn't see what was happening with Rose and Henri. The officer held Will's arm behind his back, applying pressure to make him talk. If Rose seized the opportunity to kill Henri while he was within striking distance, Will was going to miss the whole scene. Given her skill with a dagger, he knew that she could kill the king in a heartbeat. The Bard's only hope was that she would take her sweet time. He'd seen a terrier toy with a rabbit before slaughtering it, reveling in hearing its mournful squeak. Will was certain that Rose would be even more merciless.

"We went separate ways to avoid you," he said. "We were supposed to meet here, but I have no idea where he's gone." The officer increased the pressure on Will's arm until he thought it was going to break. To his credit, he didn't tell the truth, partly because he didn't think the officer would believe him, but also because Will didn't want to betray Rose. Why, he wasn't sure, for she was the one who put him in such a predicament. The officer seemed to know that he was wasting his breath, so he tied Will onto his donkey facing backwards, which he gathered was the local custom for treating criminals.

As they descended the hill, he finally caught sight of Henri standing next to Rose, evidently admiring her painting. Even from a distance, the king cut an impressive figure, tall and handsomely dressed in an azure jacket. Will realized that the officer had actually done him a favor by turning him backwards, and he thanked heaven for the turn of events. Seeing the king's bodyguard retreating to spit over the wall, he realized that Rose had a golden opportunity to slay the king on the spot. The Bard could almost see the look of surprise on Henri's face when she raised her dagger—but she must have decided to play the long game. She was going to disarm him slowly, biding her time to pounce when she was good and ready.

The officer was clever enough to refrain from spoiling Henri's pleasure by parading the horse thief he had apprehended, so he turned Will over to a soldier at the back of the pack. That ruined Will's view, of course, and he would have done anything to have heard the conversation between Rose and Henri, but that was not to be. He took small consolation in being able to get a glimpse of Rose resuming her painting, as Henri's retinue headed down the trail towards Pau. She didn't bother to look up, and Will still wasn't sure if she had forgotten all about him, or was trying to pretend that they'd never met. He confessed to some ambivalence, for he wouldn't have been in this predicament without her, but he would remember her for the rest of his life, short as it looked to be.

CHAPTER 5

As they entered the city of Pau, Will couldn't help being
surprised by how small it seemed. He thought to himself,
'Henri deserves a larger stage.' Though he hadn't even met
the man, Will sensed that he was destined for greatness. In
that respect, Henri's chateau seemed shabby, but the Bard
arrived at the back of the building, after having to run a
gauntlet of schoolboys while passing through the city gate.
A couple of the boys threw rocks at him, laughing at his
absurd situation on the back of the donkey. Will thought
to himself, 'How cruel boys are to one another, when they
should stick together. C'est la vie.'

When the prison guard confiscated his possessions,
Will knew there was no point in resisting, so he said
goodbye to his donkey, Daisy, and followed the steps
down into the dungeon. Each step took him deeper into
the bowels of the chateau, hewn out of stone by the
prisoners who preceded him. How he wished that he knew
their stories, for the setting seemed ripe for tragic tales. He
promised himself that he would try to learn the fate of his
comrades, if he somehow got out alive. How he wished
that he had even a crust of bread, because Will knew he'd
be lucky to get a cup of weak soup. It was one of those
times when growing up in England prepared him for
adversity. He pitied his French peers, who weren't used to
boiled turnips.

Will only mentioned turnips because that's all he had to

eat. Day after day. Unwashed, unpeeled, unappetizing, to say the least. However, he had to admit that it could have been worse, for he had a cell to himself, without having to listen to some foul-mouthed criminal talk his ear off.

While Will wouldn't have called it a window, some light appeared in a slit outside of his door, so he could at least tell day from night. Otherwise, he might have gone berserk. By the seventh day he recalled that God had created the entire world in the same amount of time, so Will was deeply disappointed that so little had happened to him. Not even any temptations. However, it occurred to him that the powers-at-be might just have forgotten about him, which meant he could live a little longer. Cold consolation.

As far as he could tell, Will was the only prisoner, so he couldn't see any reason why he hadn't been charged with anything. He doubted that complaining would make things any better, so he bided his time. He would have given anything for a scrap of paper and a piece of charcoal, so he could at least write to pass the hours. He might have mustered the courage to ask for paper if he had ever seen a guard, but the Bard seem to have been abandoned.

They must have waited until he was asleep before shoving a bowl of cold soup under his door, because he heard next to nothing. From time to time, he thought he heard someone coughing, but the tell-tale sign that he wasn't alone was the sound of snoring. How anyone could sleep so well in such a dismal place, with rats scurrying everywhere, was beyond even Will's imagination.

Unable to write or talk with anyone, he began to make up stories about his predecessors, until he had the chilling thought that there were none. Someone had to be the first person ever imprisoned in Pau. Perhaps he was the first. Although the city struck him as a backwater, it seemed hard to believe that there was no criminal activity, unless criminals were simply dispatched, rather than imprisoned. It seemed reasonable to Will that Henri didn't want to waste any space in his modest chateau for a prison. But it didn't seem fair that someone so harmless as himself was in jail, while a madwoman like Rose was running loose.

As you can imagine, he was relieved when the door to his cell was unlocked and a guard appeared. "Come with me," he said in English, so Will knew that someone had deduced his nationality. He was annoyed, of course, because he had anticipated that he could use his time in prison to practice his French. So speaking to him in English seemed like a slap in the face. As he climbed the stone steps Will counted them in French, out of spite, just to demonstrate how much he had already learned. Fortunately, they arrived on the ground floor before he reached a hundred, because he wasn't sure that the French simply started over again with two hundred; they had their own logic.

The guard blindfolded him before leading Will across a courtyard, and he feared that he was going to be shot without a trial. But he was whisked into an entrance at the back of the chateau, if you can even call it that, because it was just a huge, sprawling house. Although the blindfold was removed, his hands were still tied behind his back, and he was afraid that he was going to be hanged without being able to say a thing.

A distinguished middle-aged man who Will took to be a magistrate spoke to him. "You have been charged with resisting arrest, stealing a horse and concealing the identity of your accomplice. What do you have to say for yourself?" He spoke quickly in French, so that's what Will thought he said. He replied, "I fell into bad company, your honor, hoodwinked by what I thought was a priest."

"Another variation on the devil made me do it, but do you deny stealing a horse? Let me remind you that we have several witnesses who saw you ride off."

"Your honor, I admit that I borrowed a horse, but I never had any intention of keeping it. I would chalk it up to youthful folly, having been misled by an imposter."

"Nonsense," the magistrate replied. "You did nothing to stop your partner from assaulting an officer, stealing a horse, and evading the King's guards. I have sentenced men to death for less."

Will replied, "I'm sure you have, your honor, but what a waste of life to condemn me for a simple mistake of judgment. I came here with a business proposition that could benefit the King." When he explained his idea for putting the king's likeness on decks of cards, the magistrate seemed to have second thoughts.

"What proof do you have that you work for a maker of cards?"

"All of my belongings were confiscated when I was arrested, but I am certain that my employer would vouch for me. However, I need to consult with him about producing cards, so I request an audience with the king."

The man countered, "I'll give you credit for daring, but you have already admitted that your judgment is questionable. If the king is willing to hear you out, then you have a prayer of being saved. If not, I see no reason for providing you with free food and lodging. It's been awhile since the citizens of Pau have seen a hanging, so an Englishman might tickle their fancy."

Having had a brief taste of freedom, it was doubly hard for Will to return to his cell. He broke into tears when the door was locked behind him. The only thing he had to look forward to was more watery soup. Death seemed more palatable. He thought to himself, 'If there is an afterlife, surely the food will be better than in prison or England. If there is only oblivion, at least I won't have to suffer any longer.' Finding himself plunged into a depression, he was startled to hear the door being unlocked. This time the guard didn't bother saying anything, but dragged him from his cell.

Remaining behind him, the guard prodded him up several flights of stairs, leaving Will winded. Having been confined so long, he had lost any muscle tone and found it difficult just to walk. When he finally emerged from the staircase, he was almost blinded by the sunshine. After being in the dark so long, the bright light was painful to his eyes. He followed the guard along the ramparts of the chateau, which had a commanding view of the Pyrenees. While the chateau itself was nothing to look at, the view was magnificent, and he began to understand why the kings of Navarre had picked the spot. In addition to being beautiful, it provided sweeping views of the countryside, lending it strategic importance. Henri was a shrewd man.

Indeed, Will was startled to see the king making his way towards him, as if he were inspecting the premises, accompanied by a couple of guards. As they approached, the guard told him to kneel. Will was afraid that the guard was going to kill him right there, perhaps to amuse the king, but he obeyed the order. Will heard Henri say to the guards. "Leave us. He is a mere boy. Stand up, young man, so I can look you in the eye." Will thought to himself, 'They don't call him Good King Henri for nothing.'

As he stood up, Will was surprised to see that Henri was such a rugged, athletic looking man. Having seen him from a distance, the Bard knew that he was a large man, but he was truly larger than life. If ever there was a man who looked the part of a king, it was Henri. There was a magnetism about him which was utterly compelling. Had he asked Will to jump off the wall of his chateau, he might have done so, because the king exuded authority. While he did nothing to intimidate him, Will was simply awed by his presence. Which left the Bard practically speechless. Not a good sign for a budding playwright. All he could do was say, "I am honored to meet you, your highness."

"You should be, for I hold your life in my hands. I'm not interested in your petty crimes, so do not plead for mercy. I'm only here to discuss business, so tell me what you propose."

To Will's relief and surprise, Henri seemed receptive to

the idea of having his picture on playing cards, so the Bard saw no reason to tell him that he had borrowed the idea from Rose. That would have meant admitting that he had met her, which would have belied his claim that he didn't know her. He was already in enough trouble as it was.

Henri said, "At it happens, I have just commissioned an artist to paint my portrait, so your timing is remarkable. Naturally, I shall expect a commission for using my likeness, so I need to know what your employer can offer."

When Will assured him that he would contact Maréchal right away, the king put the matter aside, and surprised the Bard by mentioning Queen Elizabeth. "A little bird told me that your queen is fond of theatre and is endeavoring to make London a beacon in the darkness. I have long thought that it was just a matter of time before theatre came into its own. In this time of plague and despair the people need make-believe more than ever. Most people outgrow their imaginations when they become adults, but I never have. Being a king is a lot more work than most people think it is, which is why make-believe is my refuge."

While Will found Henri's musings interesting, he wanted to ask, "But what has this got to do with me?" However, he soon discovered that the king needed little prompting, and seemed to enjoy hearing himself talk. "As you are not yet a man, I have some hope that you are still capable of flights of fancy. More to the point, I intend to capitalize on Queen Elizabeth's passion for theatre for my own purposes. The kingdom of Navarre is virtually unknown to the world, nor have my exploits received the attention they deserve. I'm ready to step onto the world stage. For that, I need someone who knows English to chronicle my life. You have already demonstrated your daring and imagination. The question is, can you write?"

Will took his cue, "Look no further for your scribe, your highness, for I can spin tales out of thin air, so imagine what I can do with the stories of such a monarch as you are, your eminence, a king among kings. 'Tis true that you are not well known in England, where envy of France continues to blind the citizens to the paradise across the channel. Were they to admit that the cuisine, wine, weather and women are vastly superior in the Kingdom of Navarre, the English would descend upon your country like rats from a ship. I must confess that I am a remarkably gifted gambler for someone my age, or any age if I may say so, but only because it affords me the opportunity to study human nature. An oxymoron if there ever was one, for our species defies nature."

Henri replied, "Very astute, young man, but you haven't answered my question. Are you a gambler or a writer? I know that you can bluff, but can you look me in the eye and tell me you can write?"

Will replied, "Honestly, I have all the makings of a writer, but I haven't had time to bear fruit. I have written and acted out some stories for young ladies, who told me I had a knack for nonsense, but that doesn't mean I can do justice to a king of your stature. Having seen players enact skits to please a ship's captain, I must admit that I thought I could do better. I know not where my confidence comes from, but I note that many politicians believe themselves to be leaders without the slightest evidence. All I can say is: put me to the test. Give me a challenge, so we can both find out if I'm a writer or not."

Even Will was impressed by his own boldness, but you'd be surprised what one is capable of when staring death in the face. At this point, he had nothing to lose, since Henri had good reason to champion his success. The king clearly needed someone to help him realize his ambitions, and here Will was, a native speaker of English with enough wit to gamble for a living, and a gift for embellishing the truth. The part was practically written for him. So when Henri gave him seven days to write a short play to entertain his court, the Bard counted himself lucky to survive another week.

What saved him was his genuine admiration for Henri,

who seemed like an older brother to him. How many kings would have bothered with a young horse thief, especially a man who wanted to make his mark on the world? Had Will been a young maiden, he might have caught the King's attention, but the Bard was not even a pawn on the board. He resolved to return Henri's good will by warning him about Rose. But how could he reveal her murderous plot without stabbing her in the back? It came to the Bard that his play must be like a dream, merely hinting at the truth, as he had learned from Cervantes. As you can see from his attempt, Will tried to warn Henri without giving Rose away.

Winged Victory

Scene 1. A meadow.

Violet, a beautiful young woman, is walking through the countryside when she comes upon a wishing well. Reaching into the pocket of her lovely dress, she pulls out a coin.

VIOLET
How I would love to be a butterfly
If only for an hour
Flitting between flowers
Gathering pollen on my wings
Sharing my bounty with the world

As she drops the coin into the fountain, the splash echoes, and she is transformed into a butterfly.

Scene 2. Same.

Antoine, a nobleman, is walking through the meadow when he sees a beautiful butterfly among the wildflowers. Using the net that he is carrying, he sneaks up on the butterfly and deftly catches it, before putting it in a jar.

Scene 3. Antoine's drawing room.

Taking the butterfly out of the jar, Antoine carefully places it on a corkboard and puts a pin in its wing. As he is about to impale the butterfly, it suddenly morphs into Violet, whose hour is up. Looking around the room she spots crossed dueling foils above the fireplace.

VIOLET *(grabbing one of the swords)*
En garde.

The startled nobleman grabs the other foil and turns to defend himself.

ANTOINE
You have me at a disadvantage, mademoiselle,
For I do not recognize you
Nor am I aware of my fault,
If I have given any.

VIOLET
How can you protest?
When you have deprived me of my freedom
And were about to take my life
For what is to you mere sport.

Offended by her charge, Antoine attacks her in earnest, drawing blood on her shoulder.

ANTOINE
Touché, mademoiselle.
Admit that you are beaten.

Touching the blood on her shoulder, Violet finds a fury in herself that she didn't know she possessed. Charging him with lightning speed, she disarms him, his sword clattering on the floor.

ANTOINE *(continued)*

I am at your mercy, mademoiselle.
You might as well kill me,
For I cannot bear the shame
Of losing to a woman.

VIOLET

All the more reason for me to spare you.
You need to ask yourself why you are so surprised
To discover that you met your match in a woman.
What a fool you are
For failing to see your destiny in front of you.
If you miss your destiny
You meet your fate.

With that, she slashes his face with her sword, scarring him for life.

~

Will knew there was no point in offering to play the part of Antoine, because he couldn't be trusted with a sword with Henri present; he felt fortunate to be seated in the audience, flanked by two guards. "I doubt if any playwright has awaited the reaction of the audience as much as I did, but suffice it to say that I had butterflies in my stomach." Indeed, the moment he saw Rose enter the chamber, he knew that he faced danger on all sides. Had she seized the opportunity to kill the king in dramatic fashion with so many witnesses, Will had no doubt he would be implicated. And if Henri was disappointed in his effort, he could be dispatched with a wave of his hand.

In that respect, no one in the room was more eager to see the two actors succeed than Will was. So he was pleased that the woman who portrayed Violet was not only lovely, but lithe. Just the way she moved made her credible as a match for Antoine during the fight scene. Indeed, the Bard was so riveted by her performance that he barely looked at Rose, who never made eye contact. He felt certain that she could have withered him with a look, deadly as a dagger, but her attention was focused on Henri. Yet seeing her watching him so closely, Will thought he detected a change in her demeanor. Not the hatred that he expected, but an attraction that defied her intentions.

In truth, the change in her demeanor was too subtle for him to observe, so it must have been intuition that prompted him. Yet his hunch was borne out by Rose's portrait of Henri, which, if anything, flattered the king. Somehow she had captured the virility of the man, who looked as if he could have stepped off the canvas and engaged the viewer in conversation. 'How did she do it?' he asked himself, because there was no hint of the malice the Bard knew she bore him. Looking closely at the painting, he was struck by the slyness in Henri's eye, so different than the usual vapid look in a portrait. The chemistry between the subject and the artist was undeniable.

Will obviously survived his ordeal, which proved to be a rite of passage for him, setting the Bard on a course that changed his life. Henri seemed to relish taking his time to render his verdict, perhaps because he sensed there was a grain of truth in it. He couldn't have missed the connection to Rose, yet he said little about the piece itself. "I confess that I expected lighter fare from you, as a comedy might have been more entertaining. Yet you managed to rivet the audience with your pointed melodrama. Obviously you're still green, but you show more promise as writer than a horse thief. I'll have a word with the magistrate."

That was Will's reprieve, which he took as a gift from God, though he didn't consider himself religious. Dogma left him cold. Perhaps he was simply thankful, but he needed to address his thanks to someone. He knew that he didn't deserve credit for his good fortune, but he didn't blame himself for his mistake. Rose turned out to be a blessing in disguise, quite literally. True, she had almost cost him his life, but the Bard would never have met Henri if he hadn't fallen under her spell. Ironically, she continued to act as if they had never met, disappearing after his play without giving the slightest indication of her reaction.

When no one came to take him back to prison, Will had half a mind to escape before Henri changed his mind, but such thoughts vanished as soon as Marie, the woman who played Violet, complimented the Bard on his play. "How is it that someone so young could write such a powerful work? Surely you must have borrowed the story, which sounds like something out of a legend."

Will responded, "I would like to tell you that I just made it up, but the idea just came to me, like a melody for a musician. I just pulled it out of the air."

"Your modesty becomes you, young man, and I hope you retain your innocence as long as possible. In my experience, most men are full of themselves. I find you refreshing, and I wish I were closer to your age. Hang onto your youth, which will be gone before you know it."

"Surely you are not serious, mademoiselle, for there's not a wrinkle on your face. Nor would I dare to face you in combat, for your reflexes are remarkable. You have no idea what it was like for me to see you bring my play to life with such zeal."

Thus began a torrid affair that swept away what little innocence Will had left, for he soon discovered the reason actors love being on stage: they need someone to put words in their mouth. While many people envy actors for their good looks and self-confidence, these gifts are offset by the kind of shallowness that one finds at a beach. The warm water draws you into the sea, but you quickly find yourself pummeled by waves and caught in an undertow. Appearances are deceiving, especially when it comes to actors who often lack any depth of character.

In that respect, Marie's conversational gambit took him in like the neophyte he was at age sixteen. Her compliment overcame any reservation he had about getting involved with an older woman. What he didn't realize at the time was how little they had to talk about. Yet she was perfectly happy to teach the Bard how to please her, which had little to do with language. She had already memorized enough dialogue to last most people a lifetime, so when she ran out of original material, she recited whatever came into her head. As she seemed to think that nothing excited Will more than hearing her speak his words, he heard Violet's part ad nauseam. Like Antoine, he was scarred for life.

Thanks to Henri's generosity, Will was provided with food and lodging, albeit modestly, as he was treated as one of the servants. While such accommodation made it difficult for him to carry on with Marie, she had her own apartment near the east gate of the city. He enjoyed her view of the moat, but it was a reminder that the world was a dangerous place. He preferred the security of Henri's chateau, where he was treated with the kind of ambivalence most people have toward writers. Unfortunately, his good fortune did not go unnoticed by the officer who arrested him, Lieutenant Adolphe, who became the Bard's first enemy. He persisted in calling Will the king's "pet monkey," doing everything in his power to harass him.

As you can imagine, Adolphe was especially perturbed by Will's liaison with Marie, who had no business consorting with a peasant, let alone a horse thief. Any success Will had only made matters worse, as he discovered when Adolphe heard about his card scheme. According to Marie's sources, Adolphe even requested a private audience with the king to try to dissuade him from having his portrait used by "mercenaries." However, he underestimated the king's vanity and business acumen.

Nonetheless, because of Adolphe's objections, Henri didn't entrust Will to go see Maréchal on his own, so he had to send a copy of the portrait along with a letter, detailing his proposal. Will complained that writing the letter proved to be much more challenging than writing a play. It would have been so much simpler to talk with Maréchal in person. However, when Will thought about all of the trials and tribulations of travel, he realized that he was better off learning about lovemaking from Marie, who seemed to enjoy breaking him in. "You're not a stallion, yet, my darling, but you have good instincts."

While Will waited for Maréchal's response he began gambling in earnest, for he was practically destitute. Even though he had a roof over his head and could count on the king's hospitality for his meals, he needed spending money, for Marie was fond of eating in fancy places. She seemed to enjoy teaching him about the finer things in life, and he soon developed a taste for the kind of gourmet cuisine that doesn't even exist in England. Just learning to use the right silverware was almost as hard as mastering conjugations.

Unfortunately, Pau was a pretty small place, so Will's reputation as a gambler made it difficult for him to take advantage of his youthful appearance to fool anyone. Indeed, Adolphe's reference to him as the king's pet monkey caught on among the soldiers in the garrison, probably because they envied his position as a kept man. Being a playwright is a questionable occupation in the best of times, and all he had to his credit was a playlet. He knew that he needed to write something with more substance in order to make his mark on the world, but he also understood that gaining more life experience was his only hope for becoming a real writer.

While Will wouldn't say that Marie became his muse, he could tell that she was counting on him to write something with a role for her. Truth be told, they had run out of things to talk about, and even their lovemaking was starting to seem repetitive. He wanted to create a story that would put her boundless energy to good use. The answer came to him in a flash. Instead of a play about a man who meets his fate, what about the tale of a king who meets his destiny? For all of Henri's success, he had no queen. If only the Bard could write a play for Marie that would let her find her tongue, he could catapult Henri onto the world stage.

In retrospect, Will should have anticipated that Rose might resent the presence of another woman in Henri's life, but he thought that he was just dealing in make-believe. Knowing that she wanted him dead, how could he have understood how love and hate are intertwined? While he labored on his play, Rose was gradually falling in love with the object of her scorn. Spending time with him on a daily basis while he posed for her, his kingly bearing grew on her.

Will was sure that the simple magnificence of the man had much do with Rose's change of heart, but he suspected that their small talk was also a factor, because Henri was well spoken and engaging. No doubt Henri turned his interest in butterflies to good advantage with Rose, because in a convoluted way, they shared the same passion.

Rather than waiting for Henri to invite him to write something more substantial, Will took it upon himself to paint on a large canvas, as it were, verging on the grandiose perhaps, but he wanted to make a splash. At the same time, he understood that this would entail learning everything about his kingdom that he could, including the tiny details required for verisimilitude.

Mindful that Rose painted her portrait of Henri with a series of brushstrokes, Will knew that he needed to do the same for a whole host of characters. Like a composer who learns enough about each instrument to create music for it, he vowed to learn enough about each of the characters to do them justice. Looking for motives for the king wasn't hard, since he could tell that Henri was not content with ruling such a tiny kingdom as Navarre. The king wanted to have a seat at the table with Elizabeth and the major players in Europe.

When he began working on *Love's Labour's Lost*, Will

gave King Ferdinand a lofty ambition, making Navarre the equal of Elizabethan England. The Bard thought it would be amusing to turn the king into a male version of the virgin queen, especially in view of Henri's reputation as a ladies' man. What better way to poke fun at Henri that to paint him as a celibate scholar? Of course that meant having an attractive woman to test his resolve, so Will conspired to have the neighboring princess pay a visit. But he soon realized that that simple complication didn't do justice to Henri's ambition, so he added a trio of her ladies, picturing the former Princess Anne as the Queen of Hearts.

Indeed, the Bard was at a loss to match the four leading ladies with their equals, for besides Henri, there weren't many men of the same caliber in Navarre. Casting about for models for his characters, Adolphe came to mind as a villain, who would have been better suited for a tragedy. Try as he might, Will found few figures in Navarre who he could use as models for heroes. In his mind's eye, the Bard saw Henri's courtiers as Jacks in a deck of cards, but he knew that he needed more than face cards to create the cast.

Will made a point of getting away from Henri's chateau to find characters for minor parts, which is how he came up with so many buffoons, which Pau had in spades. Indeed, setting the play in a university town provided ample fodder for comic relief, for the place was lousy with pedants. In that respect, Will counted himself lucky for growing up in a backwater like Stratford, which doesn't lack for fools, but they don't pretend to be learned. Indeed, you don't have to look far for the universal character embodied in Dull, perhaps the easiest part to fill.

If anything, Will may have gone overboard in peopling his play with those who lacked common sense, including Henri's courtiers, who were lucky to be matched with the ladies from Anne's court. As he wrote the nonsense that the suitors spouted to their lovers, he began to see that he was like a juggler who had launched too many objects. It seemed too much to hope for that all four gentlemen would succeed in their quest. Though he never considered killing off any of the courtiers, he was tempted to have one of them turned away at the altar. Instead, he altered the story so that none of them marry, leaving several balls in the air.

In retrospect, Will could see all of the warts in *Love's Labour's Lost*, but he managed to please Henri, which is all that really mattered at the time. Nonetheless, his first effort suffered from the king's interference, as Will had to downplay the romance because of Rose's jealousy. As suggested earlier, Rose found herself falling in love with the man she meant to murder. While Henri had no way of knowing what was in her heart, he made the mistake of showing her a copy of the Bard's play. When she discovered that the part of Princess Anne was practically written for Marie, she could barely contain her fury.

So intense was her jealousy that Henri asked Will to re-write his piece, so that Rose wouldn't have to witness King Ferdinand marry Princess Anne. In fact, Rose wanted Will to kill her off, ideally with a dagger, or at least to have the princess poison herself like Socrates. As the Bard knew that he couldn't simply refuse her command, he opted for a delaying tactic, which Henri suggested, based on his experience on the battlefield. "If I cave into her at this point, I will have given her the upper hand. Anathema for a king, as you must understand. Our best bet is to leave the outcome hanging in the air. For in battle, as in bed, delay is a very useful tactic when used sparingly."

Will jotted his remark in his memory, in admiration for Henri's wisdom. It reminded the Bard of what a schoolboy he really was, with so little experience of love and war. He wished that he could have retained that innocence. While Henri must have realized that Rose was consumed with jealousy, he knew that she was quite capable of killing anyone who crossed her. Perhaps Will could have found another way to warn Henri, but he had already done his best with his short play. Will liked to think that he helped save the king's life, but not even the Bard's cleverness could save Henri, who seemed to collect enemies like butterflies.

Had Will known that Henri would show his play to Rose, he might have dragged his heels, but he did his best to accommodate her, for fear of bringing her fury upon their heads. He liked to think that appeasing her was justified, knowing what he did about her motives. Once she knew that Marie wouldn't marry the king in front of her eyes, she was at least able to sit through the premiere of his play. However, she drew considerable attention when the French messenger, Mercadé, delivered the news of the death of Princess Anne's father, the King of France. While there were audible gasps from some members of the audience, Rose began clapping.

The Bard admitted that it was one of the worst moments he had ever witnessed during a performance of one of his plays, which includes seeing curtains on the stage catch fire at the Globe. The flames created a huge distraction among the audience, even for those who thought it was part of the play. But in this case, Rose's response to the death of Princess Anne's father was so unexpected and incongruous that everyone in the audience was shocked. It was abundantly clear that there was a madwoman in their midst. Not just any lunatic, but the artist who had been entrusted to paint Henri's portrait.

In truth, it could have been worse, because the portrait had already been unveiled, to much acclaim. Indeed, Rose had become a celebrity, and everyone knew that Henri had discovered an artist whose future was now assured. In that respect, her irrational behavior during the premier of *Love's Labour's Lost* made her applause even worse. For a moment, the Bard was afraid that Henri was going to call one of his guards to take Rose away, but he must have known that she was quite capable of putting up fierce resistance.

"I must confess that it crossed my mind that I might be able to use the scene in one of my plays, with an audience member who disrupts the performance, but I'm saving it for a rainy day. More like an ace up my sleeve, which I can use if I find myself in a pickle. I'm not sure that most people understand how useful stagecraft can be, because there's only so much you can achieve by stringing words together on a spare stage. If I live long enough, perhaps I'll create a scene with a disruptive patron and a curtain fire, which would at least generate some press."

As you can imagine, the ending of *Love's Labour's Lost* only added to the consternation of the audience, who had been set up to expect a spectacular wedding scene. Having established that love was in the air, and the time for merry-making was at hand, the Bard blind-sided the audience by ushering in the scene of mourning at the end. It occurred to him that the spectators might have concluded that Rose knew something that they didn't, which was true enough, but it was almost as if she was determined to have a happy ending. Having been lauded for her artistic prowess, she continued the applause even in the face of death. Well, staged death, but our pulse still beats faster even if we pretend that theater is only make-believe.

Will suspected that Rose lived in a world cobbled together with reality and fantasy, making her doubly dangerous. Henri eventually realized it as well, but it must have been difficult to understand how someone who did him justice on a canvas could hate him. As the Bard admitted: "I have never been sadder to be right about someone than I was with Rose. Had I not found a way to extricate myself from our strange relationship, I have no doubt that I would have died a long time ago. I find some consolation in knowing that my clumsy attempt at drama helped save Henri's life."

The Bard was still basking in the modest success of *Love's Labour's Lost*, and had had too much to drink, when

Henri came to his room to tell him the news. Will was fast asleep, so he was startled by the knock on his door. He was too surprised to even ask "Who's there?". Flanked by two guards, Henri told them to wait, closing the door with a grim look on his face. "I owe you a debt of gratitude, and perhaps my life, though I suspect that you have concealed what you know about Rose from me. Yet you had the presence of mind to warn me about her, as you did so skillfully in your first play.

"Of course I didn't understand the implications until I began spending time with Rose, who is the most amazing lover that I've ever had. Yet it took so long for the ice to thaw between us, which made her passion even more remarkable when she let down her guard. You have no idea what it's like to have anyone, especially a beautiful woman, begin to draw your face, seeing facets of yourself that are beyond your purview. She captured my soul. There is no other way to put it. Yet in doing so, she was altered herself, and I witnessed what I can only describe as a change of season, from winter to spring.

"Sadly, her growing love for me ended up consuming her, and she became obsessed with portraying me with absolute perfection, revealing not who I am, but who I could become if I embraced love fully. It soon became apparent to me that Rose was jealous of anyone who came between us. She wanted me all to herself, and I began to wonder what she would do when she finished my portrait. Indeed, she began to linger as she worked, becoming more interested in conversing with me than painting me. While our conversations helped pass the time, I suspected that she would find a pretext to continue our sessions together.

"I suppose that I fell under her spell, for I agreed not to look at what she painted until she finished, which didn't seem unreasonable for an artist. Despite being curious, I began to see that we were engaged in a strange courtship, for I don't think either of us ever foresaw that we would become lovers. As you may imagine, I am not at a loss for female companionship, so I can honestly say that I agreed to have Rose paint my portrait because I believed that she possessed talent. Her beauty simply made it easier to look in her direction.

"If anything, I found her to be frosty when we first met, even when I complimented her on her remarkable drawings of butterflies. I doubt that she knew that I am also fascinated by butterflies, nor did she seem interested when I told her that we shared the same passion. She flinched at my words, making me feel like an intruder. Yet I must say that I found her demeanor refreshing, for she did not try to pander to me, like most people do. Being a king makes it doubly difficult to distinguish friend from foe, so I had taken to looking at everyone as if they were wearing a mask.

"I didn't plan to tell you all of this, but I wanted to let you know that I heeded your warning, even if you didn't fully understand that Rose was a femme fatale. Although I tried to dismiss my suspicions, her volatility became apparent to me when we became lovers. Suffice it to say that she is a volcano, capable of consuming everything in her path. Despite our efforts to alter your play to spare her feelings, she could barely contain herself when she saw the King of Navarre on stage with another woman, especially such an attractive one. I feared that Rose might bolt during the play. Worse yet, I realized that she could have rushed the stage in an instant, scratching out the eyes of the actress who threatened to eclipse her.

"In that respect her ill-timed applause was especially alarming, because it made it clear she had lost her reason. Had she tried to attack Marie in the theater, someone might have been able to restrain her. So her bizarre response sent chills down my spine; I knew she would find a way to pursue her revenge behind the scenes. Rose has patience in spades. I have seen her spend an entire afternoon on a couple of brushstrokes, waiting until the light was just right. I have also experienced the frenzy of her passion, and I can tell you that her lovemaking knew no bounds when we got home from the theater. I thought she might devour me like a spider that kills its mate.

"In the middle of the night, I awoke to find her gone. Suspecting the worst, I accompanied two of my guards to Marie's apartment, but was relieved to find that she was safe. Yet I was surprised to discover that she was sleeping with the actor who played my role. Although I was glad to find that Marie wasn't alone, I took no chances, leaving one of my guards to keep an eye out. Returning to my chambers, I passed a fitful night, afraid that Rose would return with blood on her hands. There was no telling what she would do if I confronted her.

"I arose at first light and was startled to find one of my guards asleep. For a moment I feared that Rose had slain him to keep him quiet, so the fool's snoring came as a relief. I slipped out of my chateau by myself, which was foolish, because there were plenty of people who wished me dead. But I had an intuition that Rose would wait until dawn to confront Marie. I knew that Rose would want to look her in the eye. She would draw out the death scene, relishing the prospect of upstaging her rival. Walking along the deserted street I passed Marie's lover, who fell to his knees when he recognized me. I waved him on, seeing no reason to put him in the picture. I was glad to know that Marie was still safe.

"Alas, I was too late, for when I got to Marie's apartment I found the guard unconscious, clubbed from behind with a flower pot. I was relieved to see that he was still breathing. I knew that Rose could have just slashed his throat, but her restraint did nothing to calm my fears. Realizing that it could be fatal for me to face Rose by myself, I began shouting for help. At it happened, an old woman was emptying a chamber pot onto the street, which just missed me. But she called out to me, pointing to Marie's open window 'Someone's climbing into the window!'

"Thank God I raised a commotion, because the whole neighborhood woke up. While I was glad to have some support, I quickly realized that they were just curious to see what all the fuss was about. It occurred to me that having all these witnesses might make matters worse, because Rose would feel cornered. So imagine my relief when Marie ran out of the door in her nightdress, screaming bloody hell. When she saw me, she ran into my arms, then quickly dropped to her knees, apologizing for failing to acknowledge me as king.

"By now, all of the neighbors were enjoying the spectacle, glad to have free front-row seats, although most of them were just standing around, murmuring. Unfortunately, Rose had witnessed Marie embracing me, which pushed her over the edge. I had no way of knowing that, of course, but I was mindful that Rose might emerge any moment, armed to the teeth. I have faced many men on the battlefield, but the rules of engagement dictate how to behave. I have never faced a woman in battle, but I had seen enough of Rose's passion to know that I had met my match. I would have settled for a scarred face, but I suspected that Rose would run her sword through me up to the hilt. At least I would be spared seeing what she did to Marie.

"Someone in the crowd had the presence of mind to send for help, for it was obvious that I was unprepared to defend myself, with only an injured guard to protect me. Despite my lack of judgment in coming alone, I knew it would be suicidal to try to disarm Rose. I considered sending for a priest to intervene with her, but figured that a nun would have a better chance of getting Rose to surrender. But I didn't want to put anyone else in harm's way. It was up to me to find a way to take her alive. If all else failed, we would have to burn down Marie's apartment, but that could easily get out of hand in such close quarters.

"Having seen a cornered fox turn on a pack of dogs

with astonishing ferocity, I knew better than to underestimate Rose. It occurred to me that there might be a tunnel underneath her building, which was connected with the city's fortifications. I ordered half a dozen guards to search the area, looking for any sign of an underground passage. When one of the soldiers suggested trying to smoke her out, by catapulting lighted hay bales into the windows, it seemed like a good idea. I figured that the smoke would help detect any underground escape route. With so many people around, I was sure that we could extinguish a fire with buckets of water. But the smoke ended up obscuring our view, and we had our hands full extinguishing a blaze on the roof.

"By the time the smoke had cleared, it was apparent that Rose wouldn't have been able to breathe for long without surrendering. I confess that part of me feared she was dead, and part feared that she was still alive, for I didn't want to have to kill her—or face her half-dead. By now, the neighbors were chomping at the bit to see what happened to Rose, and I sent a handful of soldiers into Marie's apartment, using every available door and window. I waited outside, unable to bear the sight of Rose reduced to a hunted animal.

"Suddenly I saw a soldier scramble across the roof. When he got to the edge he turned around to call out to us. 'She cut a hole in the wall. Search the moat!' I accompanied a cadre of guards to the moat, where we could see the hole Rose had made by knocking out some stones in the wall. She must have used a log in the ceiling as a battering-ram, but I wasn't surprised by her strength. She had tied some bedsheets together to lower herself down, but they only went half-way down the wall. It was still a long way to the moat, which was not very deep, so it was hard to believe that she could have survived the fall.

"It took the rest of the afternoon for the guards to drag the moat, but I wasn't surprised by Rose's survival. Knowing her as intimately as I did, I was keenly aware that she made a formidable opponent. Not only was she a superb athlete, but she was extraordinarily intelligent, combined with the ruthlessness of someone who was not playing with a full deck. Her entire being was now bent on revenge. No one in their right mind would get a good sleep until she was caught."

As you can imagine, Henri's account of Rose's escape raised Will's hackles. Rose had no way of knowing that he hadn't revealed her secret, so he posed a threat to her. She certainly knew that he was involved with Marie, making him a marked man. Not only was he irked by Marie's betrayal of him, but by her thanklessness. He was the one who had written the very words that her lover wooed her with. In supplying the dialogue between Princess Anne and King Ferdinand, the Bard had unwittingly brought the actors who portrayed them together in real life.

Will admitted that he was pleased that what he'd written could have so much power, but to have his words turned against himself seemed like the unkindest cut of all. He wondered how long Marie and her consort would last as a couple without his prompts. Even if they ended up going their separate ways, they would retain the memory of their animated conversation that he made possible. It was a reminder of the tortured relationship between actors and playwrights, whose dependence on one another provokes resentment. Indeed, how quickly we forget the author of our lives.

The thought of Rose on the loose gave him pause, for Will knew that she was capable of lying low and nursing her desire for revenge. He was certain that she had already adopted a disguise, and would find a way to stay close enough to keep an eye on Henri and Marie. If Marie hadn't stabbed him in the back, he would have warned her to leave the country. She wouldn't have a moment's peace in Navarre, where Marie would have to constantly look over her shoulder. Rose would relish her role as Marie's shadow, eclipsing any happiness that she might find with her new lover. In that respect, Will found himself aligned with Rose, for as far as he was concerned, Marie and her make-believe king could go to hell.

Like any playwright, Will was already thinking about how he could turn this dramatic set of events into a play. With a melodrama and a comedy under his belt, he wanted to try his hand at tragedy. Rose's relationship with Henri, and Marie's plight, had all the makings for a dark tale. Little did the Bard know how right he was, but like *Love's Labour's Lost*, the outcome was left in the air for quite some time. As if to fill the void, the return of the messenger who went to see Maréchal provided a welcome interruption in this turn of events.

Like a hunter returning from a successful expedition, the messenger displayed his bounty to Henri with a wide grin, unloading his packhorse to present him with sacks of playing cards wrapped in silk. Handing him a deck of cards, the messenger held up the King of Hearts with Henri's portrait on it. "All that is lacking, your majesty, is the portrait of the Queen of Hearts. The whole world awaits your choice." How glad Will was that Henri was still unmarried. Yet the Bard knew that Rose would imagine her own face as the Queen of Hearts.

Coming upon the heels of the debut of his play, Pierre Maréchal's enthusiastic response to Will's idea for putting Henri's likeness on playing cards made him feel like a genius. As far as he was concerned, he was no longer a lad and itinerant gambler, but an accomplished playwright and entrepreneur. Moreover, having been jilted by a woman, he figured that he was now a man of the world. Although he hadn't killed anyone yet, he'd learned enough about heated passions to imagine that he could kill off some characters. Nonetheless, you'd be surprised how hard it is for a playwright to murder his darlings.

The Bard's fortunes improved dramatically when he began to hawk playing cards throughout Navarre. Not only did Henri's blessing open doors for him, but his policy of banning any playing cards without his likeness made Will's job much easier, to say the least. "To be honest, it felt like a racket, because I made a point of burning any other decks of cards in every place I visited. Armed with an order to confiscate unauthorized playing cards throughout Navarre, I combed every nook and cranny of his kingdom. However, my travels also made me realize how small Navarre was in the big scheme of things. Closer to a duchy than a kingdom, if you ask me. No wonder King Ferdinand was keen to court the Princess of France."

In retrospect, Will wondered if Pierre Maréchal had any inkling that Henri would become King of France, because their fortunes rose together. Indeed, the Bard's card scheme (with partial credit to Rose, of course) put Maréchal (and himself) in the enviable position of being able to capitalize on Henri's accession to the throne of France. The market for cards with his likeness increased immeasurably, making Will a comparatively rich man at a young age. He could finally devote his time to writing. Suffice it to say that Rose's bud of an idea flowered when he nurtured it, as did many half-formed notions of others that the Bard brought to fruition.

~

Will said that he sometimes wondered how his life would have turned out had he remained in Navarre, under Henri's protection, but circumstances converged to push him out of the nest. First and foremost, his good fortune had made others envious of him, so Adolphe wasn't the only one who referred to the Bard as Henri's pet monkey. In that respect, he was glad to get out of Pau and travel the countryside, presiding over card burnings and peddling playing cards. But his vigorous campaign to monopolize the market for cards alienated a lot of gamblers, who objected to having their cards confiscated. As far as they were concerned, he might as well have been a tax collector, which he was, in effect, since Henri levied a tax on playing cards. Indeed, a case can be made that Will and Cervantes were both hustlers. Let history be the judge, not I.

Although Will was glad to have a couple of Henri's guards accompany him on his travels, he knew that Rose wouldn't have been dissuaded by their presence if she were intent on tracking him down. He was counting on her obsession with wreaking revenge on Marie, but he knew that he was dealing with an irrational creature. If she got it into her head to kill him, she was clever enough to disguise herself and surprise him when he had put her out of his mind. His only hope was to stay one step ahead of her. Consequently, he flitted from place to place as much as possible, driving his guards crazy.

While Will felt safer on the road than in Pau, he quickly tired of the hassles involved in traveling. Waking up in another town everyday left him disoriented. Even though he was happy to be bringing in good money as a traveling salesman, it went against his grain to play the role of businessman. By the end of the day, he had no interest in writing, especially when drinking was so much more pleasurable. He began to wonder if he would ever find the time to write another play. Worse than that, he had already run out of any ideas for plots. He figured his best bet was an historical play, with a forgone conclusion, rather than another silly comedy. He couldn't leave the audience dangling again.

Any thoughts he had about his next play went out the window when he returned to Pau, where Will received news that his father's health and business were declining. Henri provided a vote of confidence by encouraging him to find a London producer for *Love's Labour's Lost*. Obviously, the king knew next to nothing about the London theater scene, but he was intent on getting the recognition he deserved. Will knew he wasn't a businessman at heart, but he realized that he didn't have any other cards up his sleeve. The considerable amount of money they both made by cornering the card market certainly cemented their friendship.

Most of all, however, Henri foresaw the Bard's potential for catapulting him onto the world stage. His role as King of Hearts heralded a rising star.

CHAPTER 6

Will left Navarre wondering if he would ever see Henri or Rose again. As for Marie, he rather hoped that she met her fate. Without him to write words for her, he knew she would be lost. Still, it pained him to think that she might marry her lover and spend the rest of her life quoting from *Love's Labour's Lost*. She might have had a future in the theater, until her beauty faded, but she turned her back on the Bard. Good riddance.

Having sold all of Maréchal's cards, Will returned to Rennes in triumph, eager to see his mentor. Pierre seemed genuinely pleased to see him, but also eager to have him hawk his cards in England. Maréchal must have known that his cards were vastly superior to English ones, but he wasn't sure if the Brits would even recognize Henri. That turned out to be a blessing in disguise, because the English would only have been confused by a French king named Henri. Will had forgotten how insular the British are.

~

Homecoming may be too strong a word for the Bard's return to his homeland, where he felt estranged. It was wonderful to see his mother, of course, but his father had wilted. Once an alderman in Stratford-upon-Avon, he was now a failed businessman and suspected of being a Catholic. The Bard counted his blessings that he hadn't followed in his father's footsteps, for the life of a glover would have killed him. Indeed, he almost died from

English food, which had only gotten worse when the plagues ravaged the country. Fortunately, most Brits didn't know any better, but he certainly did.

As soon as Will arrived he began making plans to return to France, but he knew that first he had to fulfill the charge that Maréchal had given him. That meant going on the road again, which at least got him out of the backwater that Stratford had become (and maybe had always been). The Bard bemoaned, "I must say that traveling the length and breadth of England almost killed me, as if I had been drawn and quartered after an English meal. In that respect, I was glad to return to Stratford again, for I knew what to expect from my mother's home cooking. Overcooking, to be exact."

Will had been tempted to pitch his play while he was in London, but he resolved to stick to the business at hand, as he was keen to remain in Maréchal's good graces. That proved to be a wise decision, for when he returned to London with his other hat on, he found himself in a labyrinth full of dead ends. Quite literally, for the streets seemed to be in a constant state of disrepair. Moreover, most theaters had been banned from the city, forcing fledgling theater companies to perform their dark arts outside the city walls. He had heard tales of travelers getting lost in Moroccan medinas, but he didn't really believe these stories until he wandered the streets of London. He ended up spending most of his time copying folios, for fear of losing the originals—or having them stolen.

Tired of being dismissed as boy, Will had grown a beard when he got back to England, which also saved him time and trouble as he traveled the country. However, he regretted this decision, for he realized that he might have been able to play the role of a young woman. It even crossed his mind that he might be able to find a job as a bearded lady in a circus, but Will was a man on a mission. Instead of pulling ideas out the air like most playwrights, he had modeled the characters in *Love's Labour's Lost* on real people. Will claimed that he used some of their names to add verisimilitude to his plays. Not only that, but he took pride in portraying a king who was born for greatness. The Bard was determined to put Henri of Navarre on the London stage.

Buoyed by the groundless confidence of youth, Will made the rounds of theaters in London, which turned out to be few and far between. You must remember that the theater scene in London barely existed when the Bard was born, so he was ahead of his time. He had penned a play that would make his name, but he soon discovered that no one in the theater business wants to back a dark horse. Unlike gambling, there is no prospect of doubling or tripling your money. You're lucky not to lose your shirt. Consequently, he had a lot of trouble just getting his foot in the door.

His break came when the barman at the Bankside Inn introduced him to some actors who frequented the place. Will wouldn't have known they were actors if the barman hadn't told him, for they struck the Bard as a disreputable bunch. Seeing an opportunity to make some money gambling with them, he pulled out a deck of cards. They were suitably impressed by Maréchal's cards, which put English ones to shame. He let them beat him a few times, to make them think he was just a dandy with a pretty deck, but he gradually took their money.

When one of them complained that he couldn't cover his losses, Will offered to overlook his debt in exchange for accompanying him to a theater. He figured having an actor read his lines might impress a producer. "Let me see your script," the actor said before agreeing to his proposal, but he didn't have much choice. Reading Biron's part out loud at the Bankside, the actor warmed to the part, and pretty soon the whole group joined in. As you might imagine, this spontaneous reading caught the attention of some of the customers, who applauded the first scene.

Will soon understood that these shady characters were not doing him a favor, but realized that his play might lead to some work. Opportunities for actors are sketchy in the best of times, and this was a low point in London. The plague had devastated the economy, and puritans had practically taken over the city, determined to root out the dark arts. Thus, the Bard's play, like fresh meat, was welcome, especially by starving actors. The long and short of it is that these unemployed actors shadowed him around London, showing Will the ropes, staging impromptu readings for the few producers the Bard managed to buttonhole.

Despite their help, Will ran into brick walls wherever he turned. After being practically thrown out of a couple of the theaters, he resorted to displaying the playbill from the performance of *Love's Labour's Lost* which he'd saved as a souvenir. He knew that he needed to prove that he had some experience as a playwright. A curmudgeon of a producer, who seemed even shadier than the troupe of actors, shot down his hopes with slings and arrows. "This playbill could be counterfeit for all I know. Even if it's authentic, it proves nothing. French tastes are all over the board. If anything, the fact that a French audience liked the play is an ominous sign. The French are notorious for their bad taste. Let me remind you that we don't parade scantily clad women on London stages. More's the pity, but it's a fact of life."

Another producer was more receptive, but gave Will some fatherly advice. "I'm afraid you've grabbed the stick by the wrong end, young man. First of all, a play set in France is not likely to appeal to English audiences, especially in such dire circumstances as we're in now. No one wants to be reminded that there's fairer land just across the sea, where the sun shines more often than not, full of beautiful people who spend most of their time making love and partaking of fabulous French cuisine. Second, any story that takes place in France is a painful reminder of what might have been, if only God had not cursed the English for losing the Hundred Years' War. At least you had the presence of mind to name your king Ferdinand, instead of Henry or William, which would have only sown confusion.

"Third, a tale about an enlightened French king will never fly with English audiences. The French are best portrayed more realistically, as villains or clowns. There must be some good reason for setting a play in France, which is fraught with conflict, especially if your play is supposed to be a comedy. From what I can tell by skimming your play, the humor derives from the preposterous proposition that the king and his henchmen have sworn off women. It is well known that the French are libertines, who take advantage of Catholicism to be forgiven for their sins. Why on earth would a French monarch turn into a puritan and scholar? Not everyone reads Montaigne, you know. You're obviously too young to appreciate that the English much prefer to think of the French as wastrels, running their country into the ground. All that British blood spilled for nothing, but don't get me started.

"Finally, you have compounded your errors by writing about a place in France that no one has ever heard of, Navarre. Does it even exist, or did you make it up? Write me a play about a corrupt nobleman with several mistresses and an adulterous wife, and I'll take a look at it. You can find plenty of material close to home, so don't waste your time writing about far-off places. Fairytales are for children. London audiences want to laugh and cry, preferably both. One more word of advice. A little rhyming goes a long way, especially in a play. Save your rhymes for poetry, which doesn't pay good money. Give your actors language of the people, not poets. The words should roll of their tongues naturally, without being gussied-up in couplets."

The producer was right, of course, and he helped Will

understand why audiences in Navarre embraced his first play enthusiastically, particularly because it made Henri look good. But also because they may not have understood much English. He'd given them just enough of a story to catch the drift, and they picked up on the laughter of the few people who understood his humor. London audiences were a much tougher crowd. They were more interested in spectacle, preferring bear-baiting and cock-fights to plays. Their idea of theater was to see some blood spilled, as well as some bawdy humor. That's hard to do when the women in English plays were portrayed by mere boys.

Will returned to Stratford with his tail between his legs. His success with peddling playing cards only made him feel worse about his failure as a playwright. He regretted coming home, and he couldn't wait to return to France, where fortune had smiled upon him. In such low spirits, perhaps it is not surprising that the tide would turn, for the Bard had seen boats stranded on the Avon rise at high tide. Moreover, though he didn't consider himself a religious man, he mocked no one who claimed to have been saved by the grace of God.

"I make no claim that I have read the Bible cover to cover, but I've scoured it in the hope of finding some levity, without success. What need have I for a religion that leaves no reason for smiles, if only from time to time? Like the sun in England, whose brief appearance comes as such relief. Yet by some cosmic law I cannot offer any comic relief in this wicked world without balancing it with tragedy. Though I be accused of being a charlatan, the only shades I have to work with are light and dark. Yet words add such breadth to my palette, allowing me to lend color to my plays.

"What I have read of the Bible makes it clear what happens to truth tellers, who are crucified, even with God on their side. I knew that I would have to shield my calling behind a mask, pretending to be someone quite different from myself. In that respect, it seems fitting that I was wearing a mask when I first met Anne, at a feast in Stratford to celebrate the Summer Solstice. I suppose some might say that it was a heathen gathering, because it was a deliberate provocation to the remaining Catholics in the area, who associated Celtic tradition with pagans."

Will couldn't help admiring and being amused by his countrymen, who gathered in the heart of Stratford despite the rain, huddled under the roof of the marketplace, pretending to be at a masked ball. He noted that the tradition of masked balls is a better fit for Mediterranean countries, where the climate is conducive to being outdoors, and where people are comfortable wearing exotic garments. There was something comic about seeing ordinary people trying to be theatrical. Yet it was a playwright's dream to see the townspeople embrace make-believe so avidly, turning his birthplace into a stage where everyone had a part to play.

Dressed as a troubadour with a mask, he spotted a woman posing as Maid Marian. As her face was likewise concealed, he honestly had no idea who she was. He approached her, remarking that if she didn't find her Robin Hood at the feast, he would be glad to keep her company. "I grew up chasing the Merry Men in the Forest of Arden, pretending to be the Sheriff. No one else wanted to play the villain, but it came to me naturally, as my grandmother was an Arden."

She replied, "You have given yourself away, then, because I know the Ardens and their kin. I once taught music to young Shakespeare and his sister, Joan. She had some talent, but her older brother might have been a frog. I can only hope that his voice will change when he becomes a man."

He recognized her immediately, for he had a longstanding crush on Anne, and knew that she had a well-deserved reputation for a sharp tongue. No wonder she hadn't married. Will didn't want to break the spell, so he continued the conceit of pretending they were strangers.

"Not only is he a man, but a man of the world, recently returned from making his mark in France and Spain, land of the troubadours, who not only coined the word for romance, but gave voice to it in their music and poetry. They fell out of fashion, perhaps for good reason, since they wasted their words on those of noble birth. I aim to right the ship, creating plays that speak of love of everyman…and everywoman. As a commoner, I have the right to breathe the same air as the nobility. Such freedom ought to apply to love as well."

Anne replied, "Daring ambition for someone so young, but what can you possibly know about love at your age? I'm glad to know that you were inspired by the troubadours, but as you observed, they lacked the common touch. What makes you think you have anything to say to ordinary mortals like myself?"

Will responded, "Having followed in the footsteps of the troubadours, I understand why they praise beauty, for the sunshine illuminates the landscape in ways no one from England can imagine. Likewise, the light reveals face and form in intimate detail. Even now, in this dim light, I can almost see the glint in your azure eyes, as if you were standing by a sun-drenched sea."

Anne was skeptical. "Flattery comes easily to you, I see, but you speak in superficialities. I have no doubt that your travels opened your eyes, but beauty has little to do with love. In truth, most of us are plain. Should love be reserved only for those who are fair? That is as unjust as confining love to nobility. Save your breath about grace and beauty. What is the point of your crusade, if not to propose that we are all equal in love?"

Will saw no way to parry her remark, so he doffed his mask, knowing that she would not be expecting to see him with a beard. Reaching into the valise that he carried on his travels, he produced his remaining copy of *Love's Labour's Lost* and handed it to her with a flourish. "I wrote this for the King of Navarre who is little known abroad, but I hope to give him the recognition he deserves. If you will do me the honor of reading my play, you will see for yourself if I have any promise. Though I have failed to find anyone in London interested in producing my play, I have resolved to turn myself into a playwright. I will face the plague like a ship's captain sailing into a storm, knowing that there is no other choice."

Will reflected that he should have given Anne a chance to respond, but he hadn't yet learned to listen, and launched into what may have been his first soliloquy: "Early on, I knew there was no point in learning to become a glover, taking over my father's failing business in the midst of the plague. I sensed that my salvation lay hidden in the cards I held in my hand. Not as a gambler or peddler, but in the stories they revealed about the human condition. The queen of hearts, of course, had a million stories to tell about love and loss, but what about the lowly two of clubs? Their suits didn't even exist in decks from most countries, yet I was sure that there were stories to discover in every card. If only they could talk to each other. The play's the thing, not just to catch the conscience of the king, but to give voice to everyman and everywoman, regardless of their station.

"I realized that playing at cards was the perfect cover story, allowing me to sharpen my observations about people, listening to their tales, as interludes in the quiet at the card table. Yet most of the time I spent in reflection, watching their fortunes shaped by the cards dealt to them by chance and circumstance. Nor did I pretend that I was above the fray, for my luck depended on my ability to pay attention. When I failed to do so, I invariably paid the price.

"So I asked myself, if not a glover, what can I make of myself in seven years, the usual span of servitude for an apprentice? The answer came not like a bolt of lightning, but an inkling. The only real skill I possessed was with words, but it was up to me to put that gift to good use. I resolved to become a wordsmith, writing verses with the ring of truth. Not just tales of kings and queens, but of knaves and fools, of poor souls without a full deck. Instead of myths and legends, I would write about ordinary mortals, with the deck stacked against them, and villains out to cheat them, hiding behind the curtains of Church and State.

"Much of this realization came to me during my travels, as if I had to leave home to put my life in perspective. I won't bore you with tales of my escapades in Spain and France, but suffice it to say that I left my boyhood behind me. Like a caterpillar crawling slowly on the ground, I had no idea that I would be transformed into a butterfly. Someday I will tell you how I met the King of Navarre, who took me under his wing and gave me an opportunity to find out if I could write. I did not distinguish myself, but I did not fall on my face. More importantly, it opened a door for me, inspiring me to write my first play. Now, that same king is keen to step onto the world stage. As he is an admirer of Queen Elizabeth and is a Protestant, I suspect that he can pull some strings.

"In the meantime, I have had some success as an entrepreneur, peddling the finest playing cards in the world. While the future is too uncertain for me to claim that my fortune is assured, I have the means to woo you with a clear conscience. I have saved enough from gambling to sustain us regardless of my future as a playwright. Writers are held with little regard in London, as I have discovered with my own eyes, but I would consider it an honor to be associated with the theater. I cannot fare worse than my father, whose toil as a glover has come to a sad end. How is it that God could create so much beauty, but so little justice?"

~

The unusually sweet summer gave Anne and Will ample opportunities to talk and walk along the Avon. He soon discovered that Anne's sharp tongue made her an ideal sparring partner, giving rise to dialogues that showed up in some of his works. When he finally got up the courage to propose to her, he tried to turn the table on her before she beat him to it.

"I have little to offer you but a good heart and a nimble tongue. Moreover, I have to warn you that I am an inveterate gambler, which is as close to a trade as I've mastered. Yet I plan to transform myself into a playwright, the biggest wager of my life. You may take some comfort in the fact that most of my time will be spent alone, scribbling down the notions that come to me as I walk, which is the only way I know how to work. Sequestering myself in a stuffy room is not my style. Between writing and gambling, I will be hard to find, making it less likely that you will be bored by my company.

"What you need to know ahead of time is that I must create a character for myself quite out of keeping with my true heart and mind. I shall have to shield myself from the slings and arrows of criticism that will be hurled against me for speaking the truth. Even this precaution will not guard us from gossip, which cannot be avoided with such a public persona. There will be times when you will regret ever knowing me. Yet you must remember that I love you with all of my heart, and always will. Given that caveat, will you consent to be my wife?"

Anne replied, "I need time to make up my mind, for your lofty ambitions give me pause. Indeed, I have seen no evidence of any deeds that prove your point. Pretending to be a troubadour requires only a semblance of sophistication. Except for a single play, I have yet to hear any poetry or music from you. I must confess that I am inclined to believe you, for you promise a life of unusual pursuits. Nonetheless, your caveat about your persona is alarming.

"Yet your words have touched my heart, and I am pleasantly surprised to find that you are no longer a boy. The boy I knew was full of life, but I had no idea that he would aim so high. My only fear is that Stratford is too small a canvas for you, and that you will leave me behind. To be clear, I will not be content to keep the home fires burning while you concoct plays to distract people from their troubles. Promise me that you will remember where you came from, honoring the neighbors that nurtured you when your family suffered misfortune."

He gave Anne his promise, and waited for her answer. Suddenly, the harsh judgment of the producers he'd seen in London meant nothing to him. If only Anne understood his words, nothing else mattered. If not, Will said that he might have drowned himself. So when he received a note from her, asking to meet him on the bridge, he realized that she had picked the ideal setting. If she agreed to his proposal, he would kiss her, handing her a rose. If not, he would drop the flower into the Avon, and throw himself into the river. If nothing else, the scene might inspire a better playwright to tell his tale of unrequited love.

Carrying umbrellas, they met on the bridge in spite of the rain. No one in England postpones their life because of bad weather. In that respect, the country will always be in the Dark Ages. He didn't wait for her reply before handing her a white rose. Her smile put him at ease.

"Thank you, William, that was very kind. How did you know I loved white roses?"

"A red rose would have been a cliché, and a yellow one seemed like something for an old lady. Besides, I thought a white rose would complement your auburn hair."

"Do you know how old I am, William? I'm practically a spinster, and if I married you, I would be accused of robbing the cradle."

The Bard claimed he didn't know her age, but realized that she was an older woman, of course. That's one of the things he liked about her. Anne seemed much more mature than the girls he knew. Will wouldn't have dreamed of showing any of them his play. When he told her that, she laughed.

"I had no idea that men could be so romantic. I didn't know what to expect, but I was surprised there were no fight scenes."

"There was one in my first play, so I'm not averse to fights, but that's not what *Love's Labour's Lost* is all about. I tried to paint a picture of a magic kingdom, where love is always in the air, with rainbows popping up everywhere."

"You succeeded in creating an atmosphere of love, filling the scenes not with one couple, but four. Yet their banter seems to miss the mark, with the characters more interested in talking of love, than in loving. In that respect you are more a realist than a romantic. I suspect that your ridicule belies your romantic streak. You tease us so much, raising our expectations so high, only to leave us dangling. 'Tis novel, I'll give you that, to turn a comedy into a tragedy, but was there some reason for freezing everything in time?"

"I'm flattered that you read my play so closely. In truth, I thought it too trite to tie up so many loose ends in a tidy bow. One wedding would have been more than enough for a happy ending, but four would have been too much for an audience to bear. I confess that the gambler in me is fond of suits, so I led with hearts. As it is, my play calls into question the empty gestures of courtship, which are enacted as if in a dream, but not of our own making. I thought it best to let the romances marinate awhile, ensuring tenderness."

Will noted that the rain didn't dampen their spirits, for the bridge seemed like the perfect place for them to carry on their dialogue, as it would have been in a play. Indeed, a sunny day might have made them uncomfortable, for they had things to talk about that required sobriety. Anne had yet to give him her answer, and if she accepted his proposal, their lives would be turned upside down. Where would they live, what would they do, and what would their parents say? All questions for which they were unprepared;

speaking for himself, at least. But everything hinged on a single word. Yes or no.

"Yes," she said, "I will marry you, but on one condition." Anne seemed to enjoy this torment, but he wasn't about to state the obvious, so he waited for her. "You must promise to write a sequel, for I can't bear the thought of such protracted love. How can we marry, leaving your characters on ice, while we enjoy the fruits of love? I want our wedding to be just the beginning, not an end. Indeed, I would prefer a quiet wedding for ourselves and our families. For the couples you have set in motion in *Love's Labour's Lost*, let there be much merrymaking. After living in suspense so long, they deserve a celebration that reverberates throughout the town."

~

In keeping with Anne's wishes, they had a quiet winter wedding in the chapel in Worcester. The few friends who came had little in common, for she was not only older, but wiser, as Will was to be reminded again and again. They honeymooned on a rented boat, taking their sweet time to work their way down the Avon, whose banks overflowed from December storms. The cold, blustery weather only brought them closer together, under the covers.

Pulled by an old, patient horse, the boat proved to be a refuge for them, as the Avon was practically deserted in winter. No one in their right mind ventured out on the river if they didn't have to, and there were no tourists to mar the misty scenery. From time to time the sky would clear, as if readying itself for the next storm, and they would stand on the deck to watch the world go by, ever so slowly.

Most of the time they ate on board, partly to avoid having to tie up the boat, which entailed finding someone to look after the horse. They only stopped for dinner a couple of times, for a change of pace, but both taverns were disappointing, serving the kind of English food that has given the country's cuisine such a bad reputation. The

Fox & Hound, for example, had nothing resembling a green vegetable. And why on earth would anyone boil a chicken when they could roast it? If nothing else, roasting the chicken would have warmed up the drafty tavern, where the fireplace just filled the chilly air with smoke.

Will said that he would have given anything to take Anne to France, but that was an extravagance a budding playwright couldn't afford. Even a gambler knows that you have to pace yourself, waiting until the cards begin to fall your way. Crossing the channel in December would have been a disaster, likely leaving them sick in bed, instead of enjoying their honeymoon. In that respect he relished the relative calm on the boat.

Compared to the *Dragon*, a horse-drawn boat on the Avon seemed like a cozy paradise, with the woman of his dreams. While he confessed that the Duchess and Rose crossed his mind from time to time, Anne was someone he could talk with. Plato had his Socrates; Will had his Anne. If dialogue is the key to philosophy, that's doubly true for theater, where the interplay of characters brings them to life. He would have been nothing without Anne.

Were it not for his gambling and the money he'd put aside from peddling playing cards, Will admitted that he didn't know how he would have supported his family. He had few useful skills, especially in Stratford, where his father's decline was well known. The prospect of living with Will's parents seemed bleak, with yet another mouth to feed, not to mention the imminence of the screaming baby. So he wasn't surprised when Anne suggested that they live with her widowed mother in Hathaway Cottage in the neighboring village of Shottery.

Anne was in her element at Hewlands Farm, where she tended the spacious gardens, leaving the smelly sheep to the men. She seemed to relish being outside, thriving on fresh air and vigorous work. Leaving her mother to run the house, Anne carved out a niche for herself. With her brother busy expanding Hathaway House, and her mother overseeing the house, Anne put her green thumb to good use. Will was quite sure that Anne inherited her independent streak from her mother, who was sensible and strong-willed.

Unfortunately, Will got off on the wrong foot with Anne's brother, Bartholomew, who was trying to fill his father's shoes as a prosperous sheep farmer. He was all work and no play. Indeed, it's difficult to imagine Shakespeare sheering sheep in Shottery, but it seems likely that working on the family farm fed his appetite for becoming a playwright.

Will supposed that her family could be forgiven for failing to appreciate his habit of reading passages from *Love's Labour's Lost*, which he hoped might liven up their dinners. As Anne's brother always insisted on reading scripture before every meal, it seemed to the Bard that some leaven would help balance a steady diet of Biblical references. Although her family humored him by listening to excerpts from his play, they proved to be a difficult audience. It was Bartholomew who suggested that Will might make better use of his time by writing historical plays, with some "meat and potatoes" as he put it. "It's all very well that you can dream up diversions for a foreign king, but most us prefer tales with some moral purpose."

Will soon realized that the sequel to *Love's Labour's Lost* would have to wait, in spite of his promise to Anne. As much as he dreaded the thought of writing a historical play to placate her parents with something of substance, he began working on the tragic tale of Titus Andronicus, the ill-fated Roman general, whose cruelty begets horrific revenge. The Bard was determined to produce a work of Biblical proportions, in which an eye for an eye is taken quite literally. If nothing else, his play quieted Anne's brother and mother, who ended up practically begging him to turn his hand from bloody murder to comedy again.

It was just as well that he managed to draft *Titus Andronicus* before their first child, Susanna, was born, for parenthood altered the course of their dinners for quite some time. He was not ready to be a father, but Anne embraced motherhood. Glad as he was to see her so happy, he feared that they would be stuck in England for the foreseeable future, which proved to be prescient. Rather than bore you with details of raising a first child, which every parent knows all too well, I can tell you that Anne and Will's troubles more than doubled when they had twins two years later.

In case you haven't seen *Titus Andronicus*, which fortunately most people haven't, it's a twisted tale of a Roman general who conquers the Goths, taking their queen and her three sons back to Rome, where one of them is sacrificed at the tomb of his slain children. Bent on revenge, the queen (Tamora) worms her way into the heart of the emperor (Saturnicus), orchestrating the assassination of his brother, and casting blame on Titus' two sons. His daughter (Lavinia) loses her tongue and her hands to prevent discovery of the murders, only to be killed by Titus, who serves Tamora's slain sons to her at a banquet. After killing her, Titus is slain by Saturnicus, who in turn is murdered by Titus' remaining son. The Bard may have gone too far in his attempt to dramatize the trials and tribulations of family life, but no one could complain that he left them hanging.

Will noted that he had often thought *Titus Andronicus* would be a good name for a star, but feared that he had tarnished it with such a bloody play. Venturing to London again, he came away from his visit with the impression that theatre was an acquired taste which Londoners hadn't acquired yet. Indeed, his brief foray into the city was probably premature, as theater had yet to take root. The few tendrils that flourished were being pulled up by Puritans, in spite of Queen Elizabeth's soft spot for drama.

Will realized that Londoners were fundamentally Romans, with the same proclivity for blood, spectacle, animal and human sacrifice. The veneer that separated

Londoners from their historical counterparts was very thin indeed. If anything, Romans were more honest about their passionate nature than Londoners, whose puritanical pretensions barely concealed their savage nature. Nowhere was this discrepancy more apparent than using male stand-ins for women in London theaters, as if the sight of actual females would have been too much for audiences to bear.

He began to suspect that this hypocrisy was tied to Protestantism, which had gone out of its way to avoid anything that resembled Catholic rites. At the same time, Catholics had a longstanding history of excluding women from their clergy, effectively banning females from playing any roles in Catholic services. Ironically, London theater continued this tradition of excluding women from the stage. In retrospect, his attempt to draw upon Roman history was ill-conceived, as he took their fascination with blood and gore too far. It was almost as if he was trying to make up for the romantic atmosphere of *Love's Labour's Lost* by rubbing the face of the audience in blood.

Mind you, the Bard was still in the early stage of his apprenticeship as a playwright, so it's not surprising that his first works were flawed. As any writer worth his salt can tell you, writing is the easy part of the process. Re-writing is the hard part, requiring not just repeated polishing, but restructuring when necessary. Like moving furniture, you can't just try to picture things in your mind; you have to actually move things around until you get it right. Needless to say, these extensive revisions delayed Will's debut on the London stage. In fact, he confessed that recalcitrant producers were the least of his problems. His harshest critic was Anne, editor, mentor and muse, all in one.

As you can imagine, Anne had strong reservations about *Titus Andronicus*.

"When you told me that you needed to create another persona, I had no idea that you were planning on pandering to popular tastes for sensationalism. While I doubt that many people in Stratford will ever see your play, word will seep out from the gutters of London, destroying what's left of our privacy. Do you have any idea what I have to go through to explain that my husband is a playwright, who has not had a single play staged in England? I might just as well tell them that you're a pickpocket who has yet to snatch a purse."

Anne didn't mince words, but made mincemeat of Will's, excoriating him for his attempts at double entendre and bawdy humor, which she blamed on his French escapades. In the case of *Titus Andronicus*, she saw no reason for writing a play "about someone nobody has ever heard of. If you're determined to write something bloody, why not a play about Nero or Julius Cesar? Who wants to see a play about parents murdering their children and cutting off their tongue and hands? If this is your antidote for cockfighting and bear-baiting, I think you're barking up the wrong tree. What on earth are people going to talk about when they leave the theater? I'm sorry to tell you, but *Titus Andronicus* doesn't lend itself to dinner conversation."

She had a point, because plays in London are always performed during the day, before audiences were too drunk to sit still. It didn't help that the city gates were closed at dark, supposedly for safety, but everyone knew that Puritans didn't want people to enjoy themselves. Will liked to think that he wore Anne down, because she finally threw up her hands after several revisions of *Titus Andronicus*. He promised her that he would take her suggestion about a play on Julius Cesar, but she reminded him that he had yet to deliver on his promise for a sequel to *Love's Labour's Lost*. Looking back, he realized that Anne had given him his head, like a horse that needs to prove it can run.

As much as Will wanted to write a sequel to *Love's Labour's Lost*, he was mindful that it would be pointless without the prequel, which had only been performed in

Navarre. Although he was counting on Henri's influence to have his first play staged in London, he didn't fully realize what an insular country he lived in. Even in the best of times, it was difficult to get anything on the London stage, let alone a play by an unknown author. Between the recurring plague and the dismal economy, the London theatre scene was in tatters. Moreover, behind the scenes, Puritans were doing everything in their power to undermine theater, which many considered inherently immoral.

Fortunately, Henri had his own reasons for getting *Love's Labour's Lost* produced while he still had an ally in Queen Elizabeth. Will reflected that he would probably never know when Henri began scheming to become King of France, but he must have set his sights on the crown well before he succeeded. "I would like to tell you that he relied on me to ensure that my play appeared on the London stage, but Henri must have known that I had no clout whatsoever. Instead, he put his faith in Queen Elizabeth, who must have appreciated having a Protestant peer in France, even if a minor one." Whether or not she ever imagined that Henri would become King of France we will probably never know.

As you may imagine, Will had no knowledge of these machinations while living in Stratford, which is a world apart from London. All he knew for sure is that he had better deliver on his promise to Anne, so he finally turned his hand to the ill-fated sequel to *Love's Labour's Lost*. Yet I see that there is no point in telling how things went awry until I describe his play, *Love's Labour's Found*.

ACT I.

King Ferdinand of Navarre has been waiting patiently for a year to pass, hoping that Queen Anne of France (formerly the Princess, until she inherited the crown from her father) will honor her pledge to accept his proposal of marriage, along with proposals to her ladies (Rosaline,

Catherine and Maria) by the King's three courtiers, (Biron, Longueville and Dumaine). In the meantime, the King's kitchen maid, Gwendolyn, took a leave of absence, claiming that she had to look after her grandparents in Aragon, to give birth to a baby conceived during a tryst with the messenger from France, Mercadé. Having no word from him since, Gwendolyn realized that she could not raise the child on her own, and leaves the foundling at the Queen's castle in Bordeaux. The gatekeeper sends for his wife who finds a wet nurse (Monica) to look after the child.

ACT II.

King Ferdinand and his entourage journey to Bordeaux to call upon the Queen and to renew their proposals. Before they can proclaim their love again, Queen Anne tells them that words will not suffice, and that they must prove their love with deeds. She challenges the four suitors to make a meal for their ladies, along with their family and friends, giving the men a month to prepare. Gwendolyn has accompanied the King to ensure that his meals are up to par, but she obviously hopes to find out what became of her child. She goes to see the priest (Father Jean) to learn if there have been any baptisms in the last three months. He tells her that he recently christened a foundling, but cannot reveal the name of the parents. Leaving the church, Gwendolyn encounters Mercadé, who informs her that he is engaged to be married.

ACT III.

Each of the four suitors attempts to discover the favorite food of their ladies, hoping to learn how to make these dishes and where to find the ingredients. The King asks Gwendolyn to snoop around the Queen's castle, to see what she can find out about Anne's tastes. On her way to the castle, Gwendolyn sees a woman (Monica) picking peaches in an orchard outside the town walls. Beside her are two cradles, with one of the infants crying loudly. Gwendolyn notes what a blessing it must be to have twins, and asks if she can hold the baby. Acknowledging that she has her hands full, Monica readily agrees.

The infant quiets down as soon Gwendolyn picks her up, and Monica comments on her calming influence. Mentioning that she could use some assistance, Monica offers to pay her to look after her children if Gwendolyn can spare some time.

Gwendolyn replies that she is only a visitor, assisting King Ferdinand in making a meal to woo the Queen. She says that she will need to consult with the King before she can agree to help look after the twins. Monica thanks her for her kindness, noting that the children are not really twins, but doesn't reveal any more. She also remarks that she and her husband are employed by the Queen to provide fruit and vegetables for the Queen's table, so Monica will be glad to offer her counsel on the Queen's tastes.

ACT IV.

Gwendolyn enters the church, glad to find it empty. Falling to her knees, she asks for guidance, for she knows that it would be too painful for her to see her daughter, knowing that she will soon have to abandon her again. Yet how can she not spend such precious moments with her child while she has the opportunity? Hearing the front door of the church open, Gwendolyn hides behind the confessional. Mercadé prostates himself in front of the altar, asking forgiveness for breaking two hearts and piercing his own. He blurts out his resolve to throw himself on Gwendolyn's mercy, and then exits the church.

Like King Ferdinand, his three courtiers are busy trying to figure out what to make for their ladies, while learning how to prepare a meal that will match their words of love. Clever Biron discovers that his nimble wit is of little use in the kitchen. Handsome Longueville has to face the fact that his appearance masks his clumsiness as a chef. While good-hearted Dumaine's noble intentions do not make up for his lack of cooking skills, his shortcomings as chef pale by comparison with the King, who is like a baby learning to walk. Indeed, Gwendolyn feels as if she's surrounded by children. When the King asks her to look for some cheese for the meal he's preparing for Queen Anne, she's relieved to be on her own, and to reflect on what she must do about her daughter.

Returning from her mission to obtain ripe cheese for the feast,

Gwendolyn encounters Mercadé walking through the orchard. Asking if he can talk with her, Mercadé tells her that he has broken his engagement and wants to make amends for losing touch with her. Gwendolyn is tempted to tell him about their daughter, but reminds him what the Queen has said about empty words. Gwendolyn tells him that if he really wants to have a relationship with her, he needs to give up his position as a messenger, and find work that will allow him time to spend with her. It occurs to Mercadé that he could procure flowers, food and wine for the impending feasts, making a name for himself as a merchant while working closely with Gwendolyn.

ACT V.

On the day of the feast, each of the suitors rise early to prepare meals for their lady, her family and friends. Trying to be clever by preparing something unexpected, Biron hosts a brunch late in the morning, managing to impress his guests with an assortment of breakfast fare and mimosas. Longueville, true to form, also avoids having to make a full dinner by hosting a lunch featuring roast pig with an apple in its mouth. Knowing that he needs all day to prepare dinner, Dumaine opts for a simple meal featuring food from the local market. King Ferdinand upstages everyone by serving a leisurely banquet on a table set up in the orchard. Introducing each of the courses as he personally serves them to Queen Anne and her family, he notes that in her honor, no animals were killed to make the meal. As he finally sits down across from Queen Anne, the King points out that the menu reflects the journey of his life, including his upbringing at the foot of the Pyrenees, and his travels to the Middle East and Provence.

He offers a toast to his sous chef, Gwendolyn, and to Mercadé, for putting him in touch with all of the people who made the banquet possible. At the stroke of midnight, the church bells begin ringing and all of the quests gather in the town square, where Queen Anne reports the outcome of the challenge. She announces that there will not be four weddings after all, but five, as Gwendolyn and Mercadé are engaged as well. With so many weddings, at least another month will be needed.

~

In many ways *Love's Labour's Found* was a godsend, particularly since it met with Anne's approval, which meant so much to Will at the time. Like his protagonists who proved their worth with deeds, rather than words, completing this play cemented his relationship with Anne. "For someone who can barely boil an egg, you have done a remarkable job of creating credible scenes of the king and his cronies as chefs. You must have learned something about cooking from your time in France, because I've seen no signs that you have any skill in the kitchen. If only your penchant for make-believe could put food on the table, we would be rich."

Will took her left-handed compliment to heart, glad to have an opportunity to bury *Titus Andronicus* like a bone. He figured that he could dig it up later, if nothing better came his way. Most of all, he was relieved to bring some closure to his romantic tale, surpassing himself with not just a royal wedding, but five happy marriages. To be honest, he thought Anne might raise an objection to his story of courtly love, which included only one commoner, but he tried to make it clear that Gwendolyn was the equal of any woman, including Princess Anne, in beauty and grace. Though not of noble birth, she was noble in spirit. In that respect, the Bard considered that he was expanding the scope of the troubadours, by showing that romantic love was open to all.

As Anne observed, "You have convinced me that you are following in the footsteps of the troubadours, William, but you still have a long way to go. As much as I enjoyed the happy ending, your play leaves the impression that festivities center on the nobility. I dare say that five weddings in a month would require a great deal of work, all performed by ordinary citizens, without any of the nobility lifting their fingers. While Gwendolyn is portrayed as a commoner, she's obviously a woman of uncommon beauty. Would you have dared to write such a role for an unattractive woman?"

There was no way he could answer her of course. Would he have married Anne if he found her unattractive? Of course not, but did that make him a heartless monster? He saw no reason to turn this issue into a Socratic dialogue, but realized that he had been outwitted. Anne had considerably more experience of the world than he did, even if she had spent her whole life in Stratford. While Will liked to think that he knew more about the wider world, he was reminded on a daily basis that Anne had a formidable intellect, which she could wield to great effect—like Rose with her dagger.

In retrospect, Will wished that his two plays about King Ferdinand had clung closer to the truth, for the parallels with Henri's life began to go askew. Indeed, even his success in peddling playing cards didn't hold up in England, where the novelty of having Henri's likeness on the King of Hearts was lost on English gamblers. Telling them that it was a portrait of the King of Navarre meant nothing to them. So the prospect of buying new decks of cards, even if there were better quality than English ones, had little appeal. When Will attempted to put them in the picture by showing them the Kingdom of Navarre on a map, they only laughed. "You call that a kingdom? It's tinier than Liechtenstein!"

He soon realized that he was casting his pearls before swine, as his countrymen lacked much aesthetic taste. Will had been spoiled by the French, whose flair for fashion and appreciation of beauty were well known. Despite the superiority of French playing cards, especially Maréchal's, the Bard made more money gambling than selling cards. There's no accounting for other people's taste, especially if they're English.

The silver lining in Will's uphill work was that it got him out of the house, where he didn't have to deal with Anne's taciturn family or his unruly children. When he explained that he needed to go further afield to find gamblers who could be persuaded to buy Maréchal's cards, no one raised any objections. He began to feel like a coal miner, who just has to get out ten tons of coal every day. No one cares how long it takes him, or what he does on the way to or from work. So no matter how much money he made selling cards or gambling, the Bard made a point of bringing home a pound of bacon or a dozen eggs. You'd be surprised how far you can stretch token effort.

As he did his best thinking on his feet, Will made habit of walking for a couple of hours each day. Arguably superstitious, he was methodical in his own way, varying his routine by heading in a different direction each day. Picking a card at random, he went north for clubs, west for diamonds, south for hearts, and east for spades. Setting out on the road running past their cottage, he tossed a coin to guide him left or right. While this method lent itself to adventure, he soon discovered that it made it difficult to retrace his steps.

Will considered memorizing each junction as he did a card, but he wanted to save his memory for gambling, where money was at stake. He made a practice of venturing from home without consulting a map, which allowed him to let his mind wander while he walked. If there's a secret to his writing it was freeing his mind from the constraints of planning his route. After getting lost a couple of times, he began carrying a map with him to make sure he got home. By then, his creativity had peaked, so following a map didn't cramp his style.

Although his methodology, if you can even call it that, led him on some wild goose chases, he covered a surprising amount of the countryside around Stratford. Between his walks and their honeymoon, Will also got to know the Avon quite well. There's something about a river that brings people together, regardless of their station in life. Walking along the Avon also proved to be a wonderful way to catch bits of conversation. Although you might think that a tavern would be a better place to listen to people, Will observed being outdoors frees people's tongues even better than alcohol. It's also a much better place to glimpse a ghost.

One might think that his frequent travels distracted him from his mission of becoming a playwright, but his experiences provided grist for the mill, sifted well by his walks. Indeed, he made a practice of retiring to his lair in the attic when he returned home, discharging his thoughts onto paper while they were still fresh in his mind. By the time he was called for dinner, Will could put aside his writing and lend himself to conversation. After listening to the idle talk of gamblers, it was a relief to hear from his children.

Indeed, Will shuddered to think what their lives would have been like without children in the Hathaway household. In that respect, Anne's prompt pregnancy was a blessing. Before her family tired of his company and could pester him with questions about what he did with his time, they were thrust onto the stage as caregivers. To their credit, they took to their roles remarkably well, allowing the Bard the distance he needed to continue writing while they changed diapers. Despite their squawking, Will suspected that they were glad to see the back of him when he left for France with his family in tow.

The Bard blamed Queen Elizabeth for the suddenness of their departure from England. He later came to know enough about the machinations of her majesty's court to understand that one of her henchmen may have been the culprit. In any case, someone must have informed the court about Maréchal's cards, because they stole Will's thunder by coming up with decks featuring the Virgin Queen—as the Queen of Diamonds, rather than the Queen of Hearts. Pointedly, there was no likeness of Henri as the King of Hearts. Needless to say, this development put a crimp in his efforts to peddle Maréchal's cards in England, as he informed him in a letter. Will admitted that he was surprised by his mentor's response:

My dear friend,

(I caution you not to use our names or addresses. The return address on the envelope is bogus, but my letter might have drawn attention without one. Please follow suit.)

Your news may be a blessing in disguise, for it helps explain why card sales have been so disappointing in England. It has been said that imitation is the sincerest form of flattery, so perhaps we can pat ourselves on the back for our ingenious scheme. Though the English have copied your idea, you have managed to sell a substantial number of cards before our luck ran out. C'est la vie. With the Queen in their corner, I see no point in trying to compete with the English on their own turf.

Perhaps it is just as well, for sources have informed me that the King is ill-tempered, so it is likely that Henri will succeed him. As you can imagine, this will open up all of France as a market for my cards. With the King of Hearts in our back pocket, we can corner the market. However, as you have seen for yourself in England, we are not the only ones who seize upon great ideas. We must position ourselves to take advantage of this windfall when the bough breaks.

If you cannot escape the clutches of England, I need to know now, so that I can find someone to replace you. Yet I hope you realize what an opportunity this is for you and your family. Not only to witness history, but to make it yourselves. Your three children could grow up speaking English and French fluently. Just imagine what your life would have been like if you had grown up eating French food. Consider the future of your young family, who could be citizens of the world. I look forward to your prompt reply.

Cordially,

X.

P.S. My family owns a vineyard near St. Emilion, with a guesthouse your family could stay in for the foreseeable future.

The devil himself couldn't have made a more compelling case, for Maréchal must have known that Will wouldn't be able to resist the offer of a refuge in France. It's unclear what he would have done if Anne had refused to go, but she must have known that this was the opportunity of a lifetime. Indeed, he feared that she might have spent her entire life in Stratford if Queen Elizabeth hadn't agreed to become the Queen of Diamonds. A reminder that when one door closes, another opens.

Anne's family, however, were livid. Listening to his exasperated mother-in-law, Will told himself that he needed to turn her into a surly character in one of his plays. "After all we've done for you, I can't believe that you have the gall to take my daughter and my grandchildren to some far-off place, leaving us to fend for ourselves. If I tumble down the stairs and break my neck, it will be on your head!" Good riddance, Will said to himself, uncharitably, when they left in the middle of the night to catch a boat to Calais.

As eager as he was to return to France, Will dreaded the sea voyage, not so much for himself, but for Anne and their children. Remembering his first impressions of France as a fifteen-year-old, he wanted his family to be filled with the same sense of excitement that he experienced. So he was disappointed when they slept through most of the voyage, which was slow-going because of the lack of wind. Every now and then, the English Channel is becalmed, just not when you need it to be. He was looking forward to feeling the wind on his face, and enjoying the sea spray, which he was sure would delight his children. Perhaps it's because they grew up on a river, which provides endless opportunities to play, but his young family seemed unimpressed by the ocean. Will stood alone on the deck as the ship neared land, looking upon France with so much nostalgia, wondering what destiny had in store for him now that he was a married man with a family to support.

CHAPTER 7

As soon as he set foot in France, Will thought of Rose, of course, wondering what had become of her, but afraid to ask. Despite his failure to find anyone interested in producing *Love's Labour's Lost*, he wanted to tell Henri about the sequel he'd written, and he was curious to see the king's response. The Bard thought it better not to mention *Titus Andronicus* because he knew it wasn't a crowd pleaser, which is what everyone wanted. In that respect, he felt he had an ace up his sleeve with *Love's Labour's Found*, but he knew that Henri had his heart set on seeing the prequel on the London stage.

The journey to St. Emilion was nothing like Will's first foray into France, not only because he had his family in tow, but because they took a carriage with all of their luggage on board. As much as he would have liked to stop along the way, to show his family some of the sights, it seemed prudent to get to their new home as soon as possible. Will reminisced that if had to do it over again, he would have broken up the trip, since the swaying coach made him sick, but his children slept through much of the bumpy ride. Nonetheless, Anne seemed stunned to see what lay beyond her childhood home.

Anne was surprised to find out how much French she remembered, for she had taken it in school, but had never had an opportunity to speak the language. Will blamed her parents for never taking her abroad. Like many English people, they dared not imagine what lies beyond their shore. Were it not for their sailors, the English might never have known they were marooned on an island. Still, realizing that they don't know any better, perhaps one can forgive the English for their food.

There is a corollary, of course, for we forgive the French for their shortcomings because of their food. Indeed, Will was certain that food was the key to making their dusty journey palatable to their children. Whenever they awoke, he made a point of stopping at the first bakery that they encountered. Recollecting his discovery of French pastry, he wanted to make sure that their children tasted the cornucopia of baked goods that are so plentiful in France. Sadly, they had no idea what he meant by cornucopia, so Will had to show them a patisserie in all its glory. He hadn't realized what a sheltered life they led in Stratford.

Imagine Will's delight in ushering his children into a cozy patisserie in Amiens, which straddles the Somme River. As they entered the charming shop, the sound of the doorbell triggered memories of his first trip to France, and the smell of fresh baked goods almost made him swoon. Their children looked about the place in wonder, pointing to pastries in glass cases and asking their names. The young woman behind the counter patiently pronounced the names of each delectable creation, while their children did their best to repeat the names. Will could almost see their little minds working, savoring the sound of the pastries, with their mouths watering at the sight of such treats. As much as he delighted in their response, he felt a tinge of envy, wishing he'd been exposed to France at such an early age.

The sight of their children in that patisserie in Amiens seemed to wash away any doubts that Anne must have had about moving to France. Indeed, the smile on her face reminded Will of the Mona Lisa, for it was a knowing smile, of someone who understands the secret of life. Just what that secret is, he couldn't say, for Anne had a way of keeping things to herself. He had come to associate such introspection with Celtic people, whose waters run deep. Yet that encounter with French culture, hitherto unknown to their children, provided a tonic for Anne, who acted as if she was coming home after a long absence.

Even their children, who had taken refuge in slumber on the long journey, began to wake up as they approached the south of France, where the scent of flowers and fruit trees was palpable. While England has its own beauty in the verdant fields and forests, it is nothing like the light in France, whose slanting sunbeams illuminate not just the landscape, but the entire atmosphere. Indeed, even their chatty children quieted down as they approached the valley carved out by the Dordogne River. The sheer magnificence of the countryside, with autumn colors their children had never seen, brought a hush to their lips. Even the driver ceased his torrent of words.

Unfortunately, their driver found his voice again when they arrived in St. Emilion, because he had to wait while Will tried to locate Maréchal's contact, who was out to lunch. The French are religious about leisurely lunches, which can extend into late afternoon, as was the case when Will's family arrived on such a glorious day. After a fruitless search for the man he was looking for, they found a restaurant near the Place du Marché, where they could sit outside near a fountain, much to the delight of their children. As you can imagine, dining al fresco was quite a treat for Will's family. Of course their children had been on picnics during what passes for summer in England, but they had never been to a place where diners spilled out into the streets.

Leaving his family to explore the town, he tried to placate the driver by buying him a good bottle of wine. Will finally caught up with Maréchal's contact, who informed him that the guest house was not in St. Emilion per se, but in nearby Castillon. While he was disappointed that they weren't going to be actually living in St. Emilion, he knew they would be close by, so he counted his blessings. Returning to the café where he'd left the driver, Will was alarmed to find that the man was too inebriated to drive. Will managed to find someone else to take them to Castillon, but that required transferring all of their luggage, taking up the rest of the afternoon.

Ironically, their new driver turned out to be even more talkative than the last, but at least he was knowledgeable. Perhaps Will should have known that Castillon was the site of the final battle in the Hundred Years' War, but the driver seemed to relish telling Will about the rout of the English.

"I have no idea how much you know about your country's history, but surely you've heard of the war that lasted for over a century. The English commander in Bordeaux, John Talbot, had a fearsome reputation, but we beat him at his own game, divide and conquer. In his attempt to head us off before we could re-take Bordeaux, he snuck up along the river, but found himself trapped by one of our regiments. To be fair, had your squabbling commanders, Lancaster and York, come to Talbot's rescue, things might have turned out differently. But they didn't. The last battle was fought in Castillon, where Talbot and his son lost their lives. If you don't know your history, your children will."

Will was tempted to ask about Agincourt, when the English beat the French against all odds, but he didn't want to be the one who re-ignited the Hundred Years' War. Nonetheless, he was thankful for the lesson in history, which was not his strong suit in school, but better than his Latin. Although the driver's boasting stuck in his craw, he had to admit that he had never heard of John Talbot, who the Bard later immortalized in *Henry VI*. Will liked to think that living in Castillon helped make up for his shallow sense of history. How could he have known that such boring information was so full of drama?

In retrospect, his time in southwest France proved to be fruitful, not only giving him ideas for future plays, but in learning about wine. "I cannot begin to tell you what a revelation it was for me to partake of such a miraculous substance. Try to imagine what it was like to grow up in a country without any grapes. No wonder so many of my countrymen gave their lives to secure a piece of France for posterity, even if in vain. To think that Henry V once ruled England and France. Alas, he died too young for his legacy to take root."

Anne could not hide her disappointment as they left St. Emilion, with tears streaming down her face. Will was touched by her response, for it showed how affected she was by France, which came as a great relief to him. For he knew that she had qualms about leaving Stratford, the only place she'd ever known, not to mention her family. Yet that proved to be part of the appeal of France, offering Anne a fresh start, away from all that was familiar to her. For his own part, Will was doubly happy to be back in France again, and to share his love of it with Anne and their children.

As they neared Castillon he was pleased to see its setting, overlooking the Dordogne River. The town itself was rather ordinary, but the spectacular view made up for Castillon's shortcomings. The guest house that Maréchal had provided was small by comparison with the thatched cottage that Anne grew up in, but they had it to themselves. Situated on the outskirts of town, the two-story house had a tile roof and a huge yard with an overgrown garden. For the first time in her life, Anne was mistress of the house, and they had their own home, answering to no one. Their children, of course, couldn't wait to get outside to play, after being cooped up in the carriage for so long.

With so few belongings, it didn't take long for them to move into the house, which was sparsely furnished. Lying down on the bed together, Anne and Will could tell that it wasn't very comfortable, but they no longer had to worry about waking up her family. As they explored the house, Will was happy to find that there was an attic where he would be able to write with a view of the river. It occurred to him that in some ways, they had come full circle, as if the Avon flowed into the Dordogne; their lives were still connected by a river.

He had hoped that they might be able to enroll all three of their children in school, which was the best way for them to acquire French, but Hemnet and Judith were still too young. Nonetheless, Susanna took to school readily, delighted to have so many playmates, even if she didn't understand them at first. Seeing how quickly she learned the language by being with other children, he and Anne took them to the park as much as possible. This also helped them meet other parents, and provided opportunities for Anne to improve her French.

As much as he would have loved to remain in Castillon and work on another play, Will was mindful that the journey had consumed much of his savings. While he appreciated Maréchal's foresight in anticipating Henri's succession, Will saw no sign that such an event was imminent. Thus, he understood that he needed to resume peddling playing cards, concentrating on the areas that he hadn't visited yet. There was an element of adventure in his plan, but he was mindful that his success in selling cards in Huguenot communities could go sour when (and if) Henri was crowned King of France. Little did the Bard know how long Henri would resist converting to Catholicism.

Although he considered following his usual habit of improvising his route, it occurred to Will that he could take advantage of the Dordogne to venture even further afield than he had in England. He soon discovered that the town's wharf was quite a busy place, for much of the wine from St. Emilion was shipped from Castillon. Wine destined for export was sent to the harbor in Royan on the

Atlantic, but most of it was routed to Bordeaux, on the Garonne River. Consequently, opportunities abounded to take different boats headed downstream.

He didn't fully comprehend the lay of the land until he caught his first boat, which clearly wasn't designed for passengers, but was filled with casks of wine. A sight to behold for an Englishman. Indeed, he felt a bit like a child asking if he could catch a ride on the boat, but he won over the dour boatman when Will told him that he was going to Bordeaux to gamble. The boatman responded, "I suppose we can make room for a gamblin' man, but there's no place to sit. So I can't sell you a seat, but some loose change will get you part way. Let's see what you've got."

Digging into his pockets to find a few coins, the boatman stopped Will before he could even count them. 'That's close enough to get you there, but you'll have to do better next time. I'm a gambler myself, so I'm counting on you to share some of your winnings if you get lucky. I follow the golden rule, and I ask you to do the same."

Will was familiar with tow paths, of course, having lived by the Avon most of his life, but the French have their own way doing things. Although the terrain along the lower reaches of the Dordogne was gentle enough to use horses to tow boats, there are sections where outcroppings of rock make it impossible for horses to pass. While boats headed downstream can simply drift along on the current, the tides play havoc with any craft left to the mercy of the river. This predicament created an occupation for crews of freshwater sailors who towed barges in the time-honored tradition of rowing.

While this system of moving cargo up and down the Dordogne and the Garonne is cumbersome, there was no alternative. The wind is too unpredictable to rely on sailboats. While it might seem simpler to transport wine by carriage, casks of wine and spirits are quite heavy, and horse-drawn carriages are easy pickings for highwaymen.

Boats, on the other hand, can carry an enormous amount of weight, albeit slowly. As much as he appreciated the genial boatman and the view of the lovely countryside, Will quickly realized that he could have walked to Bordeaux faster than it took by boat, while hanging on to the change in his pocket.

Fortunately, he soon discovered that the delays were blessings in disguise. For the boatmen who shuttle barges between tow paths were natural gamblers, with time on their hands between boats. Though rowing is quite strenuous work, it is short-lived, leaving the small crews with nothing to do between shepherding barges from place to place. The devil himself couldn't have devised a better situation for gambling, with strong young men far from any other temptations other than wine and spirits.

The long and short of it is that Will took to the river like a muskrat, turning his voyages into profitable ventures and finding that Bordeaux had much to offer. Indeed, he discovered that the riverfront in Bordeaux was a great place to find card games. When his luck ran out, he made the rounds of book stalls, where playing cards were usually sold. To his credit, he usually ignored the multitude of women in Bordeaux, most of whom avoided the waterfront.

Bordeaux' proximity to the ocean and two major rivers makes it an ideal place for commerce, but Will found little there to inspire him. He longed to find a hill where he could look out on the ocean, or see the undulating banks of the Dordogne in the distance, but there was no place to get any perspective.

Will soon abandoned his former routine of walking, mainly because the river offered endless possibilities. Instead of setting off each day in different directions as he had in Stratford, he alternated between going upriver or downriver, flipping a coin to keep things from going stale. However, Will found that he had much better luck in Bordeaux, where the place was booming, so he ended up only going upriver once a week.

Truth be told, he was reluctant to go upstream because he was afraid of encountering his cousins in Bergerac. Of course he knew that the chances of running into them were slim, but he preferred to remember the place as a turning point in his life. He was now a married man, with children and responsibilities. Bergerac would never be the same for him. Nor did he want to spoil his memory of his cousins, who would be full-grown women by now. Why put himself in a position of temptation?

Nonetheless, it was just a matter of time before his sound judgment and sense of propriety gave way to curiosity, so when sales of cards in Bordeaux began to wane around Christmas (when even gamblers begin to think of others), he spent a week heading upstream. He was rewarded for his daring by winning a considerable amount of money gambling with some English interlopers who he met on a riverboat. They were taking advantage of the wonderful weather to play cards on the deck. These dandies were glad to find a fellow countryman who could speak French, and they could obviously afford to gamble for high stakes, which suited him well.

However, when one of them accused him of counting cards, he replied, "There is nothing illegal about being observant, which I highly recommend to you. Indeed, memory is my best friend." For some reason, that set the man off, and he drew his sword, even though Will was obviously unarmed.

The hothead said, "You pretend to be a gentleman, but you're obviously a peasant with a taste for gambling. Since you can't make an honest living, you rub shoulders with men of breeding. Did you really think you could fleece me and get away with it?"

Before Will had time to protest, a woman wearing a scarlet cape came up behind his adversary and held a dagger to his throat. The Bard recognized Rose immediately, but he was still startled, especially when she spoke to him in English.

"Put down your sword, monsieur. This is no place to settle a quarrel." The Englishman's friends wisely backed away, but he was slow to put down his sword, so Rose pressed the point of her dagger against his neck. Wincing, he dropped his sword, and Rose ordered Will to pick it up. He knew better than to hesitate. The Englishman had no idea how close he was to death.

Releasing the man, Rose spun him around and looked him in the eye. "You are not welcome in France, monsieur. You never were. You burnt Joan of Arc at the stake because you were afraid of her. Yet she lives on in our hearts and minds. You English tried in vain to put down roots here, but they rotted in French soil. God placed you on an island for good reason. You are not fit to live in accord with others. If you set foot here again, I will gladly spill more English blood. But your corpse would foul our land. I banish thee!" Rose grabbed the man's sword out of the Bard's hand and flung it into the river.

The trio of Englishmen left without saying a word, leaving Will face to face with Rose, whose blood was still boiling. "Scum. I could have killed the lot of them by myself, but I don't want to attract attention. Swear to me that you won't tell anyone you've seen me."

He gave her his word, of course, but he was afraid that she was going to ask him what he was doing there. He tried to deflect any questions by offering an explanation. "As you can see, I'm still a gambler. I returned to England for awhile, but France drew me back."

Rose replied, "With a ring on your finger, I see. I don't recall that you wore one."

"Appearing to be a married man has its advantages, I find, as it disarms fellow gamblers. They think I'm just one of them."

"Such shrewdness doesn't become you. I much preferred your innocence. So where are you living now? I haven't seen you in Bergerac before."

Having learned to stay close to the truth, he responded, "I have relatives in St. Sauveur, not far from here, but my cousins are already growing tired of me. You're not likely to see me again."

Rose seemed suspicious of him, for good reason, of course. "I'm surprised that you're not in Pau, where Henri plays his waiting game. I'm a master at it, but out of necessity, rather than ambition."

He responded, "To tell you the truth, I'm counting on the King to pull some strings, as I've had no luck getting a play on the London stage. Mere ambition perhaps, but I like to think it's a calling. I can't say the same for gambling, though it's kept me alive. How ironic that what I love doesn't love me back. An all too familiar story."

Obviously, Rose didn't just happen to intervene, but was on duty when he came there to gamble, but Will realized that she had found a way to hide in plain sight. Disguised as a lady fond of gambling, she lent an air of respectability to the riverboat, while ensuring the security of the passengers. While she certainly stood out as an independent woman, no one would suspect that she was a fierce warrior. Whoever had hired her obviously appreciated her usefulness, but they could have had no way of knowing that they were playing with fire.

It was time for the Bard to leave. When he said as much, she took the opportunity to say goodbye without revealing any more. Both of them knew that it would be best if they never ran into each other again. She had gotten him out of a difficult situation, but he doubted that she stepped in out of the goodness of her heart. She was simply doing her job, allowing her to bide her time until Henri let down his guard. Will made a point of walking through the side streets of Bergerac to make sure he wasn't being followed, before making his way to the wharf to catch the next boat. Even then, he took no chances, but got off before Castillon, and walked home the rest of the way.

Will couldn't conceal his consternation from Anne, who said, "You look as if you'd seen a ghost." He saw no point in pretending that nothing had happened, and told her all about Rose. She replied, "I had hoped that you would put your past behind you, William, but it sounds as if you were drawn back to France for your own reasons, not for the sake of your family."

"I assure you that Rose means nothing to me, and never did. I was but a boy when I encountered her. I suppose that I let myself become ensnared by her, for she exerts considerable magnetism. Yet I thought I was free from her pull, so I had no qualms about returning to France. Save your jealousy for my cousins, who are much closer to my heart, but you have nothing to fear from Rose."

Having put his foot in his mouth, the Bard was forced to confess that he had done more than kiss his cousins, but Anne forgave him his trespasses. "Some things are better left unsaid, so don't expect me to reciprocate in telling you about my past. A lot of water has flowed under the bridge we stood on in Stratford. We are now very different people, with three children who are completely dependent on us. Promise me you will avoid Rose at all costs. I think it best if you avoid going to Bergerac all together. Indeed, I don't want to hear about any chance meetings with one of your cousins. I see no reason for you to head upriver anymore."

He thought to himself, 'I too, have been banished.'

Fearing that his life would become completely predictable, Will let a coin toss determine whether to walk or catch a boat, which meant that he didn't always go to Bordeaux. Instead, he reverted to his propensity for improvising his route, knowing that it would be easy to find his way home without having to resort to a map. Indeed, he soon discovered that most maps were out of date, since the area around St. Emilion was becoming a wine mecca.

Curious as he was by nature, the Bard made a point of inquiring about local legends in every place he visited. His curiosity was rewarded when he passed through the otherwise unremarkable town of Bourg, which used to overlook the Garonne, but was now situated on the Dordogne because of the shifting sands. While not a legend, he found this bit of history to be a useful reminder that things aren't always what they seem.

Further up the Dordogne, the historic town of Blaye proved to be a more fruitful place for local lore. Built on the first defensible point along the river, Will came to think of it as a kind of pressure point on an artery. As you might imagine, Blaye played a key role in the Hundred Years' War, which he found endlessly fascinating because of the shifts in power between the English and the French. Blaye was also the home of 12th century troubadour Jaufre Rudel, who made much of the theme of *amor de longa*, love from afar. Legend has it that the troubadour fell in love with a princess from Tripoli, and sailed to join her, but fell ill on the journey and died in her arms. A scene from a play, or perhaps an opera, which even the Bard admitted was beyond his range.

The old man who told him about Rudel turned out to be a font of knowledge, insisting on showing Will his chateau, which was built on the very place where Charlemagne's nephew, Roland, was buried after being killed in the famous battle of Roncesvalles in the Pyrenees. Yet not even this wise man could tell the Bard how Roland ended up along the Dordogne after being slain in the mountains. "God's will," was all he had to say; no wonder Will put a curse on anyone who moved his bones.

Mindful that history was unfolding in front of his eyes, he was eager to see Henri again, despite Will's reluctance to admit that he'd failed to find any interest in *Love's Labour's Lost* in London. Indeed, it had only been performed in Navarre as far as he knew, which did little to tell the world about "Good King Henri." Rather than leaving Anne alone with their children, Will arranged for the whole family to visit Pau, which also provided an opportunity for him to show Anne the Pyrenees—a chain of mountains beyond the imagination of anyone raised in England.

He was surprised to see how little Henri had changed, still leading a life complicated by multiple relationships that Will didn't want to know about. The king was very discreet with the Bard's family, of course, and charmed his family by taking them all on a walk along the river that runs through Pau. After the slow-moving Dordogne, his children were delighted by the Gave de Pau, with its torrent of rushing water from the snow-capped mountains. Indeed, the sound of the river made it difficult to talk, so while Anne and the children continued to explore the river, Henri took Will aside for a private conversation in a café with a magnificent view of the Pyrenees.

"You've come a long way since the boy I first met," he said. "The woman you married has brought out the best in you, but you have yet to make your mark on the world. Nonetheless, the stars are aligning for both of us, my friend. I wish my cousin well, but it's just a matter of time before I am crowned King of France. Even Queen Elizabeth will sit up and take notice, and I will be in a position to put a word in her ear about your future as a playwright. Indeed, I am determined to prove that my faith in you was well placed.

"In addition to being a shrewd gambler, you are a natural story-teller, my friend. The bits of entertainment you wrote for my court showed great promise, and you proved your mettle with *Love's Labour's Lost*. Yet you left the audience dangling, so perhaps there is poetic justice in the delay in getting your play on the London stage. Like Princess Anne, you must exercise great patience. I will use my influence to get your work staged in your own country, not only for your sake, but for mine. Indeed, I am counting on you to immortalize me.

"In truth, your scheme to turn me into the King of Hearts whetted my appetite. Although having my likeness on a deck of cards was but a trifle, I loved the irony of having so many of my subjects holding my likeness in their hands, while I hold their lives in mine. While they gamble for small stakes, their fortunes rise and fall on my own bets, where lives are at stake.

"I suppose that it was premature for you to pen a play about me while I was in the process of making history. I'll wager you could cook up some lighter fare that would help put my kingdom on the map. While you succeeded in writing something that amused my court and my subjects in Navarre, you need to have more than one arrow in your quiver."

As you can imagine, Will took his cue from him with utmost pleasure, reaching into his leather satchel to pull out his manuscripts for *Titus Andronicus* and *Love's Labour's Found*. "This is just the beginning," Will told him. "I'm working on a set of historical plays, starting with Henry VI of England, who squandered his father's success in conquering France. Of course his dream of uniting England and France turned out to be a nightmare for the English. Living in Castillon, I am besieged by the ghosts of those who fought on both sides, killing each other in the name of God. Their patriotic fervor persists, even in death, as they whisper their tales in my ear. I will do my best to bring Joan of Arc back to life, on stage."

What Will didn't tell Henri is that his expedition to London left him with the realization that English audiences really wanted to see plays about English kings, not French ones. Indeed, he was pushing his luck by reminding them that their king lost France. However, the Bard figured that it would prepare the ground for a play about Henry V, whose victory at Agincourt ranked alongside England's defeat of the Spanish Armada.

Henri couldn't have been more pleased. "Bravo, my friend. I can hardly wait to read them. How can your queen refuse to grant me a favor when you now have demonstrated your abilities? If all goes well you can leave Maréchal's cards to someone else, and turn all your attention to writing. Perhaps we can perform another one of your plays in Navarre, but we will have to select the cast more carefully this time."

He'd promised Rose that he wouldn't say anything, but Henri's life was at stake. Will said to him, "I'm sorry to tell you that I ran into Rose in Bergerac. Thanks to her intervention, I managed to elude some English gamblers who accused me of cheating. I gather that she's employed to maintain order, so perhaps she has put her grievance with you to rest."

"Far from it," Henri replied. "She lies in wait for me like a spider. For the sake of the women I know, I've had her watched closely by contacts in Bergerac. I'm glad that you were able to see her one last time, because I've had her locked up in a convent to ensure that she doesn't hurt someone and forfeit her life. We had to drug her, which was the only way we could subdue her. I'm sure she would have fought to the death."

Will responded, "What a turn of events. I saw her less than a month ago. She entreated, nay, ordered me not to tell anyone, so in good conscience I couldn't betray her. Seeing you, however, I could not conceal the truth."

"Rest easy, my friend," Henri said. "You did not betray her, for I had her apprehended a week ago, before she could disappear again. She has concealed herself for years now, managing to elude me. She seems to have a sixth sense, knowing when we're closing in on her."

"I know all too well how canny she is, so I'm not surprised that she's evaded capture. I'm glad to know that you have found a way to ensure that she doesn't harm someone. I only hope that the nuns who have taken her in understand Rose's dangerous nature. Indeed, her only hope of being tamed lies in other women. You have acted wisely, your majesty."

~

The Bard was only too happy to share his news with Anne, who was relieved to hear that Rose no longer posed a threat to their happiness. She agreed that Henri's solution was well-advised, but she didn't conceal her concern that he was still playing with fire by being involved in numerous liaisons. "It seems to me that the king should have learned a lesson from getting involved with a woman who could have murdered him. What he considers her passionate nature could turn against him. If he is to become King of France, he will find himself scrutinized in many quarters. Indeed, a good marriage might well save his life." Prescient words from Will's wise wife.

Although Pau is hardly a large city, Will and Anne and were glad to return to Castillon, where their children were thriving in the warm weather, which drew them out-of-doors in a way unthinkable to anyone raised in England. Lest he appear disloyal to his country, Will made it clear that he loved his country, which is why he felt entitled to point out its shortcomings. Indeed, he shared Henry V's vision of a United Kingdom, for he knew well what France brought to the table. Clearly, he adored many aspects of France, but never had any intention of abandoning England. He only wanted to give Anne and their children a taste of France, even if he sensed that his destiny lay in London.

Having assured Anne that Rose would no longer cast a shadow over him, he saw no need to tell her Henri's other news. Knowing that he was slated to become King of France, Henri was well aware of the opportunity to capitalize on his good fortune by promoting Maréchal's playing cards throughout France. However, to use his own words, he had "other fish to fry," and so did Will.

"While I'm pleased that your scheme has worked out well for you and Maréchal, you have better things to do than peddling playing cards. With but a simple edict I can require that Maréchal's cards be used exclusively throughout my kingdom. While this arrangement will benefit him greatly, he will no longer have need of your services. Here's what I propose. If you can arrange with Maréchal to remain in his guest house while you're in Castillon, I will pay your rent. Instead of wasting your time peddling cards, I'll commission you to write plays for the next ten years. After that, you're on your own."

Pointedly, he did not ask the Bard what he thought about his offer, but acted as if it was his royal prerogative. Needless to say, Will didn't ask him about any terms, but trusted that he would look after him. The Bard knew that if his plays didn't meet his favor, the king could terminate his offer at any time. Will chose to believe that Henri's faith in him would bear fruit for both of them. As much as he wanted to share this good news with Anne, he feared that she'd want to know the details of the arrangement. He suspected that she would bristle at the idea of a gentlemen's agreement. Will decided to keep his own counsel on the matter, which he intended to share with her when Henri became King of France. Why worry about the future before it arrived?

The only problem with this turn of events is that he had to act as if he were still a gambler and a peddler, which was still the case with respect to his writing. In truth, he didn't think that he could have written much if he'd stayed home. Being cooped up in the attic would have driven him crazy. He needed to get out in the world, to walk the battlefields, to talk with passersby, and to spend time on the river, where his thoughts flowed freely. He knew that Anne didn't want to hear about his gambling, and he'd always been evasive about how he spent his days, so he saw no reason to tell her that he'd given up everything else to write.

"I cannot honestly say that I was more productive, but I believe that the quality of my writing got better. I still gambled from time to time, of course, which I like to think sharpened my memory and my ear for dialogue. History will judge how well I succeeded, but I am certain that spending time on French soil gave body to my work. Walking among the landmarks of the frequent wars between England and France helped bring the past alive for me. At times I could practically hear the clash of steel, the shouts of battle, and the cries of despair, especially from the women who had to watch men wasting their time fighting. If only they could have plowed the fields, instead of spilling blood in them."

CHAPTER 8

He welcomed the growing rumors of Henri's impending succession with great satisfaction, feeling that Henri had finally come into his own. But Will had no idea how deep ran the schism between Catholics and Protestants. In that respect, he was wasn't prepared for Henri's request to suppress *Love's Labour's Found*. His note to the Bard was cryptic:

The premature news of my change in fortune is tempered by the realization that I now have a thousand eyes watching my every move. Although I am loath to curtail your career, I must ask you to withhold circulation of your latest play, for it strikes too close to home. Like the Bible, people will read into it what they want. Those on both sides of the fence will find fault, exacerbating the controversy that casts a shadow over me. Indeed, methinks my life was simpler before fortune smiled upon me, only to frown on my ambivalence.

I must ask you to burn this missive, lest it fall into the wrong hands. More to the point, I am afraid that you must destroy any copies of your creation, for it could threaten both our futures. To soften the blow I assure you that you shall be well compensated for your sacrifice. Know as well that I was much taken with your work, which was full of wit and wisdom. It bodes well for your future, my friend, and I look forward to seeing what else you have in your quiver.

X.

The Bard was devastated, of course, and found it hard to take any satisfaction in Henri's praise. If anything, the king's compliment added salt to his wound, knowing that he had to destroy the best play he'd ever written. Added to his dismay was the realization that *Love's Labour's Lost* would leave audiences hanging, perhaps for eternity. He'd been so proud of himself for finding a way to bring all of the protagonists together, while adding yet another romance to the story. How much he had looked forward to seeing Princess Anne accept the King of Navarre and to hear her announce the forthcoming weddings. Alas, alack, it was not to be!

Like a boy, the Bard ran to Anne for comfort, hoping she could stop the pain. But she was his wife, not his mother, and didn't mince words. "I'm afraid that Henri has a point, for *Love's Labour's Found* is too timely, touching upon issues of the day that are fresh in everyone's mind. You would do well to concentrate on your historical plays, which provide some distance on events. If I were you, I'd be tempted to make a copy, in case Henri changes his mind. However, I think you should destroy the original, so you can look him in the eye. Though audiences will never see your work, you have touched his heart, as well as mine, so you should count your blessings. God sees all, William, so your play will never be lost."

As usual, Anne's prudence carried the day, for he knew she was right. Yet it seemed a shame to waste *Love's Labour's Found* on The Almighty, for Will knew that its humor would be wasted on God, though it may be blasphemy to say so. The Bard prepared himself to burn his play, like a soldier who imagines himself scaling a wall before he actually mounts it. That is to say, he worked up his nerve to destroy what he believed to be his finest work. Rather like Abraham, when God commanded him to kill his son.

Unfortunately, God did not grant Will a reprieve at the 11th hour, so he finally had to burn his play in the fireplace late at night, so that his children wouldn't see him weeping. Despite the fact that *Love's Labour's Found* was supposed to be a comedy, Will burned it in melodramatic fashion, reading each page aloud before throwing it on the fire. "If God had read my play, as Anne assured me, he hadn't heard it read out loud by the author, who's a decent actor if I may say so, and appreciates the timing.

"While I know I can't compare the pain of having to destroy my play with the throes of childbirth, I cried out in my own way, thinking of Gwendolyn, the King's sous chef, who felt obliged to abandon her child. How I wish that things had turned out as well for me in the end, but it wasn't meant to be. It took me all night to enact every role and burn each page, my tears hindering the excruciating process of destroying the entire work. I could've sworn that I heard the cries of some of my characters as they went up in smoke, choking on their words, as I did as well, trying to overcome all I had learned about projecting my voice."

Like a parent grieving for the loss of their child, the Bard was torn by sorrow. Indeed, he had to force himself to work on *Henry VI*, which was another painful reminder of the vicissitudes of life. At the same time, he drew inspiration from living among the ghosts who inhabited the region. He expressed doubt that he could have written any of his plays about Henry VI while living England, which is a world away from battlefields soaked with English and French blood. Indeed, Will confessed that he couldn't drink a glass of red wine without thinking of the Hundred Years' War.

Will also credited his time in France for his portrait of Joan of Arc, who he considered to be one of the finest heroines he'd penned. He admitted that her character was also inspired by Rose, whose fire courses through the veins of the martyr. If you look closely, you will see that Joan's duel with the Dauphin bears some resemblance to the scene the Bard wrote for Henri, where Marie, inspired by

Rose, disarms the nobleman. Art imitates life, of course, and vice versa.

Will endeavored to put the demise of *Love's Labour's Found* behind him by burrowing into the history that surrounded him in Castillon to write *Henry VI Part I*. Visiting the place where John Talbot died was especially touching because his son was killed as well. Talbot only had himself to blame for his son's presence on the battlefield, and encouraged him to escape, but the son shared his father's strength of character. Will confessed that he found no account of the son's death. Yet in his mind's eye, the Bard saw the son die in the arms of his father.

~

Fortunately, Will didn't have long to wait before the news of Henri's ascension to the throne, which he regarded as a good omen for his career. Of course he was genuinely happy for the king, as well all as his subjects. If ever a child had been granted a good start in life, it was Henri, whose lips were rubbed with garlic when he was born before he was given a taste of Jurançon wine. Though baptized a Catholic, Henri's mother raised him as a Protestant, setting up a chain of events that would shake the foundations of France. Yet there is no doubt that he was beloved as King of Navarre, famous for his dictum "A chicken in every pot."

Nonetheless, I was not prepared for the hostility he met as a Protestant, even if I should have been from witnessing the religious strife in England. Of course I was too young to see the sudden turn of events ushered in with Queen Elizabeth's coronation, but the aftermath played out in my lifetime. In Will's case, he was aware even as child that his father was suspected of being a Catholic. That may account for the decline in his business, which had a direct effect on his life.

As much as Will hoped that Henri would use his influence with the Queen to stage *Love's Labour's Lost* in

London, he realized that such success might jeopardize his family's pleasant life in France. In that respect, he greeted the invitation from Philip Henslowe to produce his first play at the Rose, of all places, with some misgiving. While tainted by his ownership in Bankside brothels, Henslowe was known to be a daring entrepreneur, making him a good match for producing a play written by an unknown author about a little-known king in a foreign country. While the Bard's confidence was bolstered by the fact that his play had been well received in Navarre, he knew that London audiences were another kettle of fish.

More to the point, he wanted to be present to ensure that *Love's Labour's Lost* was produced in the best possible fashion, not only to establish his reputation, but to cast a glowing light on Henri. Will was also well aware that he needed to get off on the right foot with the Queen, on whom his future as a playwright was completely dependent. Without the sequel, he would have no opportunity to overcome any misstep. Nor would *Titus Andronicus* erase any dissatisfaction with his initial effort. In short, the Bard knew that his life depended on his first foray onto the London stage.

As much as Anne thrived in France, they both knew that their sojourn had to end at some point, but he suspected that their children would have been happy to live there forever. Indeed, by the time they left, they were speaking French like natives, surpassing Anne and Will in their language skills. So the prospect of returning to Stratford had little appeal to them. Of course there was no way to tell them that he would be spending a great deal of time in London, for he didn't know how things would turn out at that point. It was difficult enough for Anne and Will to face the fact that they would be living apart, without broaching the issue with their children.

In that respect, they returned to England under false pretenses, as if they were resuming the life they'd left in Stratford. Will anticipated that their children would be glad to see their grandmother, but he and Anne knew that they needed to have their own place. The prospect of living under Bartholomew's roof again, even if briefly, was daunting. You have to remember that at the time, the Bard had no profession to speak of. If anything, he was simply a gambler again, with so much more at stake.

Both of them agreed that returning the way they'd come was out of the question, especially because their children wouldn't simply sleep through most of the journey. Most of all, it seemed a shame to repeat the tiresome and dusty carriage ride through France. Although Will had qualms about going by ship, the river offered easy access to the Atlantic, making a sea voyage seem like the only sensible option. It was also just what they needed to lure their children back to England.

Their trip began well enough, and the first leg of the voyage enthralled their children, before the ship ran into foul weather off the Breton coast. The wind blew the heavy rain straight across the bow. Forced to ride out the storm cooped up in two cramped cabins, Will's family passed a miserable night until they approached the coast of England, where Mother Nature showed them some mercy. Needless to say, the awful voyage confirmed the Bard's distaste for ships, prompting him to utter the hollow promise of a drunkard, "Never again."

Suffice it to say that Anne's family didn't greet them with open arms, even if they were happy to see the children. However, the Hathaways were appalled to discover that the brood spoke French to each other, and worse yet, switched between French and English effortlessly. What Will considered a gift to their children, Anne's family viewed as a handicap, spurring him into action to find a house.

It was at this juncture that Will was forced to divulge the truth of his business dealing with Henri. Anne was outraged by the Bard's confession that he'd stopped gambling quite some time ago, but he knew it would be useless to note that most wives would be happy to hear that their husbands had given up gambling. Anne was also livid that he hadn't disclosed Henri's generosity. The fact they could afford a house of their own and a lair for Will in London didn't appease her.

"How can you expect me to greet your news happily, when you've been leading a double life? Not only did you conceal your arrangement with Henri, but you pretended to leave our home in Castillon each day as if you had to earn a living. What a fraud you are, William! It's bad enough that you spend all your time writing plays that no one has ever seen. Now you're posing as an actor, pretending to be someone you're not to your own wife. Did you really think I would never find out that you were deceiving me?"'

Will acknowledged that he probably should have taken his flogging without trying to defend himself, but he'd kept Anne in the dark for good reason as far as he was concerned. "I wanted to wait until the time was right to surprise you, that's all. I thought you'd be delighted to have our own house."

Anne didn't see it that way. "No, you waited until it was convenient for you to tell me that you were beholden to Henri. Now you inform me that you're leaving me to raise our children while you make a name for yourself in London. You conduct yourself as if I were no longer part of your life."

She had a point, of course, for she was older and wiser, but it was not ambition that drove him. As much as Will would have loved to remain in France with his family, he was being drawn to London by inexorable forces, like the pull of the moon on the tides. The time was ripe for him to help re-invent theater, breaking away from tawdry spectacle to illuminate life. What once had been divinely inspired among the ancients no longer touched the people.

It was no coincidence that two Protestant monarchs became champions of theater, as if they understood that

Catholic ritual needed to be replaced with stories that spoke to their people. Queen Elizabeth may have been an unlikely patron of the "dark arts," but she must have seen that pomp and circumstance were hollow rituals. Likewise, as an obscure king in Navarre, it is hard to believe that Henri would have any influence on London theater, but he must have understood that his destiny was not limited to the battlefield. Surely he saw that Elizabeth would look kindly on a fellow Protestant monarch in France, England's rival and potential ally.

That she did so worked to Will's favor, of course, but he gambled everything by breaking ground with a play that didn't pander to English audiences. If anything, he was going against the grain with a tale of courtship in a foreign land. Not only did he bring the curtain down with a death, rather than a wedding, but no blood was spilled. With a hand like that, who would bet on the Bard? The Queen of Diamonds and the King of Hearts, who had their own reasons for backing him. Indeed, the stage was set for Shakespeare's success when he was spared from the plague in Stratford.

The first order of business, of course, was to find a home for his family, but he thought it best to entrust Anne with this responsibility. As Stratford had been decimated by the plague and the poor economy, Anne had little difficulty finding a house that they could afford, but it didn't measure up to the charming cottage she grew up in. Nonetheless, as their new place overlooked the Avon, their children were happy to be close to water again. Anne's mother didn't share her grandchildren's enthusiasm, as they were mindful of the dangers of living near the river. All Will cared about was Anne's happiness, so he left the choice of the house entirely in her capable hands.

As you can imagine, it was a huge relief for Will to have his family safely settled, but he knew that the prospects of finding a place to stay in London were dim. Indeed, it would have been impossible for him to have found a house for his family in London even if he wanted to; the city was filled with people desperately looking for work before the plague struck again. As he had no luck finding a place to stay within the city's walls, he ended up getting a room above the Bankside Inn, in what amounted to servants' quarters in the attic.

The Bard had second thoughts about living in London, which was even more dreary than he remembered. He began to feel that he was living in a bad dream, tormented by the fact that he'd willingly left France. Each meal was a reminder of what he was missing. He drank the warm beer almost as penance, but Will also had to spend some money in order to hang out at the bar. The Bankside Inn was also the center of his social life, such as it was, for its proximity to the theater district made it a watering hole for actors. That's meant metaphorically, of course, because no one in their right mind drank water in London.

Perhaps because he was steeped in the history surrounding Henry VI, the Bard was mindful of the vital importance of winning the first battle, and he knew that even the opening night of *Love's Labour's Lost* had to encourage the troops. With that in mind, he offered to coach the boys who played his heroines, for he feared they would fumble the dialogue that he meant to be light, like a souffle. He finally ended up buying beer for the lot of them at the Bankside Inn, where they practiced their lines to great effect among the clientele.

In what proved to be a dress rehearsal for the performance at the Rose, the Lord Chamberlain's Men staged the play for the Queen within the palace. Will had hoped that Henri could be there as well, but he had his own battle to fight, or so he said. In truth, it's not clear the two monarchs could have occupied the same room, for the only thing they had in common was their royal blood. While they shared their Protestant faith, Henri wasn't known for his faithfulness; everyone understood that it was just a matter of time before his convenient conversion.

When asked to describe his feelings as *Love's Labour's Lost* was unveiled for the Queen, Will replied: "I can tell you that the mere hint of a smile on her face was like a ray of sunshine on my soul. I had seen her once before, when I was just a boy, during her visit to Warwickshire with the Earl of Leicester. I attended one of the parties in her honor with my father, and my brief glimpse of her didn't leave a good impression. She wasn't dubbed the Virgin Queen for nothing.

"In short, I was afraid that my play would go over her head, but I underestimated her. Apparently she had read the script beforehand, not only to ensure that it contained nothing offensive, but because she feared that it might glorify the King of Navarre at her expense. She is alleged to have said, 'A chicken in every pot. Why didn't I think of that?' I suppose that all royalty is prone to envy of their counterparts in other countries, but the shifting loyalties of the English and the French provide fertile ground for pettiness. Indeed, Queen Elizabeth failed to congratulate me after the play, but I counted myself fortunate to have made her smile, if only for a moment. Smile may not be the word I'm looking for, because it was so sly, reminding me of a Cheshire cat that's swallowed a canary."

The Bard was particularly pleased that the performance at the Rose actually drew laughter, hopefully because of his clever words, but also because the bevy of Princess Anne's "ladies" outdid themselves. The beer the Bard bought them was worth the expense, for they didn't pretend to be women with sharp tongues, but embodied the fair sex at their best. In fact, Will admitted that Princess Anne made his heart flutter, despite the fact that he'd seen her without her wig.

To his credit, Will didn't remain in London to bask in his success, but hurried home to share the good news with Anne, who might have been more charitable. "Of course I'm pleased for you, Will, but forgive me if I don't applaud along with the rest of the audience. For now it will be hard to pry you away from London, where people will be clamoring for more. A word of advice, my love, I'm not sure that *Titus Andronicus* is going to go over as well. You'd best have some other work up your sleeve."

As usual, his wife was a truth teller, bound to balance the Bard's flair for fiction. Yet he wasn't able to spin stories out of the air, like Marlowe, but needed some scaffolding to erect his creations. Heeding Anne's words, he began to look around for a stage for *Henry VI*, for he doubted that he could count on Henslowe through thick and thin. The producer liked comedy well enough, because it drew an audience, but it remained to be seen if they would turn out for a tragedy, bloody as it was.

Will suspected that he needed to look elsewhere for a backer for his history plays, for he foresaw that the past was the key to his future.

CHAPTER 9

It is no coincidence that their fortunes rose and fell together, for Henri and Will were kindred spirits. Indeed, it seems fair to say that they faced up to adversity like brothers when things went awry. In the Bard's case, he gained a foothold in London with *Two Gentlemen of Verona*, which proved more successful than *Love's Labour's Lost*, but revealed his muddled sense of geography. 'Twas a pity he'd never actually been to Italy, instead of relying on his overactive imagination. In that respect, his trio of plays on Henry VI benefited from his familiarity with the battlegrounds in the War of the Roses.

However, the return of the plague ended his promising start as a playwright, forcing the Bard to try his hand at poetry. While "Venus and Adonis" proved to be an artistic success, it did little to put food on the table. Forced to become a gambler again, he knew that there was no way to make a living by returning to Stratford. Remaining in London during the plague was out of the question, even if he could afford to live there, but Will couldn't eat his words.

Fortunately, Anne agreed that it made sense to return to France until the plague abated. She knew that their children would be much happier in sunny Castillon, where they could live in Maréchal's guest house. Although she had qualms about relying on Henri's generosity, Will managed to convince her that the king owed him a favor.

She didn't see eye to eye with him on this matter, but she understood that paying their rent was a mere trifle for the future King of France.

The assassination of Henri's cousin, Henri III, suddenly thrust the Bard's benefactor onto the world stage. Unfortunately, Henri III had brought this tragedy upon himself by ordering the murder of the Duke of Guise and his brother, Cardinal of Guise. Many of Henri III's subjects turned against him, and he was murdered by a monk. Henri was slated to become King of France, but his succession was strongly opposed by the Catholic League. Once again, the clash between Catholics and Protestants rent the social fabric of France.

Will witnessed this conflict play out as he and Anne returned to France with their children via ship. Although he'd spent most of his time in their cabin, sick as a dog from the heaving of the sea, he overheard heated discussions about having a Protestant king on the throne. In fact, Henri had been thwarted from being crowned in Paris, where the Catholic League held sway. Excommunicated by the Pope, Henri mustered his allies to mount a siege of Paris, lasting four years. He finally lost the battle when the Spanish joined the fray. Whether or not Cervantes had a hand in Henri's defeat, we may never know.

With Henri thus preoccupied, Will held out little hope of seeing him, but Henri surprised the Bard with a visit. Indeed, Will almost missed him, for he'd been spending his days wandering the former battlefields trod by his ill-fated countrymen. It seemed to the Bard that history was repeating itself, except that France was being torn apart by its own people, without any help from the British. Nonetheless, Henri was under suspicion for conspiring with Queen Elizabeth, who was anathema to Catholics.

Henri was consumed by his predicament. "What kind of God is it that allows a monk to kill a king with a clear conscience? Beware of anyone who claims that God is on their side. I'd sooner face someone in league with the devil than a religious fanatic, be they Christian, Jew or Muslim. As God is my witness, I tell you that I loved my cousin and bore him no ill will. Having seen him in action, I was in no hurry to rule France, which is not a country, but an odd assortment of fiefdoms eager to go their own way. What a happy man I was as the King of Navarre. Now look at me, chasing my tail like a dog."

In effect, Henri had become a king without a country, unable to take his rightful place in a divided nation. Thus, it was no surprise when the king finally capitulated and renounced Protestantism, declaring himself a Catholic. Having been baptized a Catholic helped his case, but it was obvious that his conversion was motivated by expediency. Indeed, he drew the ire of many Protestants, who objected to his lack of principle. Nor did many Catholics welcome him into the fold.

As for Will, he considered turning this pivotal event into a play, but wisely resisted the temptation, knowing he needed to keep his distance from the history that was unfolding in front of his eyes. But he bemoaned his fate. "When will I ever have another opportunity to portray the making of a king? How I'd love to put myself in the shoes of the priest who heard Henri's first confession. Knowing Henri as well as I do, I understand all too well that he's committed a multitude of sins. It might take days for him to confess, and how could any priest be prepared to listen to a lifetime of waywardness?"

Perhaps the biggest challenge would be to assign penance for Henri's transgressions, which could only distract from the multitude of decisions he'd have to make every day as King of France. The priest couldn't let Henri off the hook by virtue of his royal obligations; atonement would be necessary, if only to remind Henri that a king is a mere mortal in the eyes of God.

Suffice it to say, Will didn't feel prepared to grapple with these issues at that stage in his career. Besides, having written three historical plays in a row, he needed a change of pace. Hence, *Comedy of Errors*, borrowing liberally from a comedy about mistaken identity by the Roman playwright, Plautus. Why pull stories out of thin air, when the ancients had left so much fodder?

Henri, however, had other things on his mind, but was kind enough to invite Will to his coronation. As you can imagine, the League of Catholics resisted having a Protestant crowned in Reims, the traditional coronation site. Nor was Henri eager to return to Notre Dame, after having his first marriage ruined by the St. Bartholomew's Day massacre. (More like a week, in fact, resulting in the death of thousands of Huguenots.) Notably, it had been an outdoor wedding because Henri was still a Protestant, so he wasn't allowed in the cathedral; this prohibition didn't bode well for the couple's future.

Fortunately for Will, Henri's coronation took place in the Cathedral of Chartres, famous for its beautiful stained-glass windows. Although the prospect of a long journey in a carriage in the dead of winter was daunting, as far as the Bard was concerned anything would have been preferable to sailing in a ship. Will had gotten better about sea voyages, but it was something to be endured. In truth, he wasn't much of a traveler, but going by carriage at least afforded glimpses of the countryside and some stops along the way. If nothing else, Will knew he could use the time to make notes on his next play, *The Taming of the Shrew*, inspired by his mother-in-law.

Having suffered defeat in the siege of Paris, and mindful that he had little support from the populace, Henri went out of his way to ensure that his coronation went smoothly. Using a veritable army to maintain order, as well as a cadre of soldiers disguised as civilians, the town of Chartres was the right size for maintaining security. So Will had no qualms about attending Henri's coronation, and was pleased when the king sent a carriage to pick him up.

After checking to make sure that Will had an invitation, the driver secured his luggage on top of the carriage while the Bard bid goodbye to Anne and their children. Having travelled in crowded carriages before, he was delighted to find that he was the only passenger. Not only could he stretch out in the carriage, but he didn't have to make conversation with anyone, leaving him free to work on his play and enjoy the view.

However, he wasn't prepared for the bitter cold and snow that began to fall as they headed north. A carriage is a drafty place in the best of times, and on second thought Will regretted that there weren't any other passengers to help keep him warm. How the driver could manage, he didn't know, for the Bard was bundled up in all of the clothes that he'd brought. As he had to keep his fingers in his pockets, Will had no chance to write anything. All he could do was look out the frosted window as snow blanketed the countryside.

The only relief from the cold came when they stopped to feed the horses and grab some food for themselves. Will soon discovered that the driver was mute, as he communicated in sign language, opening his mouth to show the Bard that his tongue had been cut out. He didn't offer any explanation, leaving Will to imagine what might have happened. He resolved to find a way to use the scene in a play before Cervantes stole his thunder.

In any case, the only opportunity Will had for conversation was in the taverns along the road, where he quickly discovered that Henri's coronation was the soup du jour. Under the circumstances, the Bard thought it best to keep his mouth shut, so he sat alone in stony silence, while the driver took his supper in the kitchen; ostensibly out of deference to Will, but probably because it was warmer there. Fortunately, the heated discussions about Henri helped warm up the chilly taverns, where the food suffered from the lack of fresh vegetables. Indeed, the tavern keeper complained that the produce had been confiscated by Henri's minions to feed his troops.

Will had assumed that they would stay overnight in Orléans, where they could also get some decent food, but he soon discovered that the driver was taking them another way. When he questioned the driver about it, he showed the Bard a map, made of leather, tracing their route. Making a gesture for having his neck slit by a knife, he made it clear that he was trying to avoid the expected route. Will understood that such precautions were understandable, considering the danger that Henri faced, but it never occurred to him that he was risking his life to attend the king's coronation.

Needless to say, Will was relieved when they finally arrived in Chartres, after being stopped several times by sheriff's officers demanding to see their invitations. The inn where they stayed was first-rate, with a view of the river, and a café where they could take their meals without venturing into the town, which was overrun by soldiers. Far from seeming like a festive event, Henri's coronation felt more like a funeral. Will could hardly wait to get it over with and return home.

Having never been to Chartres before, Will was amazed by the cathedral, with the winter light streaming through the incomparable stained-glass windows. Rather than being ushered to his seat along the west wall, he was escorted by a soldier, who looked closely at his invitation, holding it up to the light to make sure it had the right water mark. Seeing a veiled woman dressed in black enter a confessional, Will thought it odd that a widow would have anything to confess. However, he was quickly distracted by the sight and sound of the military band that began to play, signaling the beginning of the ceremony.

It is worth remembering that French royalty represented an unbroken line of Catholic kings, in marked contrast to the English, where queens were entitled to rule as well, including Protestants like Elizabeth I. Despite having converted to Catholicism for the second time in his life, Henri was still excommunicated by the Pope, creating an awkward situation for his succession. Henri had seen fit to give his coronation the trappings of a religious rite, by holding it in Chartres Cathedral, with the town's mayor presiding over the ceremony. It seems likely that considerable pressure was exerted on the mayor, who couldn't refuse Henri, but must have risked the wrath of the Catholic League.

Following a procession of military officers, Henri entered the cathedral like a man walking on eggs, then took his place in front of a round table conspicuously roped off from the altar. No doubt he looked the part, with the bearing of a commander wearing his military uniform covered in medals. Will reflected that Henri's coronation would have made a great subject for a painter, who could have taken advantage of the incomparable light in Chartres. Rose crossed his mind, of course, but he knew that she was safely behind the walls of a convent.

As one of the officials placed the crown on a table, four armed guards stood by while the mayor prepared to crown Henri. Soldier that he was, Henri stood at attention with his hand on his sword, reminding Will of his portrait as the King of Hearts. When the mayor asked him to raise his right hand to swear allegiance, Henri hesitated to take his hand off of his sword. The awkward moment passed when he made his vow in a booming voice, pledging his loyalty to the people of France.

As if on cue, the widow that Will had seen burst from the confessional and dashed across the room brandishing her dagger. Before the guards could close ranks to block her way, she rushed towards Henri, crying out, "Usurper!" Before she could get to him, the mayor shielded Henri, whose assailant could not bring herself to kill such a minor character. By then the veiled woman was surrounded by the guards. "Drop your dagger," Henri commanded, with his sword drawn. Crossing herself as she handed her dagger to one of the guards, she kicked him in the groin and ran to the altar, pursued by Henri. Grabbing a votive candle, she threw the hot wax at Henri. "You are an imposter, not a king."

One of the guards pinioned her arms, while Henri pulled off her veil. Rose, of course, having escaped from the convent. "I know your heart only too well, and it defies your words. You are nothing but a turncoat, pretending to be a Catholic. Your mother shares the blame for raising you as an unbeliever, but you have compounded her folly. You are loyal to nothing but your ambition. I would rather die than watch you become King of France."

To his credit, Henri didn't kill her on the spot. Will suspected that the king still loved her, after all they'd been through. Most of all, however, he was not going to let her upstage him. After the guards managed to get her out of the cathedral, like a hissing cat, the mayor finally placed the crown on Henri's head. His coronation was greeted with a few cheers, which echoed through the cathedral hollowly, as if lacking conviction, like Henri. The deed had been done, but like a tainted verdict, there was no sense of justice. The Bard realized that he and Henri were headed in different directions, like brothers who drift apart.

~

Just like that, Will flew away like an upstart crow. After all the time I spent listening to his dubious tales, writing them down for posterity, he pursued his hot hand like the gambler he was at heart. He didn't bother to tell me where he was moving, but I heard that he was staying with a Huguenot family, for he had a soft spot for the French. Of course I was just the barman, so why should he care about abandoning the Bankside Inn for cozier quarters?

I wonder if Will had second thoughts when his gory Roman saga couldn't compete with bear-baiting, where the public could see real blood. Proof that beginner's luck doesn't last. If I sound bitter it's because I am, for I could have told him that he was wasting his time with costume drama, when he should be dazzling audiences with his gift for language.

Will did stop by the Bankside from time to time, because there were so many theaters nearby, but he had outgrown the place that nurtured him. There was no point in showing him my journal, for I hadn't kept up with his success. All that I had recorded was the run-up to his debut as a playwright. Nonetheless, just listening to him, I felt as if I had shared his adventures. I knew that it was as close to visiting France as I was ever going to get. They say that the journey is its own reward, so even if I never left London I would carry Will's memories in my mind. I tucked my journal away for safe-keeping, underneath my bed, and counted my blessings for knowing such a poet.

CHAPTER 10

I would like to claim that Will kindled my interest in theater, but it was curiosity that kept me going to see his plays. As if trying to distance himself from Henri, who had alienated Queen Elizabeth by converting to Catholicism (or pretending to), Will turned his imagination to the kings of England. To be honest, I was never a fan of his history plays, for the outcome was always a foregone conclusion, but no one could complain about the plausibility of his plots. Despite taking poetic license, the Bard managed to stick close to the truth. In that respect, he stuck his neck out by showing the monarchy at its worst in the figure of Richard III, a villain par excellence. The contrast with Good King Henri of Navarre was not lost on me, especially because I knew that Henri was beholden to Will for burning *Love's Labour's Found*.

Of course, the English kings that Will paraded across the stage left Queen Elizabeth smelling like a rose. Having ingratiated himself with the Queen, Will's fortune continued to rise. Indeed, his success eclipsed Henri, who spent almost a decade auditioning for his role as King of France. From my perspective, his attempt to pander to Protestants via the Edict of Nantes was an obvious ploy to curry favor with Queen Elizabeth. She must have known that Henri represented the last hope of uniting England and France.

In that respect, Will was lucky to have another theater-goer succeed her, for King James didn't miss a beat, taking the former Chamberlin's Men under his wing and renaming them the King's Men. Indeed, I expected that Will might drop by the Bankside to celebrate his good fortune, as the place was lousy with actors, but he had other fish to fry. While I was glad to see him turn his hand to comedy again, *Measure for Measure* had a bitter edge to it. I thought it telling that Will set the play in Vienna (another place I knew he'd never been) to deflect any comparison with London's moral decline.

Fortune soon turned her back on Will, when the plague closed the theaters in London. Once again, my job at the Bankside dried up, and I was forced to return to my parent's farm in Devonshire. Though I think they were glad to see me, I had to sleep in the barn, for fear that I might be carrying the plague. They had never forgiven me for moving to London, which they considered the cesspool of the world. They exacted their revenge by working me to the bone, as if to make up for all the time I had wasted in London, promoting drunkenness. Suffice it to say that I come from a family of puritans, who considered the theater as the playground of the devil.

With nothing to occupy myself besides toiling on the farm, I finally got around to reading my journal, which I found sketchy, so I began to fill in the gaps. Realizing that I was privy to stories about Will's early life and his association with Henri, I knew that I had to be careful about having my journal fall into the wrong hands. So by the time I was able to return to London again, much against my parents' wishes, I thought it wise to show Will that he wasn't the only writer worth his salt.

Knowing Will's habits, I made the rounds of the taverns frequented by actors, and found him sitting at a bar at the Bull Inn; a step up from the Bankside, I suppose, in the heart of London, but too crowded for my taste. The Bard seemed oblivious, scribbling away at the end of the bar in his own world. Indeed, I hesitated to interrupt him, so I ordered a beer and bided my time. When he finally came up for air and ordered another beer, I took the opportunity to speak to him. "You may not remember me, but I'm the barman from the Bankside. I knew you before you became famous."

"Such flattery suggests you want something from me, but I don't believe I owe you any money, so I take it that you have something else on your mind, Horatio."

I was amazed that he remembered my name, as I thought it boded well for telling him about my journal. "I thought you might like to know that I wrote down much of what you told me, chronicling your colorful life. How many people can claim they know the King of France." Reaching into my satchel, I pulled out my journal and opened it to show him. As he began to read, he turned white as a sheet.

"If this is your idea of blackmail, you are a fool, for we are surrounded by witnesses. I should warn you that no publisher would touch this with a ten-foot pole. What I told you was in strict confidence." Before I could say a word, he took my journal over to the hearth and flung it into the fire. His rashness caught the attention of several customers, but no one dared to ask him about this melodramatic deed.

I was dumbfounded, of course, because I thought he would appreciate what I had done to preserve his memories for posterity. My shock soon gave way to anger, when I stopped to think how much time and effort I had spent on this ungrateful upstart crow. When he returned to the bar I gave him a piece of my mind. "Sir, I believe you owe me an apology. My journal represents an enormous amount of time and trouble. Indeed, I spent several months during the plague copying my recollections, which I thought you might appreciate. Blackmail never crossed my mind. But now that you mention it, I believe you owe me for the copy you destroyed."

"Copy?" he said. "Are you telling me that you still have

the original?"

"Indeed I do, and you've just given me an idea for auctioning it off to the highest bidder. I'm sure that there are a lot of people who would be interested in learning more about the man of mystery who has made such a splash on the theaters of London. I dare say that readers of 'Venus and Adonis' would lap it up."

He replied, "Mark my words, if your journal ever sees the light of day your life will be in jeopardy. Our company is not called the King's Men for nothing. And there's no telling what Henri might do. Loose lips sink ships." With that, he stalked out of the Bull Inn through a back entrance. I made no effort to follow him, for I was stunned by his ingratitude.

When I finally recovered from the shock of being spurned by him, I realized that he had done me a favor. It never would have occurred to me to expose Will's double life as an Englishman and a Francophile, beholden to the King of France for his debut as a playwright. The public was content to believe that the Bard had somehow catapulted onto the London stage from Stratford. Like a humble carpenter who becomes a miracle worker.

Yet I was not the only person in the world who knew Will's backstory: born in a backwater on the muddy Avon River, banished to France by his impecunious father, led astray by a she-wolf in sheep's clothing, taken under the wing of the future King of France, and virtually wet nursed by the Virgin Queen. Then bursting upon the scene, only to be dismissed as an upstart crow, before demonstrating his genius at bringing life to the stage. Like a meteor illuminating the sky, such as it is in the London fog.

There were only two other witnesses to Will's ascent, as I was certain that he had kept Anne in the dark about his youthful follies. Henri had his own reasons for keeping his own counsel. Various accounts of his coronation continued to circulate, and rumors of Rose's demise were rampant. I doubted the claim that her tongue had been cut out, for Henri was known to be merciless on the battlefield, but merciful with his sword sheathed. I also doubted that Rose had been imprisoned in a convent again, for she had proven to be too wily to be contained. The claim that she had been banished to the New World seemed most plausible to me, especially because of Henri's determination to establish a colony in the New World. If anyone could survive the winters in Acadia, it would be Rose.

As a Protestant myself, I had no one to confide in, but I thought it best to consult a solicitor, to consider my options for what to do with my journal. I suppose that it might have been simpler to see if I could find a publisher who might appreciate the value of my hard work, but London publishers were known for printing purple prose. Besides, it wasn't money that drove me to share my work, but pride in what I had accomplished in recording Will's background for posterity. For the record, Will's the one who mentioned money. My parents might have been right that I was a wastrel, but I was not a thief, nor did I know anything about blackmail. How much do you ask for? How often can you squeeze your victim? When do you count your blessings instead of your money?

I suppose that I should have shopped around for a solicitor, but if I had learned anything from my parents, it's that you can't judge a book by its cover. Having heard that Fleet Street was teeming with solicitors, I walked up and down the street, looking for an office without a fancy sign.

Spotting a place for "Perkins and Son" I liked the simple black and white letters. Perhaps because I was estranged from my father, I appreciated the idea of a business run by father and son.

Having never been to a solicitor before, I wasn't sure what to expect when I entered the office, but I liked the sound of the bell, which I'm sure was a lot cheaper than paying someone to announce every client. After waiting for a while, I began to wonder if there was anyone around, but I thought I heard muffled voices. Sure enough, moments later, two elderly men emerged from the back of the office. The older man tipped his hat, which is not something I'm used to as a barman, but I reciprocated, pretending I was a gentleman.

After the man left, Mr. Perkins introduced himself and asked me how he could be of service. As I followed him back to his office, I realized that I wasn't sure what I wanted to ask him. Remembering my father's advice about cutting to the chase, I pulled out another copy of my journal, wisely leaving the original under my bed. "I'm in a bit of a quandary, as I've recorded the testimony of a playwright who confided in me before he became famous. He's threatened me if I divulge anything he said, and went so far as to burn a copy of my journal."

I could tell I had his attention, as he reached for my journal to see for himself if the matter was of any import. I sat there patiently, watching him skim through my journal, which obviously held his interest. Raising his spectacles, he looked me in the eye. "This could make your fortune, young man, or get you killed. Whether it's true or not, I cannot tell, but that's beside the point. What's true and what's legal have nothing to do with each other, which is the first thing you learn in my profession. I have no doubt that you could find a publisher for your account, but there is nothing to prevent someone else from stealing your hard work and undercutting your profits. Timing is everything, my boy, so keep this under your hat for now. First, we need to come to an agreement about my services, for I would hate to see your work fall into the wrong hands."

I left Mr. Perkin's office with his written assurance that he would keep me apprised of his efforts to find a publisher, but I had qualms about leaving my journal with him. While I still had the original hidden away, I had taken great pains to make two copies, by hand, and penmanship was not my strong suit. Having seen one of the copies burned in front of my eyes, I was loathe to just hand my remaining copy to someone I didn't know. Especially someone who admitted that the law had nothing to do with the truth. Moreover, while I was intrigued about his comment about making my fortune, he admitted that my journal might be fatal.

As far as I was concerned, I was simply a scribe, recording what I was told as faithfully as I could. It didn't seem fair that such a benevolent act could get me in trouble. In retrospect, I suppose that I should have listened to my parents' warning about the "dark arts." Indeed, theater was considered dangerous by Catholics and Protestants alike, and even in the best of times actors are held in low esteem. Based on my own experience, I would put more trust in an actor than a solicitor, whose esteem is related to their wealth rather than their character. I found this out the hard way, when Mr. Perkins returned my journal to me, claiming that he was unable to find a publisher, for fear of being sued for libel. "I assured them that no one can sue my client for slander, since the words came from the horse's mouth."

The bill Mr. Perkins presented to me represented a week's worth of wages, when I was working, which was not often during the plague. Even fools knew that the worst place to be was in a bar when so many people were sick, and few had the money to spend on drink. We were all just trying to survive. In that respect, I took my misfortune in stride, knowing that no one was going to buy a copy of my journal, even if I found a publisher. To my credit, I understood that my account of Will's life might never see the light in his lifetime, especially if he could help it.

My philosophical attitude crumbled when I finally returned to work at the Bankside Inn, where one of my customers brandished his copy of my journal, bound in red leather, as if it were the bible. Despite being a Protestant, I crossed myself, praying that Rose never saw the book, which would have set her off. I knew there was no point in confronting Mr. Perkins, who had the law on his side. While I was outraged that he had stolen my work, I realized that my journal might never have been published if it weren't for him.

While I was irked to see that the book was anonymous, I felt a tinge of pride in the fact that I was now an author, even if the words were mostly Will's. Until you hold your book in your hand, you have no idea what it's like to see your work in print. Rather like holding your newborn baby in your arms for the first time, I suppose, for I have yet to father a child. So I was startled when a couple of soldiers entered the Bankside, perusing the bar until they spotted my journal on the bar. "We're under orders to confiscate this rubbish," one of them said, picking up the book and stashing it his satchel. "By order of King James."

"I paid good money for that!" my customer protested. I knew that Will was behind this raid, of course and had tipped them off about the Bankside. I was afraid they might arrest me, but I was just a pawn, who made the mistake of lending his ear to a playwright. Feeling guilty that my customer had lost his money because of my good deed, I bought him a beer; small consolation for losing good money.

As you may well imagine, I was curious to see if any of copies of my journals had escaped being confiscated, so I made the rounds of the taverns near the theaters on both sides of the Thames. Feeling obligated to buy a beer wherever I went, I was soon inebriated. At least I had the good sense to keep my mouth shut, for I didn't want anyone to connect me with my journal. So I was both disappointed that I didn't find any more journals in circulation, and pleased that no one else was going to profit from my hard work.

Practically staggering back to my rooming house, I came upon a group of soldiers, burning copies of my journal in a huge bonfire near a warehouse. Watching my journal go up in smoke, I took some consolation in the fact that they were Will's recollections, rather than my own. It struck me as odd that someone would have gone to so much trouble to burn a book, when there was so much gossip to go around for free. Then it occurred to me that that the book burning might have been a ploy by the publisher to drum up business. Destroying a first printing in such dramatic fashion would only fuel interest in the second edition.

Sure enough, the publisher bided his time, waiting for word to spread about Will's secret hideaway in France and his cozy relationship with Henri. The opportunity for another edition arose when Henri's mistress, Gabrielle d'Estrées, died during childbirth, thwarting Henri's plan to marry her after divorcing his estranged wife. Ironically, both of them had encouraged him to convert to Catholicism, but Henri dragged his heels before finally capitulating. Indeed, the dramatic turn of events in Henri's life resembled one of Will's plays. He must have regretted his close relationship with the King of France, which made it impossible to make Henri the subject of another play. Needless to say, Henri's conversion closed the door on any sequels.

Had Will listened to me, he would have written a play about Henri's sister, Catherine de Bourbon, who Henri appointed regent of Béarn at the age of 16, serving for thirty years. Mind you, Béarn is but a tiny province in southwest France, but so was Navarre, where Will set *Love's Labour's Lost*. What a pity he had to destroy the sequel, which some mistakenly called *Love's Labour's Won*. A misunderstanding if there was ever one, for lost and won are applicable to war, not love.

I have no doubt that some pious people viewed the death of Henri's mistress as an act of God, who must have taken satisfaction in the death of both the mistress and their ill-conceived child. Even some of Henri's supporters realized that the stillbirth did not bode well for the birth of an heir, who was desperately needed to avoid more squabbles over succession. The death of Henri's mistress seemed all too convenient to me, and I suspected that Rose might have poisoned Gabrielle d'Estrées, but I knew that I had seen too many of the Bard's plays.

To be honest, I was much more worried about Henri's next move, because he had been embroiled in his own succession for years. Spending so much time on the battlefield was not likely to give him a son. It seemed ironic that the King of France was actually a pawn in many respects, especially when it came to love. Having annulled his marriage with Margaret of Valois, it was only a matter of time before the other shoe dropped, and he married Marie de' Medici, daughter of Francesco I de' Medici, Grand Duke of Tuscany, and Archduchess Joanna of Austria. As if Henri didn't own enough land to begin with.

Converting to Catholicism proved to be a shrewd move for Henri, as did his second marriage. As if to balance Henri's struggle to become King of France, fortune smiled on him during the next nine years, when his wife gave birth to six children, beginning with the son he needed to continue the Bourbon line, Louis XIII. Not only that, but their youngest daughter, Henrietta Maria, ended up becoming Queen of England when she married Charles I. Sweet revenge for Protestants.

It was also a fertile decade for Will, beginning with the construction of the Globe by the King's Men. The success of *Much Ado About Nothing*, *Twelfth Night*, and *Henry V*, soon followed, proving Will's mettle as a gambler. After the death of Queen Elizabeth, he sounded a more somber note, with *King Lear* and *Macbeth*, stark contrasts with the Virgin Queen. However, from my perspective, Will's success began to fade with his binge of history plays, *Anthony and Cleopatra*, *Timon of Athens*, and *Coriolanus*. Had he listened to me, he would have stuck with original material, rather than trying to hang his hat on historical rehashes.

Perhaps the Bard appreciated the role of history in our

lives more than I did, for the end of the decade ushered in a darker tone. Linked together as they were by unseen forces, the tide caught Henri and Will unprepared for Fate. I say that without passing judgement on them, for I was taken by surprise as well. Indeed, I can still recall hearing the news of Henri's assassination as I crossed London Bridge close to midnight. Noting the call of the town crier, whose words were drowned out by the wind, I drew closer to hear his wail.

The tale of Henri's death, stabbed by a Catholic zealot on the streets of Paris, still came as a shock, despite the fact he had escaped death eleven times before. You cannot begin to imagine my sense of relief that he had not been murdered by Rose. Someone had finally gotten to Henri before she did. Yet I feared that would only make her madder, putting Will's life in jeopardy as well.

With these brooding thoughts on my mind, I resolved to seek out Will again, in the hope that he knew what had happened to her. Against my better judgement, I felt that I also ought to warn the Bard that my journal might be floating around London, while the publisher bided his time to reprint my revelations. Surely Will could not blame me, for I did not stand to profit from this ill fortune. Indeed, any opportunity for blackmail had already flown the coop.

Suffice it to say that as a barman, I am not a morning person, so having to spend my mornings combing London to track down the Bard seemed like wasted time. In retrospect, I should have realized that finding Will awake before noon was next to impossible, for I knew he was a creature of habit. I'd seen him scribbling plays in between bites of lunch, washing down his leisurely meals with warm beer. But I also knew that he could no longer sit at some bar without being recognized, for he was now the talk of the town. There was simply no point in searching the taverns, especially before lunchtime.

My opportunity finally came when the Bankside Inn closed during another bout of the plague, leaving me out of work. I could not bear the thought of staying with my parents again, nor was I sure that they would welcome their prodigal son. Without any prospects for finding another bartending job, I ended up taking the next best thing, digging graves. Being a gravedigger is not a plum job in the best of times, but the funeral business was booming in London. No one asked me about my qualifications for the job. Take it or leave it. Simplicity itself.

The great thing about being a gravedigger is that I could work at my own pace. I got paid for each grave I dug, so if I needed a break, no one cared. For a barman, this flexibility was a Godsend. Practically like being my own boss. Even better was the fact that I didn't have to listen to a bunch of drunks telling me their troubles. It's been said that dead men don't tell tales, and I can testify to that from firsthand experience. As a gravedigger, all of my customers waited patiently without complaint.

I suppose that I have the Bard to thank for giving the profession some grudging respect, despite referring to them as clowns in *Hamlet*. One of the gravediggers displays a kind of nobility that I found inspiring, even if I couldn't live up to it. Rather than singing while I dug graves, I was busy trying to figure out where I might be able to find Will. Recalling that he liked to take walks, I considered places he could go without being recognized. For people forget that he was also an actor, so his face was well known by theater-goers, which included the so-called groundlings, a polite word for riff-raff.

Anyone who's ever been to England can tell you that there are few opportunities to take a walk outdoors, especially in London, where there is no fresh air. One has to wait until the fog lifts and the rain abates, a rare occurrence. Another advantage of working as a gravedigger, I might add, was being in touch with the elements. Thus it was that I seized the few opportunities to venture beyond Highgate Cemetery which presented themselves, barely missing a beat as I threw the dirt over my shoulder.

While I would like to tell you that my little scheme worked like a charm, and that I found Will chasing rainbows along the Thames, I failed to find him. I found consolation in that fact that my wanderings took me to places in London that I'd never been to before, including Finsbury Fields, where I found wild strawberries. But the Bard eluded me. My luck did not turn until I listened to the advice of a fellow gravedigger, a swarthy fellow with a ring in his ear, which he claimed helped him hear better. "Let the quarry come to you, young man. Chasing the rabbit, or the maiden, for that matter, will only send them scampering."

Will would have written such words down in his notebook, of course, but I was only armed with a shovel. Indeed, the great irony is that I was busy digging when Will paid a visit to Highgate. Perhaps drawn by the sound of my shovel, or the memory of Hamlet's soliloquy, he approached the grave. Having grown a beard, and with my face smeared with dirt, the Bard did not recognize me. "What wisdom can you impart to a simple soul like myself, sir?"

I was at a loss for words, and feared that he would recognize my voice if I spoke. "Come, my man," he implored, "surely you must have learned something from being so close to death."

"Forgiveness is all," is the best I could answer. "You see before you a ghost, who never meant to wrong you, but would have sung your praises, had God given me a voice. I ask for your forgiveness. I fear that Rose will unleash her fury on both of us. Please tell me that she has found mercy in her heart, wherever she may be."

For a moment I thought Will might keel over and fall into the grave, but he soon recovered from the shock of encountering me. "Your voice gives you away, Horatio, despite your clever disguise. I am no stranger to coincidence, but how is it possible that we should cross paths here, of all places? How could you possibly know that I have come to visit the grave of Rose's child? The bitter fruit of her liaison with Henri. I share their grief, having lost my son, Hamnet."

I was stunned, of course, realizing how much I had missed since I left off recording his life's story. How could I have guessed that the juiciest part was yet to come? Evidently, the plot had thickened since Will's life took such a dramatic turn. "Rose is still alive, then?"

"Why should I tell you anything, when you'll only turn it into another tall tale. I will tell you about Rose, but only if you acknowledge that your journal was a fabrication. Whether invented by me or you is beside the point. My work stands on its own. The play's the thing. That's how I want to be remembered. Swear that you will tell no one what I'm about to tell you."

Clearly a double standard, which provided some latitude in adhering to my word. So I agreed to his terms, which he threatened to have written up by his solicitor for my signature. As far as I was concerned, I had always respected the Bard's confidences. Publishing my journal was Perkin's idea, not mine. So I swore myself to secrecy with a clear conscience. "I give you my word as a gentleman." A bit of an overstatement, perhaps, but Will was as common as I was.

Rather than bore you with Will's wordy account, I have distilled the essence of it, as one boils gallons of sap to make a jug of syrup. Suffice it to say that Henri had Rose imprisoned in the Tower of London for her own good. A favor granted to him by Queen Elizabeth in solidarity with another Protestant monarch, a rare species in the Elizabethan era. The Queen's good deed came back to haunt her when Henri acquired Catholic tastes, but turning Rose loose in the midst of such turmoil was out of the question.

Following her outburst at Henri's coronation Rose had gone stark raving mad, thinking herself to be none other than Princess Anne in *Love's Labour's Lost*, but cooking up her own subplot to account for her imprisonment in the Tower of London. For someone who was not playing with a full deck, Rose had an astonishing ability to memorize not only her lines, but virtually the entire play. While she sometimes departed from the original, even Will had to admit that her versions were remarkable. "Had I thought to set the ending of the play in the Tower of London, I would have won over the English, but I was a greenhorn."

As you may imagine, this news was music to my ears. Not only did it assuage my fears that Rose might dispatch Will or me at any moment, but it also meant that I might contrive to visit her. For all I knew, she was a figment of Will's fertile imagination, so the prospect of actually seeing her, unarmed, without her dagger, gave me goosebumps. The very fact that Will was willing to tell me what happened to Rose suggested that he had begun to forgive me.

CHAPTER 11

I daresay that most people in the world have heard of the Tower of London, but nothing can prepare you for the experience of stepping across the threshold, being searched for concealed weapons, and hearing the gates locked behind you. Not just a single gate, but a series of them, clanging shut with sounds that echo off the stone walls. It is impossible to convey the sense of history that surrounds you, almost palpable, as if you could touch the ghosts who inhabit the place.

Thus, I was not prepared for the grandeur of some of the accommodations hidden within the walls of the Tower of London, which has housed some of the most remarkable people in the world. Let's face it, England isn't known for its architecture, but some of the cellblocks within the Tower rival any suite you might find in the finest inn you can imagine. Mind you, I've never been abroad, but I've seen enough of the Bard's plays to know that there's some stunning scenery on the continent. Nonetheless, let me just say that the accommodations in the Tower of London are deluxe. Fit for a queen.

In case you are wondering why Will didn't accompany me on my visit to the Tower, he assured me that Rose would be more likely to accept my apology on my own. The implication being that she had reason to mistrust Will, whose metaphysics she found suspect. I could only hope that she wouldn't ask me about my own faith, but I was prepared to prevaricate if need be. In truth, I didn't believe that I had wronged Rose. I only recorded what Will had told me, trusting that he had no reason to lie. Which only demonstrates my naïveté.

Ushered into her chambers by two guards, I found Rose in a spacious drawing room, illuminated by a bank of high windows. She was working on a painting of a beehive in an oak tree. Not wanting to disturb her, I sat down on a divan in the corner of the room. To be honest, I was not sure that she even knew that I was there, as she seemed completely absorbed in painting, using a tiny brush to color the honeycomb. Suddenly stepping back to view her work, she spoke without looking at me, as if I were a ghost. "I understand that you have come to apologize to me, but we have never met. I can't imagine how you could have offended me."

She looked nothing like the woman I had pictured, based on Will's description of her. I had expected a faded beauty, like a wilted flower, but Rose belied her name. The image of a coiled snake came to mind, which was unfair, for she did not seem threatening to me. On the contrary, she had a magnetic presence, making me wish I could draw closer. As if reading my mind, she asked me to take a look at her painting. "It's meant to give you a sense of being outdoors, far away from London, where nature rules over all."

I replied, "I have no training in the arts, your highness, but as someone who grew up in the country, I can say that you have done justice to these bees. I like the way you've included the butterflies in the background, suggesting the harmony of nature."

I was painfully aware that our conversation was banal, like two strangers thrown together for no reason, trying to make the best of the situation. Afraid that we would remain bogged down in small talk, I wanted to tell her that her painting paled by comparison with her own beauty, which seemed to be lit from within, rather than the by the harsh sun. Instead, I came right to the point: "Without meaning to, I fear that I have revealed your turbulent past, which is likely to feed speculation about your character. Fortunately, what Shakespeare told me about you has gone up in flames, but I'm afraid the other shoe may drop. I wanted to forewarn you and to beg for your forgiveness, well in advance."

"Aside from your mixed metaphors, you have done nothing to offend me. If anything, a princess requires observant writers to chronicle her life. I have done nothing I am ashamed of, at least not yet, and if I do, I trust I can rely on you to record my deeds for posterity. A painter deserves a colorful life, if anyone does."

Up until then, Rose had shown no sign of madness, except for alluding to being a princess. Rather than ignoring her remark, I seized this opening to see how far she would go with her delusion. "Forgive me, but it seems to me that you have grieved for your father long enough. Words of love still hang in the air, waiting for you to reconvene the lovers."

Her retort was quick and to the point. "Sir, you have no right to point out my predicament unless you are prepared to do something about it. As you can see, I am a prisoner of the Virgin Queen, who has no experience of love and never will, God help her."

Apparently, Rose had not heard of Queen Elizabeth's death, or refused to believe it, since it conflicted with her delusion. As I had no reason to curry favor, I told her the bald truth, figuring that lancing the boil was the best way to heal her wound. "They have concealed the truth from you, your highness, for the queen has gone to her just reward. James VI is now the King of England."

"I see that you bait me, to watch me rejoice in her passing, only to see me wince at another Protestant on the throne. If you are here to administer slow torture, you have underestimated me. Joan of Arc is my protector."

There was no doubting her conviction, but she seemed

to have one foot in the real world and another in the Bard's counterfeit. As she chose to stay in character as Princess Anne, I was curious to see if she had read the sequel. "I have a confession to make, for I had the privilege of reading *Love's Labour's Found*, where you marry the King of Navarre. I'm sorry that the play had to be destroyed."

Rose looked at me with piercing eyes. "Burned, but burned into my memory before it was consumed by fire."

"Then you hold the key to your future, because you were born to be queen. With Henri gone, there is no longer any reason to hide the truth. I confess that I copied most of the play before Will demanded it back. Between the two of us, perhaps we can restore what Will was forced to destroy. He will never go back on his promise to Henri. Without your help, Princess Anne will remain frozen in time."

I pulled out my incomplete copy of the play, hoping that she could step into the shoes of Queen Anne. As I began to read her part, she rose from her chair and started speaking her lines without any prompting:

Welcome guests from the Kingdom of Navarre.
'Tis a year and a day since last we met,
As I went into mourning for my father,
Losing any good reason to rhyme.
Forsaking pretty gowns for mourning clothes,
My three ladies bid adieu to their suitors,
With words of love hanging in the air, like laundry,
Now tucked away in wardrobes and drawers,
Just waiting to be unfurled once again.
My father's passing brought me to my senses,
Awakening me to death's darkness.
Casting shadows over illusions of love,
Turning the tables on our banquets,
Setting the stage for an untimely funeral.
In the midst of dancing and feasting,

The curtain came down on courtship.
How I regret not being there for my father,
Listening to his last words of wisdom,
Telling him goodbye with all of my heart.
Though we agreed to your proposals months ago,
The answers to your questions remain to be seen.
Has professed love stood the test of time?
Words alone will not suffice without deeds.
Slaying dragons has been done before,
The golden fleece already found.
So I propose a timelier challenge,
To win the heart of your beloved and her family,
Whose consent depends on your chops.
Make us a meal fit for a queen and her ladies.
Though you are allowed a sous chef,
I challenge you to turn yourself into chefs.
Let us see what you can put on the table,
To match the words you left hanging on the line.
You have one month to show what you are made of,
And what you can make with your own two hands.

More than I hoped for, but the spell was not broken. The princess had been transformed into a queen. Rose looked at me forlornly. "You must know that that is not the beginning of the play. You cannot trick me, you know. Any fool can see that I'm a prisoner. If Queen Elizabeth is really dead, why am I still here?"

I did not have an answer for her, but I assumed that Will must know the truth, even if he didn't disclose it to her. My hunch is that she was just in limbo, as King James had more important matters to attend to. A holdover from the Queen's reign, Rose remained out of sight, out of mind. The question was, had Henri's death rendered her madness harmless, or was it just a matter of time before her violent streak surfaced? As far as I knew, she had never done anyone harm, even though she was capable of anything.

I took it upon myself to put her to the test, for no one else dared to, but I suppose that I was beguiled by her. When she told me that Will had mentioned me as one of the few people he could trust, I was flattered. He must have changed his mind when I told him about my journal, but up till then he had referred to me as his "everyman." Indeed, he would sometimes call me over to listen to a passage he had written, trying it out on me. After a while, he would sometimes let me read drafts of his plays, to let him know how they sounded to my simple soul.

When Rose asked if she could paint my portrait, I knew that she took me seriously. No one had ever paid me much heed as a barman, except for Will, who just needed someone to lend an ear. Not Rose, who seemed to relish the silence as she painted me, discouraging me from any small talk. All of her attention was focused on painting, which seemed to free her from the constraint of being trapped in the Tower of London. The only conversations we had were upon my arrival and departure. Thus, it took me a long time to sound her out.

Surprisingly, she never asked for news of the outside world, which probably would have upset her. Indeed, she was visibly upset when I mentioned the Queen's death. I was glad that Will had been the one who told her about Henri's assassination, for she apparently fainted. Something I had never witnessed, as I thought ice water ran in her veins. Yet little by little I came to understand that Rose knew that she was mad—for good reason.

What I failed to understand is that her love and hatred were bound together in a Gordian knot. Attempting to cut it with reason was futile. There was no point in confronting Rose with her true identity. It finally came to me that I had to catch the conscience of the queen in order to free her. I suggested that we surprise Will by piecing his lost play back together, using her memory and my notes. "To what end?" she asked me pointedly. Having put me on the spot, I grasped for an answer. "Let us propose a performance for King James, of a play that Will has kept secret. How could the King refuse?"

I was relieved when the King took the bait, intrigued by the prospect of turning the tables on Will, who had always been the puppet master. Now the King could pull the strings. Such conspiracy appealed to Rose, binding us together as we pulled the play out of the fire, as it were. The King could not ask the King's Men to perform the piece without revealing our hand to Will, so I contrived to recruit a cast from the actors who frequented the Bankside; a motley bunch, but eager to catch the attention of the King.

Mind you, keeping this under out hats was quite a challenge, as actors can't keep their mouths shut. If Will had an inkling of the surprise that was in store for him, he didn't show it when I told him that Rose urgently needed to meet with him. We contrived to stage the performance near the East Gate, where the ramparts offered considerable room for the actors to remain concealed until they had to speak their part. Cleverly, King James asked Will to join him on the watchtower that guards the gate.

As you may recall from my synopsis of *Love's Labour's Found*, it opens with the discovery of a foundling. I'm glad to report that Will rose to his feet when he saw the heroine, Gwendolyn, ride through the gate and leave her babe on a cart, before dashing off on her horse. He must have known the jig was up, so he did not protest when the scene he had written unfolded before his eyes, for the first time. So try to imagine how he must have felt when Rose made her entrance and Queen Anne welcomed the guests from the Kingdom of Navarre.

Yet even this dramatic turn of events did not dispel the question of Rose's madness. Inhabiting the part of Queen Anne, she displayed the composure and regal grace of a queen. While I waited with bated breath for Rose to stumble in her speech, her performance was not just flawless, but inspired. It was if all the fire in her nature had turned to slow-burning embers, giving her acting a steady warmth.

Watching King James absorbed in the play, I thanked my lucky stars that this lark had turned out so well. My plot could have easily gone awry. Yet I was never worried that Rose might try to escape, for she relished the opportunity to shine. In so many ways, she had always been on stage, but now she had an audience. Having displayed her power to captivate, she no longer had to threaten anyone. She had used Will's words to win her freedom.

While I confess to some lingering doubts about Rose's sanity, there was no question of imprisoning her any longer. Having seen and heard Rose with his own eyes, King James ordered her release. She certainly seemed clear-headed, remarking to Will, "I now know that I can become anyone I want to. Why think of myself as Princess Anne, when so many other roles await me? Yet I hate to admit how much depends upon your words, monsieur. If only I had your gift, I might be a true queen. Yet you and I are both commoners, so why aspire to royalty? As you have shown in so many plays, royalty are merely pawns in the big scheme of things."

Will responded, "Then I have succeeded in shedding some light, rather than creating hot air, mademoiselle." Unfortunately they began speaking in French, so I was utterly lost, but I could see that they were enjoying themselves. Indeed, from the sound of her laughter, I was assured that Rose had recovered her wits. While I do not take credit for her recovery, without my notes I doubt that we could have reconstructed the play. Although certain passages were burned into her memory, some were merely singed. My notes were sometimes sketchy as well, but between the two of us, I believe that we did justice to the Bard.

~

Sadly, Will's star soon began to fade. Despite finally

writing a genuinely original play, *The Tempest*, with a plot of his own making, his pace began to slow and he soon retreated to Stratford. Or at least he pretended to. Why return to his hometown, where theater had been banned by the Puritans? Why trade the liveliness of London for a backwater village filled with dullards? Would any man in his right mind remain on a dreary island if given the chance to flee? Having heard Will's tales of France, I knew that he would not be able to resist its pull for long.

I suspect that his pretended retirement was merely a dress rehearsal for his next stunt, designed to evade the many people who wished ill of him. Indeed, there were growing complaints that Shakespeare was being quoted more often than the Bible. So I was not surprised by the news of his sudden death, on his 52nd birthday, more or less, since the records are sketchy. It was just the kind of subterfuge that I expected of Will, who understood the importance of making an exit. He wasn't about to squander the opportunity of staging his own departure.

Master of stagecraft that he was, the Bard reportedly went to a tavern with some friends (including Ben Jonson), then keeled over in the middle of a card game in front of several witnesses. To lend authenticity to his death, he left money on the table, as if to dispel any doubts about his sudden collapse. Having recently updated his will, repeatedly claiming to be in "perfect health and harmony," his sudden death added the drama that was in his blood. As if that weren't enough to color his death scene, he omitted any mention of Anne in his will, adding mystery to his demise. He knew very well that villains often make the most memorable characters.

It is well known that Will was knowledgeable about poisons, which he used to great effect in *Romeo and Juliet*. So I wouldn't put it past him to have used the potion that the priest gave to Juliet, which only put her to sleep, while giving the impression of death. Whether or not he fooled his fellow card players, it would not have been hard for

Will to bribe the undertaker, using a few rocks to weight the casket, or substituting someone else's cadaver—which were plentiful during these dark times.

I was curious to see his grave, of course, having a professional interest in these matters. As I expected, Stratford-upon-Avon wasn't worth the trouble of getting there, especially as I was stuck in a carriage with a young family. Spending time with them only fortified my resolve to remain a bachelor, for the constant bickering of this ill-begotten brood almost drove me over the edge. I was never so glad to bid farewell to anyone in my life as I was to see the back of this family of Puritans, who claimed they were bound for the New World. "Good riddance," I wanted to say, but held my tongue until I remembered the one French phrase I knew: "Bon Voyage."

My qualms about Stratford were confirmed when we came to a tollhouse on the outskirts of the hamlet, which was too small to be called a village. But when do you call a rock a boulder? The truth is in eye of the beholder. Indeed, the coachman complained that the toll was "highway robbery," which gave too much credit to the rocky road we were on, but I took his point. However, the toller replied, "There's only one road to Stratford, as you ought to know. If you aren't willing to pay for privilege of riding through the King's country, then take a boat! A shilling a piece if you want to pass through my gate."

For a moment I was afraid they were going to get into a heated discussion of taxes, which was a sore point in the countryside, for most of the money flowed to London. Fortunately the coachman was in a hurry to get to Stratford and find some lunch, so he handed over the toll while holding his tongue. A better man than me. As far as I was concerned, the toll keeper was just a mosquito, sucking the blood of every passerby. Like a good barman, I thought it best to keep my thoughts to myself.

My resolve to keep my own counsel soon vanished when I saw the first signs attached to trees along the road.

"Stratford-upon-Avon only two miles ahead." This was soon followed by another sign, hanging from a branch of a huge elm tree. "See the house where Shakespeare was born." Turning to the other passengers I said, "You're leaving for the New World just in time. The Bard is barely buried before they turn him into a cash cow. The world is going to hell in a handbasket."

The father upbraided me for my language. "Watch your tongue, sir. There are women and children present." I thought Puritans were conversant with hell, but I saw no reason to get into an argument. One of the children asked, "What's a hand basket, father?" There was no time for him to answer, as we crossed the bridge over the Avon. I couldn't wait to get out of the stuffy carriage.

My relief was short-lived, however, for Stratford was the very definition of a hamlet, a little cluster of houses in the country. In this case, strewn along the muddy banks of the Avon. I was amazed to think that such a backwater could produce a consummate playwright like William Shakespeare. Not even the river running through the hamlet could redeem the place. Indeed, "running" is too good a word for the sluggish body of water that constitutes the Avon. The bridge over the brackish river was in desperate need of repair, with yet another sign that read: "Welcome to Stratford-upon-Avon, birthplace of William Shakespeare, world's greatest playwright." Bombastic, to say the least.

The irony of the situation was not lost on me, for theater was banned in Stratford, as it was in most communities where the Puritans had taken over. Having driven out the Catholics, some Protestants had gone overboard, determined to root out vice at any cost. I doubted that even the theater could have enlivened Stratford. I realized that Will had to dream things up to keep from going stir crazy. Anything to take Will's mind off the routine of country life, completely unaware of London, where his future lay.

Had I not suspected subterfuge, I would have been sad to see Will's grave in the churchyard, and to think that he had ended up where he began, as if the remarkable journey of his life was all for naught. Even the bust of him failed to do him justice, for though a rogue, he was a handsome one, I have to admit. Obviously, he must have conspired with Anne to hire a sculptor to create a monument that would baffle his biographers. For the caricature of him looks more like a notary than the rakish man I knew. Even the quill in his right hand seems posed. Anyone who knew Will could verify that he was left-handed, so why go to the trouble of concealing the truth on his grave?

Any doubt I had about his death was put to rest by the inscription on his gravestone, putting a curse upon anyone who "moves my bones." Clearly, Will's way of ensuring that no one discovered that his body was missing. I was certain that the upstart crow had flown to France, where he could pick up where he left off. By now, his two remaining children were grown up, so there was nothing to keep him in England. Cleverly, he had co-written quite a bad play, *Two Noble Kinsmen*, since retreating to Stratford, to suggest that he was going to seed. All part of his exit strategy, no doubt.

Having heard that Will owned one of the largest houses in town, New Place, I asked for directions from an old woman who was pruning her rose bushes. She didn't bother to respond, but simply pointed at the huge three-story house at the end of the street, as if any fool could see the Bard's house. "Mind you, it's just for show, because he rarely set foot in Stratford. Too big for his britches, if you ask me." I thanked her and walked down to the house, where I was accosted by two boys who were selling hand-made maps of Stratford.

From the way that they fought with each other, I suspect that they were brothers, like Cain and Abel, trying to outdo each other. The bad one waved a map in front of my face, demanding two pennies, while the good brother just handed me a map; "Donations appreciated, sir." I gave them both two pennies, just to get rid of them, and looked at the map to see if I had wasted my money or not. The town council had obviously figured out that Will could be turned into a cottage industry, with a dubious map of everyplace he had ever set foot, which included just about every building in town.

I didn't have time for such nonsense, for there was no way to tell if the "William Shakespeare slept here" signs were genuine or not. Figuring that few people would be interested in seeing his school, I went to see where Will received the education that served him so well. Honestly, it could have been anywhere, as King's New School is just a room with some maps, a poster of the alphabet and multiplication tables. The only indication that Will had ever been there was a quote written on the blackboard. *All's Well That End's Well.* It would have been more apt at the cemetery.

I was afraid that the house where Will grew up would be crowded with visitors, so imagine my horror when I saw the obnoxious family from the carriage entering the ramshackle house on Henley Street. What they were doing in the home of such a false idol I can't imagine, but perhaps the Puritanical parents wanted to warn their children about the dangers of the theater. In any case, their brood ran out of the house as if it were the birthplace of the devil. Oh, if only it had been that interesting, for in truth there was little to see in Will's birthplace. His bedroom looked more like a linen closet, but I was surprised to see how many brothers and sisters he had. More evidence that his father had Catholic sympathies.

While I was put off by the crowds of tourists seeking souvenirs of the Bard, it dawned on me that my journal would sell like hot-cross buns in Stratford. So I was startled to see an old man standing on a soap box on a street corner, brandishing my work. "Read all about it, the secret life of William Shakespeare from the horse's mouth." Instead of being bound in red leather, my journal had been printed on what looked like a ledger. Probably pirated from the copy I had loaned to the crooked solicitor.

I protested, of course, good Protestant that I am. "I object to being called a horse, sir, and you have no right to peddle my journal." To which he replied, "Finders, keepers, laddie. I paid good money for these folios, and I have the receipt to prove it." I saw no reason to call his bluff, for I knew I didn't have a leg to stand on.

Although I was eager to leave Stratford, the prospect of being cooped up in a carriage again was repugnant to me, so I inquired about catching a boat down the Avon. Having discovered that I could catch a boat in late afternoon, I had time on my hands, and I can tell you that time passes slowly in the English countryside, where pigs and cows seem more at home.

I couldn't leave without seeing Anne Hathaway's cottage in neighboring Shottery, if only to see the window that inspired Will to write the balcony scene in *Romeo and Juliet*. So I was startled to discover that the place where Anne grew up is actually a huge farmhouse. Indeed, it's the handsomest building in the area, which is riddled with flimsy houses that make London look prosperous in comparison. No wonder Will took a fancy to Anne, who might well have lured him by pretending to be Rapunzel, lowering her tresses for him.

From the look of the place, I could tell that the Hathaway residence had seen better days, but I suppose that the same could be said for most of us. Nonetheless, I was surprised to see the clothesline at the back of the house hung with black dresses, which seemed staged to me, as if to demonstrate that Anne was still in mourning. I realized that I didn't have any idea how long widows dressed in black, but there must come a point when wearing black dresses is unseemly. Was Anne trying to cast herself as a nun? Part of the Bard's plot to feign his death, no doubt. Yet Anne's display of grief only piqued my curiosity. I couldn't help knocking on the door, to see who lived there.

Nothing could have prepared me for the shock of seeing Rose, clad in black, like the apparition I had seen at Henri's coronation. "What on earth are you doing here?" I blurted out.

"I could ask you the same question," she replied. "I'm surprised it took you so long to try to track Will down."

I suppose that I must have sounded defensive. "I would have liked to come to the funeral, but by the time I heard about it, there was little point in visiting Stratford. As dull as dull can be. It would have been better to leave his birthplace shrouded in mystery." Little did I know that I would live to regret this remark when I made my debut as an actor, playing Dull in *Love's Labour's Lost*, but I see that I'm getting ahead of myself again.

"Come in before anyone sees you," Rose commanded. "There are eyes everywhere in Stratford. The whole place is full of voyeurs, without lives of their own."

I had expected that Rose would remove her veil when she closed the door, but she seemed to take her role of widow quite seriously. "It's time for me to hang out the laundry again," she said, as if I understood her charade. "I promised Anne that I would stay for a while, pretending to be her, but I'm not sure I can keep my promise." Without any more explanation, she went out the back door, carrying a basket full of black dresses, which she began to hang up on the clothesline. I was sure that she had gone mad again, thinking she was Princess Anne in mourning.

Rose returned with an empty basket, and looked at me accusingly, as if I should have helped her with the laundry. "Now that you're here, maybe you can make yourself useful. As you can see, I'm a prisoner again, having agreed to give Anne and William time to get away from this wretched place. I was better off in the Tower of London, where I could spend my time painting, instead of hanging up laundry, like a married woman. Heaven forbid that I would ever make such a bargain. Indeed, I want nothing more than my freedom back. What a fool I was to help out a couple of Protestants. So much for Christian charity!"

I couldn't help thinking 'methinks the lady doth protest too much,' but I tried to steer her in another direction. "I thought King James would recognize your talent and open doors for you. Surely he must have been impressed with your performance in *Love's Labour's Found*?

"You're even a bigger fool than I thought. First of all, kings don't open doors for anyone. Even the King couldn't overcome the English aversion to women. The very thought of a woman on stage is anathema to Puritans, who hold the purse strings in London. I had to resort to pretending to be a boy to get on stage, but my curves betrayed me. With no way to make a living in this Godforsaken country, all I could do was to help Anne and William with their charade."

I said, "I'm afraid that my journal reveals their hideaway in France, so I hope they don't return to Castillon. How was I to know that Will would fake his death?"

Rose was unforgiving. "I know better than to trust you with the truth, so don't bother to ask me where they've gone. We agreed to go in separate directions, which is more than you need to know. If I catch you writing down anything I tell you, I'll scratch your eyes out."

I had no reason to doubt her, so you must forgive me if my account of what happened next is sketchy. Suffice it to say that we left Stratford together on a barge, with Rose still dressed as a widow, and myself as her valet—a fancy word for servant. I spent most of the trip leading a horse along the banks of the Avon, well aware that we were retracing the route that Will and Anne took on their honeymoon. Far from being a honeymoon, I slept on the floor of the boat, with only a blanket under me, rather than Rose. The horse was better company, always willing to listen, and never telling me what to do.

To be honest, I was actually looking forward to visiting some of the places along the way that Will had told me about, but the plague had taken its toll on the area, with most taverns shuttered. Indeed, I began to wonder if the Fox & Hound wasn't just a figment of Will's imagination. I saw neither hide nor hair of the place. I ended up knocking on doors in the few settlements we passed, offering to buy bread and cheese, which is about the only thing we lived on during the voyage, if you could even call it that.

We had better luck when the Avon flowed into the Severn River, where we left the barge and caught a boat to Cardiff. I was almost sad to say goodbye to the horse, which had been so endearing; if only I could find a woman with such patience, I'd marry her in a heartbeat. Patience wasn't Rose's strong suit, nor did she show a spark of interest in me as a man, with a couple of exceptions that don't bear mentioning. Indeed, I dared not write anything until the end of our voyage, which, as you will see, turned out longer than I ever imagined.

Despite their reputation as friendly folk, the Welsh in Cardiff proved the exception to the rule. Even Rose's disguise as a widow did not dissuade some sailors from peering through her veil. By this time, of course, I began having questions about where we were going, but I knew there was no point in asking. I could tell she was a woman on a mission, who answered to no one—especially not me. To her credit, she finally put me in the picture as we walked up the gangplank of the *Dragon*. I recognized the name of the ship, of course, for I had included it in my journal. I was disappointed to find that Captain Montague has been replaced by Captain Cardenio, who was merely a puppet installed by the East India Company.

As I soon discovered, Cardenio was a captain in name only, delegating his nautical responsibilities to his minions so he could concentrate on directing plays. As you may recall, the crew of the *Dragon* doubled as actors, performing *Hamlet* in West Africa with the kind of missionary zeal that would warm the heart of any theater-goer. From what I could gather on the voyage that I have only alluded to, King James appreciated Queen Elizabeth's prescience on the power of the English language. The way I heard it, he saw the East India Company as the vanguard of the Royal Navy.

"Let's face it, we import just about everything in this bloody country. We have no tea or wine to export, except from our colonies, and you can't count on them for long. The only thing of any value in Great Britain is our language, which needs to be our chief export. Who better to represent our native tongue than Ben Jonson and William Shakespeare, our ambassadors to the world? Under the guise of doing business, the East India Company can conquer the world with theater, harkening back to the Greeks."

If you're wondering what this has to do with Rose, you're forgetting that she was a woman to be reckoned with. Having seen her act in the Tower of London, King James appreciated her potential to perform on the world stage—but not in England, where she was a clear and present danger. So I suppose it's fair to say that Rose was banished from England, but it turned out to be a blessing in disguise for her, and for me, if you must know. Rather than spending the rest of my life pouring beer and listening to drunkards pour their heart out to me, I was given a new lease on life.

Just imagine how you might have felt, finding yourself on a ship sailing around the world with a skeleton crew who were actors first, and seamen (and seawomen) second. It's a wonder we didn't sink, of course, but imagine performing plays to audiences who didn't understand English, but didn't care. They would eventually, or at least their children would, thanks to Queen Elizabeth and King James, who saw the handwriting on the wall. Admittedly, Will's gift for language was lost on many audiences, who couldn't begin to grasp his subtlety and wit. Yet I would argue that his true genius was his stagecraft, his use of visual cues to keep the story flowing. In that respect, Rose was a natural, because she didn't just deliver lines, but embodied them.

I can say this with some authority, because as a complete novice on the stage, I quickly learned how much the bit parts contributed to performances. For reasons I don't fully understand, I ended up playing the fool, Dull, in *Love's Labour's Lost* and Wall in *Midsummer's Night's Dream*. If I may say so, I hit my stride when I played a grave digger in *Hamlet*, for which I was uniquely qualified. Why Will called the pair of gravediggers "clowns," I'm not sure, but my singing drew some laughter. Who but Will could find so much humor in a graveyard?

I see that I have failed to set the scene for you, dear reader, for we were stuck in Cardiff for some time, while the *Dragon* underwent repairs from an attack by Spanish pirates. Suffice it to say that Captain Cardenio put this misfortune to good use, rehearsing some plays by Cervantes, but I fear they lost something in translation. Quickly discovering that Cervantes should have stuck to writing novels, the Captain went back to Shakespeare, much to my relief.

~

By the time we set sail, I considered myself ready to take on any role, provided that the lines would fit on my hand. Despite the formidable powers of recall that made me such a valuable scribe, I found myself tongue-tied on stage. Much of the blame falls on Will for his flowery language, which bears little resemblance to natural speech. In short, with so few roles suited to my talents, I was soon put in charge of the props. In that respect, I found my calling behind the scenes. I was perfectly placed to witness history in the making, as you shall soon see.

You must remember that I had never ventured beyond the sceptered isle before, so try to imagine my excitement when the *Dragon* sailed into the port of Bordeaux. Especially after spending most of the voyage across the channel standing on the ship's rail, heaving into the wind. No wonder Will had learned to fast before boarding a ship. The fact that English food is so bad was no consolation while watching it spill overboard.

I would like to regale you with my experience of seeing France for the first time, but nothing can compare with Will's description of finding paradise on earth. Moreover, it was dark when we approached Bordeaux, whose port is located near the confluence of the Dordogne and the Garonne rivers, which was news to me. While the sky began to lighten as we sailed up the bay, the fog obscured my first glimpse of France. Indeed, if you called me into court, I would be hard-pressed to testify that we had actually landed in France. The judge would have to coax my impressions out of me, and I would have been tempted to fall back on Will's version of events, which were so much more vivid than my own.

To make matters worse, Captain Cardenio had issued orders to have me blindfolded, to ensure that I didn't reveal the ship's destination. Apparently, my reputation as someone who couldn't hold his tongue had preceded me. While Will may have forgiven me for my trespasses, he knew better than to entrust me with a secret. So I suspected that he was counting on my acute powers of observation to record what I was about to see with my own eyes and ears for posterity. Lest you think I exaggerate the importance of the events that were about to unfold, I will cut to the chase and do my best to put you in the picture.

Still blindfolded, I was lowered from the ship into a small boat, along with Rose, whose scent betrayed her presence, even if she refrained from saying anything. Even at the time, I thought it a shame that she didn't say something memorable. By then, she must have memorized hundreds of lines of dialogue, so surely she could have thought of something to say. While it would have been comforting to hear her melodious voice as a sailor rowed us to our destination, no one said a word, except me, of course, wondering out loud, "Where are we?" Once again, I seem to have been relegated to playing but a minor part in life, but I was determined to leave some mark on life, small though it might be.

My question remained hanging in the air, though the fog seemed to have lifted, as I could tell from the current of air on the back of my neck. I was led up a steep staircase made of stone, judging from the hard echo of our footsteps as we climbed what turned out to be a tower, as I could see when my blindfold was removed. Initially blinded by the light, I found myself in a sun-drenched room with windows facing in every direction. To the east, I could see the Dordogne, curving through the countryside like a giant serpent.

But my initial impression of the spectacular scenery was swept aside by the sight of the people in the room, sitting around a round table that might well have accommodated King Arthur. In his place was an empty chair for the French philosopher, Michel de Montaigne, whose portrait was displayed above the table. Although his commanding visage left no doubt that he was there in spirit, it was his wife, Françoise, who hosted the gathering. It was a great relief to see Will alive and well, confirming my doubts about his death. He sat next to his winsome wife, Anne, I presumed, and a striking woman I'd never seen before, her face powdered like a Parisian I supposed—despite the fact that I'd never been there.

I had heard of Montaigne, of course, but I'd never had much interest in essays. And to tell you the truth, I had no idea that he knew Will, who had never mentioned him before. I wondered who else Will had failed to acknowledge to me. No doubt part of his plot to remain a man of mystery. In that respect, Montaigne's visage on the wall contributed to my sense of him as a cipher, concealing a secret. For a man of so many words, he was even more impressive in his silence. Perhaps a lesson for all of us.

Even to me, it was obvious that everyone in the room knew each other, despite the fact that they didn't all speak English. Indeed, Françoise began the proceedings, which were still a mystery to me, speaking in Latin, which was apparently Montaigne's first language. I later learned that he was raised by peasants during the first three years of life, which sounded more like Henri to me. I had a lot to learn about French customs. I noted that Will interjected a few Latin and Greek aphorisms from time to time, as if to engage Montaigne's wife, who smiled knowingly.

Having never met Will's lovely wife before, I was surprised that she spoke French, frequently making remarks to Françoise, who simply laughed and continued sewing, without missing a stitch. What a pity that I don't speak French, for I would have loved to know what they were discussing. Just as well, I suppose, for I still had no idea what this gathering was all about. Indeed, even before any introductions, it occurred to me that I had chanced upon the Tower of Babel.

Consummate hostess that she was, Madame de Montaigne understood that I was out of place at this gathering, so she endeavored to put me at ease. Turning to me, she said, "As was his custom, my husband liked to celebrate his birthday by surrounding himself with artists, musicians and writers. He understood the importance of conversing with people with different points of view. A philosopher himself, he noted that there's nothing duller that a room full of philosophers, who aren't sure that anyone besides themselves even exists. While we used to have visitors from the court in Nérac, everyone seems to think that Paris is the center of the universe these days. Henri exceeded himself. How I miss the presence of such fascinating people as Cervantes, who called our home a citadel of light."

I bristled at her remark, of course, knowing that the

Spaniard had pulled the wool over Will's eyes. "I'm glad to say that even I have heard of Cervantes, though few English have read *Don Quixote*, which was burned when the Spanish Armada attacked us."

Madame de Montaigne replied, "As you can see, our guest knows his history, which is why we invited him to this gathering. A modern Plutarch if you will. As much as I've enjoyed our conversation, I'm a realist, unlike the maestro of make-believe in our midst. William has entangled us in his plot to become a ghost, but his dilemma only confirms my fears about fiction. Any fool can pretend to be a writer.

Will took the opportunity to interject. "If I may interrupt, I'd like to say that your realism, and that of your late husband, has been like cold water splashed on my face. Not dampening my spirits, but awakening me. For I have spent so much of my life dreaming, which is the only way words come to me, as if someone were whispering in my ear. It is not my own voice that I hear, but a woman's voice. I have never seen her face, nor can I even imagine what she looks like, for I understand that she takes many forms. She speaks to me not like a lover, but a sister. When I listen carefully, my plays take on a life of their own. When I fail to heed her, my lines fall flat, like a singer who is tone deaf. Yet like the singer, I hold myself blameless, for I sing with all my heart."

It was at this point that Marguerite de Valois, Henri IV's first wife (Margo), revealed herself. Having never seen her in her prime, I can only imagine how beautiful she must have been before her family ruined her life. She was still alluring, with a sonorous voice and lively green eyes. As if responding to Will's remarks, she said, "I would like to take this opportunity to thank you for your loyalty to Henri, who thought the world of you. As much as he appreciated your work, he valued your honesty above all else. Honesty is not something a king can count on. Almost everyone told Henri what they thought he wanted to hear. I have often reflected that he would have been much happier as King of Navarre, where he felt at home and was appreciated by his people. He much preferred dogs to people, and was never happier than on a horse.

"For a young man who obviously knew so little about love, you were remarkably eloquent, William. However, your attempt to ignore Henri's horrendous wedding forced you to abort your comedy. To his credit, he didn't blame you for your flawed play, for he saw some potential in you. Likewise, you must have had some inkling that he was destined to become France's most beloved king. Even if you failed to foresee that Henri was fated to be felled by hate.

"I don't blame you for feeding Henri's ambition, for you were trying to make your mark on the world. Yet it was your play that called attention to him. Without Queen Elizabeth's interest in his future, Henri might well have remained in obscurity—and might still be alive. I only wish I could have encountered him before we got caught up in events beyond our control. Our lives were written for us like characters in one of your plays. But even you must have been surprised to see what befell King Ferdinand, whose prospects seemed so promising. You left him dangling, like the hanged man in a Tarot deck."

Rose had been very quiet up till then, but could no longer restrain herself. "If anyone is to blame for this turn of events, it is me, for I unwittingly brought Will and Henri together. I would like to tell you that I saw something in young William which boded well for his future, but I just needed someone who could help me get closer to the king. Were it not for Will, I might have died trying to kill Henri, for I was bent on his destruction. He represented everything I detested: arrogance, blasphemy, and privilege. For my hate to be transformed into love wasn't alchemy, but nothing less than a miracle. In this respect, I owe my life to you, but we both know that your encounter with Henri was a gift from God."

Margo didn't give Will a chance to respond. "Forgive me for interrupting you, Rose, for I admire your piety, but I think God has little to do with human affairs. I expect that you will consider my views to be heresy, but I believe that God has much to answer for. Indeed, I look forward to Judgement Day, because I think I have the right to some answers. Having barely survived the honeymoon from hell, I want to know how anyone could condone so much hatred in the name of God.

"I saw the devil in the eyes of my own brothers, who ordered the slaughter of all of the Protestants at our wedding. How could any of the murderers look themselves in the mirror ever again? They destroyed whatever innocence I had left as a young bride. They succeeded in ruining any hope of love that Henri and I ever had. Do you have any idea what it was like for me to see my husband hiding in my closet, cowering under our bed? Henri was a man of heroic stature who deserved respect. I am happy to see him immortalized astride his horse on the Pont Neuf, the most beautiful bridge in the world. Henri wanted it built not just to span the banks of the river, but to connect people of all faiths and walks of life.

"When I first met Henri he told me, 'Paris is a pigsty, the Seine an open sewer fouling the air.' He was determined to transform Paris into not just a great city, but the greatest city in the world. Some people have observed that Henri surrounded himself with beauty, but he insisted that beauty by itself was meaningless. He wanted Paris to become a memorial for the thousands of victims of the Saint Bartholomew's Day massacre. From my perspective, it's a miracle that Henri and I finally became friends later in life."

Rose was quick to reply, "We don't have to see eye-to-eye for us to be friends, Margo. I continue to find inspiration in your *Memoirs,* which I turn to more often that the Bible, which I hope surprises you. I like to think of myself as daring, but I could never bare by soul as you have. Henri must be thanking his stars that he is still loved by both of us, in our own ways. What a blessing that you were reconciled before he died."

As if sensing the need to lighten the atmosphere, Madame de Montaigne spoke up, impishly. "My husband has reminded me that we're here to celebrate his birthday, so let us have some tart and Armagnac on the terrace. Let's take advantage of the beautiful day to bid farewell to the ghost in our midst before he disappears."

How I wished that I could have written down the cascade of words, but I had already used most of my ink. So I simply let the words wash over me, trusting that I could remember the gist of their remarks for my journal. In the meantime, I had spotted a dessert the likes of which I've never seen in London.

~

Hearing so little from Anne so far, I was pleased to see her propose a toast to William. "Having seen so little of my husband while he was in London, I'm looking forward to having him to myself, if only as a ghost of himself. But before I put my foot in my mouth, my remarks are not meant for posterity, so I trust that the Plutarch in our midst will set aside his pen and have another sliver of the lemon tart that Madame de Montaigne baked for the occasion.

"Since you're all sworn to secrecy, I can tell you that honesty is not William's strong suit. As a young man, he learned the importance of keeping his cards close to his chest. He trained himself to dissemble, concealing not just his cards, but what was on his mind. He might have been a gambler, had he not met someone who saw through him. Although my husband claims that he's indebted to Cervantes for calling his bluff, I'm the one that first saw behind his mask.

"I'm the real gambler, for I took the chance of marrying Will, practically a boy without means, with no skills other than a way with words. When he dared to show me his play I realized at once that it was flawed, but it showed so much promise. It revealed a side of him that I'd never seen before, wearing his heart on his sleeve instead of concealing what was in his hand. I thought to myself, 'The journey we take together won't be easy, but we will never run out of stories to tell each other.'"

At this point Will interjected, "I'm not sure where Anne is going with these remarks, but it's starting to sound like a memorial service. Let me remind you that I'm still very much alive, even if I have to pretend otherwise in order to regain my privacy.

"Besides, I've made a habit of pretending most of my life, so playing a ghost comes naturally to me. Cervantes gave me the idea, but I expect that the tradition of counterfeit death can be traced to the Greeks. Having used it in several of my plays, I hesitated to feign my own death, but I loved the idea of life imitating art."

Will's remark reminded me of Plutarch, of course, so I seized the opportunity to put the Bard on the spot. "What say you to those who claim that no one man could have written such a body of work by himself?"

Will replied, "Consider the birds if you will. Anyone who has ever observed a pair of birds building a nest can tell you they don't create it out of thin air, but use the resources available to them in their milieu. It is only by working in tandem, taking turns while one bird forages, and their partner weaves twigs and twine together, that the pair builds their nest. Even after the female lays her eggs, they share responsibility for feeding their young and guarding the nest. In short, I have created nothing by myself, and could have produced nothing of note without Anne."

I trust that Plutarch would approve of my success in pinning the Bard down on this important point, which settles the matter once and for all.

Anne managed to redirect the conversation, "I think we should also toast our hostess, who has demonstrated the patience of Ariadne, putting her fingers to good use while the rest of us brought only our appetites."

~

After we devoured the fabulous tart and washed it down with Armagnac, Will seemed intent on making his farewell speech. "I trust that you understand why I've chosen to step away from the stage at this juncture in my life. Of course I had no clue that Cervantes would upstage me by dying the day before I feigned my own death. Off the record, I didn't stage my death on my birthday to baffle my biographers. My birthday provided a perfect excuse for gambling with friends, who weren't in on my plot, by the way. I did have an accomplice, who helped me fill my coffin with stones after the sleeping potion wore off, taking a page from Romeo and Juliet.

"Leaving Anne behind to go through a suitable period of mourning, I made my way to France on a fishing boat, pretending that I was smuggling whiskey, which made the venture quite expensive. I lucked out with the weather, an unexpected benefit of being born in April, so the crossing was uneventful. Nonetheless, I was glad to set foot on land and soon found a farmer willing to sell me a horse, even if he gouged me. I figured that my freedom was worth every penny, as I could go anywhere I wanted to and could avoid traveling in carriages, where I'd have to endure endless questions.

"As much as I wanted to return to our hideaway in Castillon, I didn't want to run into any of the people who knew us. So I headed for Pau, where I figured the weather would be warm, and it seemed like a good place to hunker down until Anne could join me. While passing through Poitiers, I came upon a group of pilgrims returning from Santiago, which is how I heard about Cervantes' death. There was no way I could have made it to his funeral, of course, but I was determined to pay my respects.

"To make a long journey short, I rode as fast as I could to Madrid before my horse was stolen near Segovia, so I had to walk the rest of the way on foot. Speaking no Spanish, I had to rely on gestures to make myself understood, but I eventually found the cemetery where Cervantes was buried at the convent of the Barefoot Trinitarians—who had been instrumental in coming up with the ransom money that freed him from his captivity in North Africa.

"I learned these details from one of the nuns, a sturdy young woman who spoke remarkably good English for someone born in Paris, despite her quaint Canadian argot, which doesn't distinguish between literal and figurative use. Explaining that she had emigrated to Canada during Henri IV's campaign to colonize the New World, she claimed 'I was seduced by the king, for he made America sound like the promised land. He took advantage of my love for dogs, singing the praises of Labrador and Newfoundland as the land of milk and honey. He failed to mention the snow and ice, which proved to be my undoing. After a long, miserable winter, I swore to God that I'd become a nun if I could return home again. When my prayer was answered, I decided to move to Spain while I was at it, where I knew I'd never be cold again.'

"I saw no reason to tell her that Henri had inspired two of my plays, for I wasn't sure that they were appropriate for a nun's ear, and I was afraid of wandering off on a tangent. I told her that I had traveled all the way from England to visit Cervantes' grave, a white lie, but close to the truth. She said to me, 'As it happens, we have a letter to one of your countrymen which was found under the maestro's bed. It's addressed to the Bard of Stratford-upon-Avon. Does that ring a bell by any chance?'

"For someone with a way with words, I suddenly found myself tongue-tied. I'm used to choosing my words carefully, revising what I've written as I go. However, speaking out loud leaves little latitude, for one can't tinker with one's utterances. If I admitted who I was, I obviously couldn't be a dead man. But I was dying to find out what was in the letter. Delving into my bag of tricks, I said to her, 'What a remarkable coincidence, for I'm the Bard's twin brother. I'd be happy to deliver it to him when I return to England. In the meantime, is there any possibility that you could translate the letter for me?' I realized that claiming I was a twin might complicate matters, but my audiences have always enjoyed the twins trope.

"Suffice it to say that the nun took me at my word, another small miracle, and led me to Cervantes' grave. I knelt in prayer, regretting that I was too late for his funeral, but thankful that I had made the pilgrimage. Then the sister read me his letter while we sat beside the burbling fountain in the courtyard:

Dear William,

Death has finally caught up with me, my friend, as foreshadowed in my dream. I now understand that most of the tears will be from the sisters in the convent where I will be buried for eternity. Their cascade of tears will cleanse my soul. We have much to learn from our dreams, which continue to bear fruit. Remember the words of the Talmud, "A dream uninterpreted is like a letter unopened."

As I have always wanted to go to Greece to see the theaters of the ancients, I am asking that you go in my stead. You of all people could benefit by being re-acquainted with the ancients, since you often flout Aristotle's unities of action, time and place. While the current occupation of most of Greece makes it difficult to visit many of the theaters, I am enclosing a letter of introduction which should open doors for you in the area controlled by the Venetians. Having spent five years in Italy, I am well known in Christendom. Indeed my success in defeating the Ottoman Empire at the Battle of Lepanto has not escaped the attention of the Pope. Likewise, there is a price on my head among the Turks, so make sure my letter of introduction does not fall into the wrong hands.

In vino, veritas
Miguel de Cervantes Saavedra

"In the evening I returned with flowers for Cervantes' grave, and was glad to find the cemetery deserted. As I put the bouquet on his tombstone, I felt the tears well up in my eyes, then fall onto his grave. I said to him, 'In your dream you spoke of a beautiful young woman who wept for you. Now you have found a deeper meaning. Yet I wonder if you might have foreseen my presence as well, for my tears fall like summer rain, clearing the air, allowing us to part as the best of friends despite our differences."

CHAPTER 12

The next few days of our voyage on the *Dragon* were dull by comparison with our farewell to the circle of the remarkable people that I had barely met. Indeed, time passes very slowly on board a ship, even one as colorful as the *Dragon*, filled with misfits confined to a floating prison. Small wonder that actors and sailors rank so low on the ladder of life, but as they say, misery loves company. And the crew of the *Dragon* had nowhere else to go. Indeed, they should have counted their blessings, because how many people in the world get to sail the seven seas for a living, despite the boredom and the danger?

To Captain Cardenio's credit, he was not as ambitious as King James to spread the King's English to the whole wide world, but limited himself to just one sea, the Mediterranean. Arguably the best food in the world, but certainly the best wine, as I can testify myself, if you'll take the word of an Englishman. However, as our captain well knew, wine takes up a lot of space on a ship. By comparison, ouzo contains a lot more alcohol, is inexpensive and is plentiful throughout Greece. Indeed, I suspect that we visited most of the countless Greek isles, where *The Tempest* was well received.

As much as I enjoyed the islands, they began to look alike after awhile; white stucco houses with tile roofs and goats wandering about like sacred cows in India. I was also disappointed that the Greek islands didn't have many historical sites. The few that did had already been ransacked by British archeologists. So I was delighted when Captain Cardenio announced that we were going to spend a week on the Peloponnese peninsula, where the Spartans once ruled. What I know about the classical world would fit in a thimble, but even I had heard of Mount Olympus.

As we entered the harbor in Nafplio on the west coast, I was sobered by the sight of the Venetian encampment guarding the lovely city. A chilling reminder that sovereignty is "more honored in the breach than in the observance," in Will's words. How anyone could attack the place seemed impossible to me, because intruders would be seen well before they could mount an assault. I would have been happy to spend the week in this charming seaport, but the captain was a man on a mission. He had arranged for us to perform in one of the great theaters of antiquity, at Epidaurus. In Greek legend it was the birthplace of the healer, Asclepius, son of Apollo.

Honestly, I had no idea that such places still existed, but its saving grace is that it's located in the middle of nowhere. Too far from the coast to be looted by pirates, and well beyond the reach of Athenians, Epidaurus is not only the site of an outdoor theater dating from the 4th century, but was once a center for healing. Imagine if you will, a semi-circular theater carved out of stone with seating for 14,000 spectators. Set in a forest, the theater looks toward the mountains in the distance. How many people must have watched Greek drama play out there over the centuries?

Unfortunately, my first impression of Epidaurus was clouded by the torrent of rain that greeted us, along with thunder and lightning, as if the gods were displeased. The Captain's plan to rehearse before our first performance on the Greek mainland was washed away in the deluge. Given liberty for three days, I was determined to see Mount Olympus, but Captain Cardenio had other plans for me.

Taking me aside, out of hearing of the rest of the crew, he told me that he was entrusting me with a secret mission. He refrained from telling me that Anne and Will were heading to Epidaurus on horseback. Perhaps he was afraid of letting me down if they missed the rendezvous.

Handing me a knife, the captain showed me the scroll concealed in the handle, before inserting it in a leather sheaf attached to a belt. "You must guard this with your life, for the message you are to deliver is urgent, as you will understand when you meet the monk for whom it's intended. Do not entrust it to anyone else, no matter what happens. If you fail to find him, return immediately. Time is of the essence." Without offering any further explanation, he showed me my destination on a map, drawn on a piece of parchment, with ink the color of blood. "There is a monastery in Mystras, not far from Sparta, where you will find Brother Pyramus, who is a hermit, so he will not be expecting to see you."

As you may well imagine, the sound of such an adventure dispelled my disappointment at missing Mount Olympus. And having already seen the mountains near Epidaurus, I doubted that any mountains could be much higher. Once you've seen one mountain, you've seen them all, I wager, and I wasn't eager to encounter any more thunder and lightning. Best of all, I now had good reason to visit Sparta, which every schoolboy has heard about, as the epitome of fortitude. I couldn't have dreamed up a more challenging mission on my own.

With no time to waste, I set out on my quest, determined to uphold Captain Cardenio's confidence in me. But I soon found that my map was practically useless, as the only writing was Greek to me, nor could I pronounce any of the places on the map. Even in the unlikely event that I managed to say something intelligible, I would be unable to understand any reply. Thus, I concluded that my only hope was to point to the place that the Captain had marked with an X. However, remembering that we were also on a mission for King James to spread the word among the masses, I resolved to at least speak some English when asking for directions.

My first test came when I lost sight of the river I had been following, which I knew must have its source in the mountains. I reminded myself, when in doubt, head for higher ground. Sound advice in morality, I believe, and in this case, higher ground would provide some perspective. Seeing a farmer plowing his field behind a donkey, I waited until he came to the end of a row and hailed him as best I could, without having the slightest idea of how to say hello in Greek.

Evidently taking me for a fool, he ignored me and began plowing another row. Anticipating his route, I waited for him with my map unfurled, hoping that he would understand that I was lost. Seeing his dog running toward me from the other side of the field, I reconsidered my strategy and began to run. I would have climbed a tree, but the grove of olive trees offered no refuge. I considered drawing my knife, but it didn't offer much protection when confronted with a beast.

Fortunately, the dog lost interest in me when a rabbit ran across his path, so I returned to the road, which was really more of a path in the wilderness. Indeed, it soon petered out in a field of rocks that were strewn over the barren landscape. Faced with this impasse, I looked up to see the sun, hoping to get my bearings. But the sun was directly overhead, suggesting that it was close to noon, as my stomach confirmed. So I sat down and ate the lunch that the ship's cook had prepared for me, a crock of gruel with piece of dried cod. Just what I needed to make me feel at home, which couldn't have been farther from the truth.

Under usual circumstances I would have taken a nap after lunch, but I was mindful of my mission, so I piled up some rocks to stand on, providing a vantage point. As luck would have it, I saw a figure in the distance, riding on a donkey, so I began waving, hoping that they would see me. Whoever it was waved back, but went in the other direction, as if they had spied a fool or a peddler.

Yet I reckoned that they must have come from somewhere, not out of the blue, so I did my best to find the trail which the stranger had used. I thought to myself, if a donkey can find a way through these rocks, then I can, too. In retrospect, I suppose that animals possess instincts that humans don't have, for I spent the rest of the afternoon trying to find a trail. Chasing my tail is more like it. My salvation finally came in the shape of a shadow, when I realized that the sun must be going down in the west. That meant I needed to head in the other direction, as I could tell from my map. Apparently, even the Greeks use four directions, like the English, so all I had to do was keep the sun at my back to get to Mystras.

Mind you, I had yet to meet a living soul on my Greek journey so far, which was both a blessing and a curse. Anything they said might have led me astray, but I longed to at least see someone face to face. As if in response to my unsaid prayer, I finally encountered what must have been a Roman road, judging from the width of it, probably to accommodate their chariots. My hunch was confirmed when I came to a bridge over a river, which I found on my map. Seeing the well-hewed stones in what I took to be a Roman bridge, it dawned on me that the fields of stone which I had encountered must have been quarried in this area. No doubt the poor farmer I had seen earlier spent most of his life digging stones out of his fields before he could plant anything. No wonder he didn't have time to stop for me.

So imagine my delight in encountering a crone walking down the road towards me, carrying a basket of olives. Afraid that I might startle her, I stood on the side of the road, in a gesture of respect for an elder. Summoning my courage, I addressed her in English, like the loyal subject of King James that I am. "Good day to you, madame. I would offer to buy your olives, but I have no money to speak of, unless you would like an English penny, which bears the likeness of Queen Elizabeth."

The old woman didn't miss a step, but kept walking as if I were a mere phantom. Yet I could have sworn that she winked at me, offering a grin that showed her two teeth to good advantage, for they were white as snow. The contrast with her black dress, black hair and black eyes was striking. Not to mention the dark brown olives in her basket. Not just any olives, but Kalamatas, for those of you who know what I'm talking about.

It soon dawned on me that I didn't really need directions, since I could now see where I was on the map, even if I couldn't read the words. Had I been in Scotland, I would have been in the highlands, for the perspective afforded a glimpse of the sea in the distance. Indeed, I found myself in mountains beyond the wildest dreams of an Englishman, with views worthy of a landscape painter. What a pity that I had no one to share this magnificent countryside with, but my adventure had hardly begun.

The sight of a woman carrying her baby on her back only added to my sense of being in a reverie, which quickly vanished when I heard the child's cries. From the scowl on the woman's face I gather that I was the cause of the crying, for I suppose that the sight of a stranger was unusual in these mountains. I tipped my hat, which only made things worse, as the child wailed even louder. Never have I been so glad that I am not a father. Indeed, from the stern look on the man who followed them, I gather that he was the child's father, for regret was written all over his face.

Consulting my map again, I was pleased to see that I was making good progress, and without anyone's help. So I was startled to find that the road ahead of me was closed by a landslide, which may have accounted for the distress of the family I had encountered. I suppose that landslides must be a frequent occurrence in the mountains of Greece, but you may recall that I have spent most of my life in London. Suffice it to say that natural disasters take different forms in England, where steep is a word associated with tea, rather than terrain.

The long and short of it is that I had to backtrack to get to Mystras, forcing me to have to ask for directions, and leading to disaster. For as luck would have it, I slipped on a rock while crossing a stream, stubbing my toe and soaking my map. Opening my map as carefully as I could, I watched in horror as the bloodred ink dissolved in front of my eyes. I took some consolation in the fact that I couldn't really read the map anyway, but it had at least provided a sense of direction. As the sun began to set, I knew that I just needed to keep going in the opposite direction.

In retrospect, my inability to read Greek proved to be a blessing in disguise, for if I had seen the sign for Sparta, I'm not sure that I could have resisted going there, if only to set my foot in ancient history. Realizing that a monastery would likely be set high in the mountains, I headed upwards at every turn. In the fading light I kept going until the road became a path, and the path ended in a cul-de-sac. Before me stood what could only be a monastery, rising to the heavens. But I was mistaken. Seeing a woman dressed in black, I realized that it must have been a convent.

Unable to communicate with the nun, I startled her when I unsheathed my knife. But when I pulled out the scroll from the handle, she must have understood that I had good intentions. Showing her the writing on the scroll I realized that she couldn't read English, which is just as well, as I was sworn to secrecy. Yet she seemed to understand that I had come to the wrong place, and gestured for me to follow her. This was easier said than done, because the chasm we had to cross to get to the other side of the river was formidable, with spray from a waterfall drenching us as we made our way across the bridge.

I couldn't help thinking that the chasm between the convent and the monastery seemed symbolic, mirroring the dualities of male and female, heaven and earth, love and hate, thick and thin. I was particularly perplexed by the juxtaposition of the convent and what turned out to be the monastery. Why put them so close together when nuns and priests were forbidden to communicate with each other? For me, it would have been torture to be so close to women without ever seeing them. As I was to discover, there is a reason that the Greek Orthodox Church doesn't adhere to Catholic doctrine, even if I can't grasp the nuance that keeps them separate.

As I followed the nun across the bridge, she suddenly stopped, as if there was an invisible line, which there was. Pointing towards the monastery on the other side of the bridge, she didn't bother speaking to me, but turned and walked back toward the convent. I felt a fool for having no way to say thank you. I considered thanking her in English, but it seemed impotent under the circumstances.

As I approached the monastery I could see that it was perched high in the mountain, as if to be as close to heaven as possible in this life. Seeing that there were no steps to climb, I made my way to what appeared to be an entrance to a cave. Foolishly, I called out, hoping that someone would hear me, but the only response was my echo. As my eyes adjusted to the darkness in the mouth of the cave, I noticed a rope hanging down. Giving it a tug, I had the impression that I was ringing a bell, but I heard nothing. It occurred to me that I might need to spend the night in the cave, hoping to rouse someone in the morning. The prospect of spending the night in the cave gave me pause, but I doubted that the convent would take me in.

Hearing a sound above my head, I was startled to glimpse what appeared to be a basket attached to ropes. As the basket descended, I wondered if I had the courage to trust myself to an unseen puppet master. There seemed to be no choice in the matter, so I climbed into the basket and waited to meet my fate. My fortitude was rewarded when the contraption began to rise. To my surprise the basket passed through a hole in the ceiling of the cave, affording a spectacular view of the river and the convent, which was illuminated from within by candles. Looking up at the sky, I could see stars which looked close enough to touch.

Enthralled by my ride in the basket, I was almost disappointed when it stopped, after passing through a gap in the rock which served as the foundation of the monastery. I didn't dare to look down, for fear of getting vertigo, so I sat still, admiring the view. Even at night I could tell that I was sitting on top of the world, and I wondered what it must look like in the light. How I wished that I had come when the moon was out, but I counted my blessings. I had arrived at my destination.

All I had to do was to deliver the scroll.

After a while I began to wonder if I would have to spend the night in the basket, but that seemed more preferable than remaining in the cave. I recalled from school that Plato had written about caves, but I sat in the back of the class, caring little for philosophers. I expect that Plato would have been happy to spend time in the monastery, with few distractions, but I was getting ahead of myself, for I had yet to set foot in the place.

I was not prepared to be greeted by a leper, especially not one who spoke French and English, but it was a relief to finally be able to talk with someone, even though I couldn't bear to look at his face. Having no idea what to say to the disfigured monk, I blurted out the name of Brother Pyramus, hoping that the name might ring a bell. He said, "What brings you here, my son?" Clearly, he was not a native speaker of English, but his accent was pretty good.

It didn't seem like a good time to tell him about King

James, so I reached for my knife to give him the scroll. This foolish move almost cost me my life. Drawing a sword, he knocked the knife out of my hand, sending it clattering to the floor. Raising my hands to show him that I was unarmed, I said to him, "Don't kill the messenger. I am merely an errand boy for Captain Cardenio, who has sent you a secret message concealed in the handle of the knife. As God is my witness, I have no idea what message he has for you, but he told me it was a matter of life and death."

The mention of the captain seemed to put the monk at ease. Indeed, after putting his sword away, he removed the mask that he was wearing so that he could inspect the knife and retrieve the scroll. Naturally, I was startled to discover that he had been only posing as a leper, but as he told me later, the brotherhood had assigned him to be guardian of the monastery for good reason. In his former life he had proven himself in battle and was adept at disguise, crediting Will for some pointers about stagecraft. A bit of an understatement, as I was soon to discover.

While Brother Pyramus perused the message on the scroll, I tried to put him in the picture. "As it happens, I am a man of many missions. I signed on with Captain Cardenio on behalf of King James, who is intent on making English the lingua franca of the modern world."

I realized too late that my revelation might have offended him, since he was obviously French, but the cat was out of the bag, as we like to say. Before he could object, I continued my explanation of our quest. "While it may seem like a fool's errand to spread the word, I hope you can see the King's wisdom in tapping the genius of William Shakespeare to promote English."

"You are even a bigger fool than I took you for," he replied. "How can you win people over when you can't even speak their language?"

I was quick to defend myself, deftly, if I may say so. "I may be a fool, sir, but at least I know it. There are even bigger fools who are blind to their foolishness. 'Tis a pity that you don't know Shakespeare very well, for he appreciates the value of fools like me, who often get the best lines. Indeed, it's frequently the fool who gets the last laugh."

Noting that he lacked a sense of humor, I continued in this vein, "You, yourself, belie the truth, as you obviously have learned some English. How is it that even a masked monk in the mountains of Greece speaks the language of the future? While it may seem a waste of the Bard's wit to perform his plays throughout the world, consider the birds. You don't need to understand them to appreciate their songs or to enjoy the sound of their banter. Nor to marvel at their nestbuilding, which they accomplish without saying a word. Where do you think Shakespeare learned the value of dialogue? Not from humans, who like to hear the sound of their own voice, but from birds, who understand flights of fancy."

Brother Pyramus interjected, "I see that you are astute for a fool, able to read between the lines."

To which I replied, "Only when God chooses to smile upon me, but you might be surprised how much a fool can tell. Your mask, for example, clearly aimed to frighten people, didn't fool me for long. You must have reason to hide, as if retreating to a monastery weren't enough to protect you. Your secret is safe with me, sir, unless you happen to reveal it, for I cannot hold my tongue for long. I share all that I am given, for better or worse. In that respect, I am a monk like you, giving of all I have. But unlike you, I am not concerned with my own salvation. As I said, I am here to spread the word of King James, who has seen fit to let Shakespeare speak for him."

He parried my remark; "Then I fear that William Shakespeare would be rolling over in his grave, if he were truly dead. For all of his wit would be lost on those who do not know English."

I responded, "Then let a fool enlighten you, sir.

Whatever meaning he means to convey is beside the point. Language is the message."

At this point I thought it prudent to tell the monk that I needed some proof that he had read the message contained in the scroll, in order to assure Captain Cardenio that I had delivered the goods. Brother Pyramus reached into his robe and produced a signet ring attached to chain around his neck. He said, "While it might appear that I have been unable to let go of the trappings of my former life, I wear this chain around my neck to remind myself that I can never escape my past while I am still in this world."

I would have done anything to hear about his former life, which I'm sure must have been more colorful than his present self-imprisonment, but he didn't volunteer any details worth recording for posterity. I thought to myself, what a pity that this striking man has no stories to share with me. For he obviously has no idea that I am the Plutarch of my age. Indeed, he showed me to my sleeping quarters, fit for a dog rather than a scribe.

In what seemed like the middle of the night, he roused me from my troubled sleep and sent me on my way, asking me to convey his regrets to Captain Cardenio. "There is nothing I would rather do than to see Shakespeare's lost play performed at Epidaurus, and to see Rose in full flower. That is precisely how I know that I need to deny myself such a pleasure. The devil himself could not have contrived a more cunning temptation. The captain has outdone himself, but I have renounced the world."

~

Returning to Epidaurus was simpler than I thought, as all I had to do was reverse my strategy, heading downhill instead of uphill. Having managed to find the monastery on my own, without any help from the unhelpful Greeks, I was determined to get back without having to ask for directions. To make sure I didn't get lost, I simply followed the first river that I came to, which I knew would lead me towards the sea. However, I didn't anticipate the river would disappear underground, in the labyrinth of caves below.

I thought I was quite clever to follow the sound of the rushing water beneath my feet, until the noise disappeared. I then found myself utterly lost, for I had come to a broad plain, without any view of the sea. Had this been a scene from one of Will's plays, a shepherdess would have appeared to complicate the plot. Alas, the author of our lives had other plans for me. I encountered an old woman, who might have been the older sister of the crone I had seen before, but this poor creature had no teeth left at all. She took one look at me, as if sizing me up for dinner, and handed me the bundle of wood that she was carrying.

I understood immediately that she wanted me to relieve her of her burden. Although I had no idea of her destination, I didn't see how I could refuse. Curiously, she said not a word to me at first, as if I were a donkey rather than a man. Yet as we made our way through the lovely countryside, she began speaking to me, in Greek, I gather. After awhile, I began to feel awkward just listening to her prattle away, and I was mindful that I wasn't holding up my end of the conversation, so to speak.

So when she stopped to catch her breath, I began speaking to her in English, of course, remembering that I was a missionary. My speech seemed to amuse her to no end, but she finally interrupted me and continued babbling again. After a few minutes she stopped talking and looked at me, as if letting me know that it was my turn. And so we passed a couple of very pleasant hours.

It finally dawned on me that conversation is just an excuse to hear yourself talk. The point is not to communicate, but to listen to the thoughts that cross your mind. I suppose that there is nothing to stop us from speaking our minds by ourselves, but other people would think us quite odd for talking without anyone else around. Appearing to hold a conversation gives us permission to pretend we're listening to someone else.

Noticing that the sun was starting to set in the west, I decided that I needed to pick up my pace to return to Epidaurus, to report to the captain. So when we came to a dirt crossroad I stopped and drew a picture of the theater, scribing a semi-circle in the sandy soil. I saw no way to represent the seating for 14,000 spectators, so I sketched a few lines to get the point across. The old woman pointed towards the crossroad, holding up five fingers. I had no idea what this meant, of course, but it was clear that she was pointing me in the right direction. How far I had to go, I couldn't tell. Whether it was five miles or five leagues didn't matter. At the very worst, I would end up at the sea, and I was confident that I could retrace my steps from the port.

Bidding my companion farewell, I handed her the bundle of sticks, which she dropped on the ground. Then she started wailing, and her cries were so loud that I was afraid someone would think I was robbing the old woman. As soon as I picked up the bundle of firewood, she began walking again, so I had no choice but to follow her. Five minutes later, we came to the hut where she lived with her fetching daughter, Aphrodite, but by then time was slipping away.

Returning to the crossroad, I soon spotted the theater in the distance, and found the cast rehearsing for the next day's performance. There was no sign of the Bard yet, but I wasn't expecting him anyway. Producing the scroll with a flourish, I showed Captain Cardenio the seal and conveyed the monk's regrets. Fortunately, my only role was to play the horse bearing Gwendolyn, Queen Anne's maid, who leaves her baby at the gate of the castle, before riding away just before dawn. While I thought the horse looked more like an ass, I had no lines to memorize. All I had to do was to carry the lovely actress on my back and whinny a couple of times. There are advantages to being a fool.

~

I would like to tell you that the theater at Epidaurus was filled with spectators, but you have to remember that at the time, Will's plays were not well known around the world. So I was quite happy to see members of the audience trickle in, taking their seats on a beautiful afternoon, with just a few clouds in the azure sky. Indeed, I have never seen such a blue sky in England, perhaps because the skies in Greece reflect the color of the Mediterranean. In any case, it was a perfect day for the performance of a play that might have been lost to history.

I noticed that the front row had been roped off, evidently for dignitaries, but the places remained empty until the first act. As I was in the opening scene, I had to put on my horse costume, so the front row was still empty when I pranced onto the stage. I must admit that this was one of those times when I wished that I had a speaking part, because the acoustics at Epidaurus are famous. An actor standing in the middle of the stage can be heard throughout the theater, even in a whisper. Although it was thrilling for me to know that my whinny reverberated throughout the theater, it would have been nice to utter a memorable line or two.

Having already played my part, I shed my horse costume and looked for an empty seat, which were plentiful. Seeing that the front row was almost empty, with only three spectators as far as I could tell, I took a seat nearby, leaving space for any other dignitaries, who are frequently latecomers, in my experience.

As you may recall, Rose had already distinguished herself by portraying Queen Anne in the Tower of London. She possessed the kind of gravitas that the role calls for. Thus, it was such a pleasure to hear her opening lines again in such a spectacular setting, a world away from London. Yet as she greeted the guests from the "Kingdom of Navarre," someone in the front row gasped in surprise. Looking over at the cloaked figure, I was startled to see

Brother Pyramus, wearing his leper mask.

I hoped that there would be an intermission, so that I could take a closer look at him, but the Greeks are known for their staying power, as evident in the Marathon. Consequently I found myself glancing at this mysterious man to gauge his reaction to the play. So it came as a huge relief to see him rise with the rest of the audience for three standing ovations, joined by a couple of dignitaries wearing hoods. Brother Pyramus turned towards me, put his finger to his lips, and then sat down while the rest of the spectators began to leave the theater. Apparently, none of them had seen his face when he sat down, for I'm certain that he would have created quite a stir.

Even I can take a hint, so I didn't try to engage him in conversation, or ask him why he had changed his mind. I realized that he had made a momentous decision in attending the play, but I was in no position to plumb his depths. In truth, I'm no Plutarch, but I'm persistent, which covers a multitude of sins. So I waited patiently, to see what his next move would be.

I didn't have to wait long, for I saw him turn his head when Rose approached him. Even I was not prepared for her fury. "Did you really think that your disguise would deceive me? I, who studied your face for days while I painted your portrait. I know every feature of your face, your body, and your soul. I must admit that I could not bear to see the face of a leper, and turned my gaze away. But not before I saw your eyes, which I painted with a thousand brushstrokes.

"How could you possibly let me believe you were dead? Did Shakespeare put you up to the deception, or did you think of it yourself? No matter. You pierced my heart with your sword. You may not have died, but I did, when the news of your murder reached my ears. I have every right to kill you. I have no doubt that God, himself, would forgive me."

Pulling off his mask, Brother Pyramus fell to his knees,

begging for forgiveness, but imploring her to kill him if she must. "The man you knew died years ago, knowing that he could never have a moment of peace while he was alive. All that I did for my subjects was held against me. Even my reputation as Good King Henri came back to haunt me, as Catholics and Protestants alike called me a traitor. I was a marked man, Rose, whose life was not my own.

"It took me years to become King of France, but once I occupied the throne, my days were numbered. Getting wind of another plot to assassinate me, I feigned my own murder. Protected by a vest of chainmail, I concealed a sheep's bladder filled with chicken blood under my coat. I completely fooled the assassin, who thought that he'd succeeded in stabbing me in the heart. A piece of stagecraft worthy of Shakespeare, if I may say so. I promised myself that I would exchange my royal robe for the vestments of a priest. Not a Catholic priest, but a monk in the Eastern Church, which isn't ruled by the Pope. This may be heresy to you, who are so devout, but I have made my peace with God. If you cannot forgive the man that I once was, I understand, but I am born again."

Rose only shook her head. "Then why disguise yourself as a leper, if you can look God in the eye with a clear conscience? And what are you really doing here? Have you come out of vanity, for the King of Navarre that you once were, or have you come to see me? Surely you can't imagine that I can forgive you."

Rising from his knees to look at her, he said, "The fool who found my refuge startled me with the truth. He pointed out that I was only concerned with my own salvation. I have found a way to elude death, but my heart is empty on my own. Despite my new life with God, my prayers have gone unanswered. If only you will forgive me, all will be right in this world."

"Right for you, perhaps, but what about me? Am I to content myself with the knowledge that you are still alive, but shut away in a monastery? Do you really think that I can go on with my life as if nothing had ever happened between us? You seem to forget that I was prepared to kill you when we first met, but the tide turned, and I found myself falling in love with you—only to see you win and lose your fight to become King of France. I have earned the right to slay you or breathe life back into your body."

Henri took her in his arms, saying, "Then let us spend the rest of our lives together, Rose, even if they are short, for I am too old to let fear cast a shadow on my soul." With that, they kissed each other, in a scene worthy of Epidaurus, where love has prevailed for centuries, at least on stage.

It was at this point that I realized that the scene had been witnessed by Will, who was unrecognizable with his beard and shaggy hair. Without his earring, which he'd left on Cervantes' grave, he looked like an abbot or a pirate, I wasn't sure which. Anne could have passed for a headmistress, commanding attention with her distinguished demeanor. As she pulled back the hood of her disguise, I saw that she had cut short her hair, which had gone completely white. She made no pretense of being younger, nor did Will try to conceal the lines etched into his face.

Will told me later how delighted he was to have fooled me. I told him he owed me a favor. I asked him to speak a couple of lines, from the horse's mouth. He told me to climb to the top row, to see if the theater lived up to its reputation.

As I walked up the steps, I tried to guess what play he'd pick. *Hamlet? Romeo and Juliet? Love's Labour's Lost* seemed like a longshot, especially after the sequel. I waited and watched as he looked out onto the deserted stage and whispered:

The quality of mercy is not strained.
It droppeth as the gentle rain from heaven
Upon the place beneath. It is twice blessed:
It blesseth him that gives and him that takes.
'Tis mightiest in the mightiest. It becomes
The thronèd monarch better than his crown.
His scepter shows the force of temporal power,
The attribute to awe and majesty
Wherein doth sit the dread and fear of kings,
But mercy is above this sceptered sway.
It is enthronèd in the hearts of kings.
It is an attribute to God himself.

~

I was especially pleased that Anne and Will were there for the wedding, but they didn't reveal their plans to me, nor was I fool enough to ask about their future. I had hoped that Captain Cardenio would marry Henri and Rose on board the *Dragon*, for I doubted that the Pope would condone such a marriage, but I gather that Rose chose not to ask. After all, Greek Orthodox was a far cry from Protestant, so she must have made her peace with her decision to marry a married man--even if he had given up his wife and children to become a monk.

Unfortunately, the Captain couldn't wait until the wedding, as he had performances lined up throughout the Mediterranean. I knew that I couldn't leave Greece without seeing Mt. Olympus. It was an opportunity of a lifetime. As I said to Captain Cardenio, "I trust that you will have no problem replacing me, for fools abound. Nor does it take a fool to impersonate an ass, for almost anyone can learn to whinny. Having come all this way, I cannot leave Greece without seeing Mt. Olympus. And although I think we have fairer maids in England, I am drawn to the dark beauty of Greek women. Indeed, I have already encountered a young woman whose mother saw fit to introduce us. A good omen in any land."

Having discovered on the way back from Epidaurus that the old woman and I could enjoy each other's company without understanding each other's language was an inspiration to me. If Aphrodite is half as agreeable as her mother, I would be well advised to join the family. For I now understand that there is a comprehension that needs no words. It is music that we can't live without.

I must confess that my missionary zeal has cooled. I would rather learn Greek than proselytize for the British Empire, bent on expansion for its own sake. Moreover, having tasted the local cuisine, I'm not sure that I can ever settle for English food again. So please forgive me if I stay behind, for it may take me a lifetime to retrace the steps of Plutarch, who has become my patron saint, so to speak.

Indeed, though I have no idea what he looked like, I seem to see Plutarch's face everywhere, most often in the shrines strewn across the landscape. I light a candle in his honor, searching for his likeness in the icons hanging on the wall. I have yet to learn the names of these saints, but once again words do not matter. It is the look in their enlightened eyes that speaks to me.

~

Aphrodite and her mother brought the flowers to the wedding of Henri and Rose, which was held in the ruins of the Sanctuary of Asclepius, not far from the theater at Epidaurus. It was an intimate wedding, and I wish that I could tell you the vows that they exchanged, but I vowed to remain silent. Indeed, Greece has been good to me. I have learned to hold my ouzo and my tongue.

EPILOGUE

While doing research in the Vatican on Henri IV's assassination, an alert graduate student in history from the University of Glasgow discovered a letter written to the Pope by a French priest in the 16th century:

Your Holiness,

I hesitate to bring this small matter to your attention, but I must advise you that I heard the confession of one of Henri IV's servants who we managed to place within the king's retinue. As a Catholic, the servant had great difficulty in coming to me amidst a community of unbelievers, but his confession was so startling that I did my best to write down what he uttered:

Forgive me, but I pride myself on being a faithful servant to Henri of Navarre, and pray that he will see the light. Be that as it may, he recently asked me to burn a play about a king who bears a striking resemblance to Henri, and is likewise a blasphemer. I confess that I only know this because curiosity (or the evil one) led me to peek at the play before I burned it. Forgive me, but once I started, I could not avert my eyes, despite, or perhaps because of the blasphemy, which would burn the ears of any good Catholic.